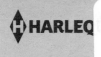 **HARLEQ**

SHIPMENT 5

Dalton's Undoing by RaeAnne Thayne
Rustled by B.J. Daniels
Gage by Delores Fossen
In Their Footsteps by Tess Gerritsen
In the Dark by Heather Graham
Home in Carolina by Sherryl Woods

SHIPMENT 6

A Measure of Love by Lindsay McKenna
Stampeded by B.J. Daniels
Mason by Delores Fossen
Night Watch by Suzanne Brockmann
Yesterday's Lies by Lisa Jackson
A Place to Call Home by Sharon Sala
Susannah's Garden by Debbie Macomber

SHIPMENT 7

A Cold Creek Secret by RaeAnne Thayne
Corralled by B.J. Daniels
Josh by Delores Fossen
Thief of Hearts by Tess Gerritsen
Honor's Promise by Sharon Sala
The Best Man by Kristan Higgins

SHIPMENT 8

Solitaire by Lindsay McKenna
Wrangled by B.J. Daniels
Sawyer by Delores Fossen
Obsession by Lisa Jackson
King's Ransom by Sharon Sala
Woodrose Mountain by RaeAnne Thayne

The More I Love You

NEW YORK TIMES BESTSELLING AUTHOR

brenda novak

Previously published as *Coulda Been a Cowboy*

Recycling programs for this product may not exist in your area.

ISBN-13: 978-1-335-40578-4

The More I Love You
First published as Coulda Been a Cowboy in 2007.
This edition published in 2021.
Copyright © 2007 by Brenda Novak

This edition published by arrangement with Harlequin Books S.A.

For questions and comments about the quality of this book, please contact us at CustomerService@Harlequin.com.

Harlequin Enterprises ULC
22 Adelaide St. West, 40th Floor
Toronto, Ontario M5H 4E3, Canada
www.Harlequin.com

Printed in U.S.A.

New York Times bestselling author **Brenda Novak** has written over sixty novels. An eight-time RITA® Award nominee, she's won the National Readers' Choice, The Booksellers' Best and other awards. She runs Brenda Novak for the Cure, a charity that has raised more than $2.5 million for diabetes research (her youngest son has this disease). She considers herself lucky to be a mother of five and married to the love of her life.

To my sister-in-law Angel, who is as beautiful as her name suggests. Thanks for your enthusiasm for my books. You've provided me with a great deal of support and inspiration. Thanks, too, for your pure heart. It's been a blessing to the entire family. May you find your own Prince Charming...

Chapter 1

Grandpa Garnier: If you find yourself in a hole, the first thing to do is stop digging.

She seemed ideal: slightly overweight, older than the typical groupie and definitely on the frumpy side. All of which would keep things as simple as Tyson Garnier needed them to be.

"What was your name again?" he asked. But he kept his voice down. God knew he didn't want to wake the nine-month-old monster in the other room. He'd just spent twenty-four hours alone with said monster and would rather suffer the roughest tackle imaginable than flounder helplessly through another fifteen minutes.

"Dakota Brown. I didn't send you a résumé, if that's what you're looking for. Gabe posted a flyer at the grocery store, saying you'd be staying at his cabin for a couple months and needed a good nanny while you're here, but I didn't consider applying until he called me." The woman met his eyes, but he had no idea what she was thinking. She certainly didn't seem impressed with him or his fame—didn't smile coyly, unbutton the top of her outdated blouse or bat her eyelashes. She treated him as he imagined she treated anyone else, which made Tyson even more hopeful that he'd found the right candidate. It was a major point in her favor that she hadn't turned into an idiot just because he played football on TV.

He set aside the stack of résumés he'd been studying. The name Brown was as ordinary as she seemed to be. But Dakota. That was unusual. Especially for a woman who looked to be of mixed race. Was she part Polynesian? Native American? Mexican? Tyson couldn't tell. But her creamy *café au lait* skin was clearly her best physical asset.

"And you have no children of your own?"

He'd told Gabe Holbrook, who'd talked him into coming to Dundee in the first place, not to send him any potential nannies with children, but it didn't hurt to double-check. The last thing Tyson wanted was more motion and chatter. He'd come to Idaho to get his mind and body ready for training camp at the end of July, barely two months away. Considering the recent changes in his life, that was going to be hard enough without any added distractions.

"No children," she said.

She had no discernible accent, nothing that would give away her heritage. "Are you married?"

"No."

"Do you nanny for someone else right now or…?"

"I work at the pharmacy behind the counter in the gift shop and soda fountain."

That was pretty ordinary, too. "You realize you won't be able to keep that job and work for me at the same time. I need someone who's available—" he nearly said "twenty-four/seven" but quickly amended it to something slightly more reasonable "—almost every day."

"I understand."

"Good, because I have to be able to rely on you a hundred percent."

"Of course. This is your son we're talking about."

He tried not to wince at the reminder. He wasn't ready for a child, for fatherhood. He'd never had much of an example. His own father had been killed trying to land his private plane in San Jose when Tyson was only two. His mother had married and divorced four times since, and he hadn't liked any of her husbands. But Rachelle had circumvented his usual defenses, had set him up so perfectly....

Reminding himself to unclench his jaw, Tyson cleared his throat. "That's right. He's my son." Maybe if he said it often enough, he'd believe it. *My son. I have a son. A baby.* He had a paternity test to prove it, along with a stack of canceled checks he'd given the child's mother as a result. He'd been hoping the money would be enough until an anonymous caller, a woman who was probably a neighbor or acquaintance of some kind, made him aware that Rachelle wasn't taking proper care of Braden. Then he'd been forced to hire a private investigator to take a closer look—and, ultimately, to make a life-changing decision. He'd seen his son for the first time only two days ago, when he took over as primary caregiver.

Stifling a groan at the tremendous responsibility behind "primary caregiver," he rubbed his face. It was all so damned ironic. There wasn't another member of the Stingrays more religious about avoiding the groupies that congregated wherever the team went.

But Rachelle hadn't been a groupie. She'd been a down-on-her-luck waitress without a place to stay. And he'd felt sorry for her.

The pencil in Tyson's hand snapped in two, which caused Ms. Brown's eyes to widen.

He tried to smile. It probably came across more like a pained grimace—he didn't feel particularly lighthearted these days. After the injury that had benched him last year, he was hanging on to his football career by his fingernails. Grandpa Garnier, his father's father and a central figure in his life, had just died. He had a baby he didn't want or know how to care for. And he had the media hounding him at every turn: Would he sign for another two years with the Los Angeles Stingrays? Or would he move to another team when he became a free agent at the end of the season? How was he handling his grandfather's death? Would his grief hurt his ability to play? Was his knee fully healed? Was he considering an early retirement? Who'd watch his baby once the season was underway? Would Braden travel with him?

Even the details of the arrangement he'd made with Rachelle had been splashed across newspapers all over the country: Stingray Wide Receiver Tyson Garnier Pays $1,000,000 for Custody.

Who the hell told the press? he wondered. It had to have been Rachelle. She loved the attention. Which was a whole other issue, one he'd have to deal with later. He'd headed for the hills the day he saw that headline, hoping to disappear and regroup—before the paparazzi could surround his Malibu home in an attempt to get a picture of him caring for his million-dollar baby.

"You realize I won't be here long, that the job is only temporary?" he asked, struggling to stay focused on the interview. He'd been up most the night, pacing with a crying Braden, and hadn't had the chance to shower or shave. A day's growth of beard covered his jaw, and his eyes burned from fatigue.

"Gabe explained that to me, yes," she said.

"And the job still appeals to you?" He

hated to ruin his chances by driving home the negatives, but he didn't want to lie to her. She was giving up her current job for an eight-week stint as a nanny. How wise could that be?

"Actually, it's an ideal situation for me," she explained. "I've been working at the pharmacy since high school, so I have a lot of vacation time saved up. Mr. Cottle—that's my boss—told me I had to take it or I'd lose it."

"And you're going to spend it working for me? You don't want to see the ocean? Go to Disneyland?"

Her eyes slid away from his, appeared to focus on the edge of the desk. "I can't. Not right now. Anyway, I don't want to miss this opportunity."

Who considered such a brief job as a nanny an *opportunity?* "It's only two months of work."

"But it pays well."

Tyson hadn't decided on a salary yet. He'd been waiting to ascertain the expectations of his applicants. "It does?" he asked in surprise.

"Gabe said you'd pay me at least three times what I make at the pharmacy."

Tyson's eyebrows jerked up. *Thank you, Gabe! That's some sympathy, buddy.* "He did? *Three* times?" God, hadn't he been taken for enough already?

She twisted the handle of her worn leather purse. "He told me you were looking for the best and were willing to pay for it."

When she put it that way, what could he say? "How much is three times?" he asked, still a bit skeptical.

"Forty-five hundred a month."

She stated the amount quickly, as if she was afraid he'd object. But he was actually relieved. Was that all? He'd have to pay at least that much in the city—for probably half as many hours. "That's fine."

She smiled self-consciously. "We could use it."

He caught her choice of pronouns right away. "I thought you weren't married."

"I'm not. I live with my father. He…he can't work right now."

"Is he injured?" If so, Tyson immediately identified.

"No." She tugged at one sleeve, seeming a bit selfconscious. "He has…health issues."

"I'm sorry to hear that. I hope it's not serious."

"He'll be okay." She lifted her chin.

"Does he need constant care?"

"Not *constant*. A neighbor, Mrs. Duluth, looks in on him every now and then while I'm at work, and that seems to be enough until I get home."

"So he'll have what he needs while you're here?"

"Yes."

Tyson had hoped she'd explain what kind of health issues her father faced. When she didn't, however, he had no choice but to move the conversation along. There were only so many questions he could ask without invading her privacy beyond what was reasonable in a job interview. "Have you had any experience with children, Ms. Brown?"

"Nothing official, but I've been babysitting since I was twelve." At the mention of children, her face lit up with enthusiasm and, just like that, she seemed far less average than before.

It was her eyes, Tyson decided. Large and luminous and one shade darker than her skin, they seemed exotic. How old was she, anyway? Twenty-four? Twenty-five?

"I know most all the kids in Dundee," she added, smiling wistfully. "I *love* babies."

That made exactly *one* of them. At this point, Tyson was too angry to love anything. Even himself. "That's encouraging."

"I can get references if you want."

"You already have the best reference you could get. Gabe thinks very highly of you."

A squawk from the other room caused Tyson's stomach muscles to cramp with tension. The monster was awake....

"When can you start?" he asked, anxious to make the final arrangements. Forget the rest of the résumés. He needed someone *now*. Maybe she was only the second person he'd interviewed, but he liked her better than the starstruck Ms. Davie he'd spoken to earlier. Dakota hadn't even *mentioned* football. With her, he was just a man hiring a nanny, and she was just a nanny looking for work.

Perfect.

Her lips parted as she stared up at him. "I've got the job?"

"You've got the job."

"That's wonderful." Smiling in apparent relief, she clasped her purse to her side and stood. "I can be here first thing tomorrow, if you like."

He stood, too, and instinctively moved to cut off her path to the door. She couldn't leave him alone with what was in the next room. He wouldn't survive another hour. "Any chance you'd consider starting today?"

Her step faltered. "It's almost two o'clock in the afternoon."

Braden was just working himself up into a full wail, but it was enough to shred Tyson's last nerve. "Is that a problem?"

She raked delicate-looking fingers through her dark hair. "How long do you need me?"

He wondered how many hours he could get away with. "Four hours? Five?" he asked hopefully.

"I hadn't expected to start quite so soon. I need to notify my current employer."

The crying was growing louder by the second. "There's a phone." He pointed at it.

"I was also going to check on my father."

"Can't you call the neighbor and have her do that?"

Her teeth sank into her bottom lip. "I could try, I guess…"

Tyson needed a more decisive answer. "I'll give you a five-hundred-dollar bonus if you can make the arrangements," he promised. Surely a pharmacy clerk would be willing to briefly impose on a neighbor in order to earn five hundred dollars! She could even share the money with the neighbor to make it worth his or her time.

He could tell by Dakota's expression that she was tempted, but she still took a moment to respond. "You're serious?"

"Completely." He wished he could slap the cash down on the desk, but he didn't have that much in his wallet. Maybe that wasn't the best approach, anyway. She seemed almost as spooked by his eagerness as she was relieved to get the job. "What do you say?"

She glanced around the office, at the action photos of Gabe Holbrook from the days when he could still play football. "How long have you known Gabe?"

"Years and years," he assured her. "We used to play together when I was a rookie and he was MVP. Before the accident that... you know." He couldn't say it, wouldn't jinx himself that way. What had happened to Gabe was every professional athlete's worst nightmare. "Gabe likes me," he went on. "Really, he does. You can call him if you want. On that phone there." *God, stop the crying!* "Then you can start."

"No one pays five hundred dollars for one afternoon of babysitting," she murmured. "I—I couldn't accept that much."

Her response threw him. "Sure you can. If you'll stay, I'm happy to pay it. I can't give it to you until tomorrow, though. After that I'll pay you weekly."

"Gabe mentioned that you're going through a hard time right now, that you're not quite yourself."

Tyson couldn't help being offended. Who'd be normal after what he'd been through? "I'll have to remember to thank him for that."

"He meant it well," she said earnestly. "He's worried about you. And… I'm not the type to take advantage of someone."

What? Almost everyone he met wanted *something* from him. Sometimes he felt besieged, as if the whole world was crowding him, forcing him farther and farther into a corner as they pleaded for a photograph, an autograph, an interview, a donation, an endorsement—even sex. Some women did all they could to sleep with him just for the bragging rights.

"I'm fine. Totally…fine," he said. It was a lie, but he figured it didn't really count because the quality of his life was a matter of perspective. By most people's standards, he had it all. If he couldn't say he was fine, who could?

Her shoulders finally lifted in a shrug that said she'd let him be the judge. "Okay."

Thank you, Lord. The baby was making such a racket he could scarcely think. "Great. Follow me."

Tyson led his new nanny through Gabe's cabin to the bedroom where he'd spent better than three hours trying to assemble the crib he'd had delivered from Boise. It wouldn't have taken nearly so long except he could only work in short bursts, in between patting, bouncing and cajoling the child he'd unwittingly fathered that fateful night eighteen months ago. "There he is," he said, waving her into the room.

He felt a little guilty, as if he was throwing her to the wolves. But she said she loved children. Doing the baby thing wasn't torture for those who loved children, right? He just had no affinity for babies, had never been around one. An only child, he'd had a mother who was about as nurturing as an iron chair and had spent his summers at his widowed grandfather's ranch in Montana. He'd been happiest there—but even then he'd been surrounded by cowboys, not children.

When he didn't come into Braden's room with her, Ms. Brown glanced between him and his child, who—amazingly enough—had quit squalling the moment the door swung open. A pair of chubby fists gripped the slats of the crib as Braden hauled himself to his feet, then stood there, wobbling, and deceptively quiet.

"What's his name?" she asked.

"Tyson."

"And you call him…"

Monster… "By his middle name, Braden. I guess," he added as an afterthought. Rachelle had named the baby without any input from him. She'd used his name to strengthen the link between them.

"I guess?" Dakota repeated in confusion, but the baby interrupted with a squeal. Bouncing in anticipation of being picked up, he offered them a drool-laden smile, and she melted quicker than a Popsicle on hot cement. "Look! He's darling! You must be so proud."

"Just make sure you take good care of him," Tyson said gruffly and hurried back to the relative safety of the office before the truth could come out.

What kind of man couldn't tolerate the sight of his own baby?

Chapter 2

Grandpa Garnier: Good judgment comes from experience, and a lot of that comes from bad judgment.

It was the first time Dakota had ever been inside Gabe Holbrook's cabin. She'd brought him a homemade carrot cake when he'd been holed up out here a few years ago, but he hadn't invited her in, hadn't even answered the door. That was before they'd become friends. Ten years older, he'd been one of the best quarterbacks in the NFL by the time she reached high school—already a legend, and the best and brightest Dundee had to offer.

Until the car accident that had robbed him of his ability to walk.

She remembered the details of that earlier visit as she carried Braden outside and walked around the property with him. Gabe had left her standing on the porch holding her cake, even though she knew he was home. She could feel him watching her from inside.

His lack of response didn't offend her, though. She hadn't expected a warm greeting. Adamant that the doctors were wrong about the permanency of his condition, he spent every minute of every day doing therapy in his upscale weight room, and was scarcely willing to talk to his own family. So she'd set the cake on the patio table for him to enjoy when he felt safe enough to retrieve it, and hoped he understood the gesture for what it was—not the hero worship he'd encountered so often in the past, not the pity that others expressed in hushed tones whenever his name came up, not the gawking of those who remained fascinated by the tragedy, but rather, a simple, "I understand."

Their situations were very different—she had no idea how horrible it'd be to lose the use of her legs—but she could relate, at least to a certain extent, to what he'd been feeling in the months immediately following the accident. She'd had to put a brave face on her own misery. She was just less visible, which made it easier, and she'd been doing it longer. Experience had already taught her how to smile serenely to cover her pain: *I'm fine. Really. We're doing okay, don't worry.*

"Da-da-da-da," Braden cooed, shoving his fist in his mouth and gnawing on it.

Dakota pressed her lips to the baby's soft round cheek. "You are the cutest thing I've ever seen," she told him. His father wasn't bad, either, but she admitted that only grudgingly. The rest of the world made a big enough deal about Tyson Garnier. Nearly six feet four inches tall, he had greenish-blue eyes, golden skin and dark brown hair with a cowlick that made it stand up on the right side of his forehead. But it was his high cheekbones and strong jaw that really set him apart. And his body, of course.

She remembered the layout she'd seen in *People* magazine a year or so ago. Some movie director had been offering Tyson the lead in a romantic comedy, which had brought him into the Hollywood spotlight. He'd eventually refused—saying he was a football player, not an actor—but that only made this director, and others, want him more. The photographer had shot him on the beach, coming out of the surf like some sort of water god. His eyes, in stark contrast to the darkness of his hair and eyelashes, matched the green-blue of the waves in the background, and his teeth gleamed in the sun as he laughed. He looked like leading-man material, all right, and contrary to what Dakota had expected, seeing him in the flesh was no disappointment.

But she suspected he wasn't a very nice person. He seemed rather standoffish. And she'd read all about his situation with Rachelle Rochester. Because she couldn't leave her father for any length of time, Dakota escaped the drudgery of her life through magazines—fan magazines, decorator magazines, food magazines, even science magazines. Most recently, she'd read an interview with poor Ms. Rochester in *The Lowdown*. Braden's mother was upset that Tyson didn't love her as much as she loved him. She also said she couldn't believe how vicious he'd become during the custody battle: "How can I stand up against a man with the kind of money and influence he's got?" At that point, according to the journalist doing the interview, she'd broken down in tears. "He won't let me be part of my baby's life. Can you imagine anything so cruel?"

Dakota couldn't. She knew Gabe liked Tyson, and she trusted Gabe's opinion, but friendship could be as blind as love.

Kissing Braden again, she shot a dirty look at the window to the office where she'd left Tyson a few minutes earlier. As far as she was concerned, taking a child away from a loving mother was unforgivable.

"Okay, okay—you were right," Tyson told Gabe on the phone.

Relaxed for the first time in three weeks, he leaned back in the leather office chair and stretched his legs in front of him. He'd considered going to bed—his eyes felt so grainy he could barely open them, and his knee was aching again—but he was afraid he'd encounter Dakota and Braden on the way. Then she might want to talk about what he expected of her, and how could he tell her when he didn't know what a baby's care entailed in the first place? Maybe, like the rest of the world, she understood that he was new to parenting Braden full-time. But Braden was nine months old. At a minimum, she'd expect him to be prepared for his son's most basic needs.

He just wanted her to keep Braden healthy and happy. That was all there was to it.

He supposed he could say that much, but if she asked specific questions—what to feed the baby, how his meals should be prepared, what his naptimes were, whether or not she had his permission to administer medication if needed—he wouldn't know what to tell her. They'd have to figure that out, as well as her hours and her duties, as they went along. He was enjoying this brief respite too much to risk losing it.

"I knew she'd be ideal," Gabe said. "Dakota's great. And unusually smart. There's no telling what she could've done with a college degree."

"She doesn't have one?" Tyson doodled on the clean, white desk calendar, which was turned to February instead of May. According to Gabe, he'd been too busy to visit the cabin over the past few months, but Tyson knew his friend hadn't worked since finishing coaching high school football last season. He'd been traveling all over the world, hoping to find a specialist who could help him regain the use of his legs—something no one had been able to accomplish yet.

"Family problems."

Tyson drew a football in a man's hand. He could understand family problems. Since his grandfather died, his mother hadn't been the same. Neither was he. "She mentioned that her father is unable to work."

"He was in an accident something like fifteen years ago. She's been taking care of him ever since."

"What kind of accident?"

"Hang on a sec."

As Gabe took care of whatever it was that had called him away from the phone, Tyson added a Super Bowl ring to one of the fingers he'd drawn, and an arm tattooed with the words *The Duke*. Grandpa Garnier had loved the old John Wayne movies. Tyson was thinking of getting such a tattoo on his biceps in memory of his grandfather. Problem was, his grandfather had never really liked tattoos. "Why'd you do that?" he'd said when he spotted Tyson's only tattoo—his jersey number etched on the inside of his forearm. "Think y'might forget?"

The entire team had done it before a big game, but Tyson didn't bother to explain.

Grandpa Garnier didn't understand following the crowd. He also didn't understand why Tyson wanted to play football—something that would afford him such a short career—instead of becoming a cowboy like him.

Some days, Tyson thought he would've been better off taking over at the ranch.

"Sorry," Gabe said, coming back on the line. "Hannah needed the car keys."

"You were telling me about Dakota's father," Tyson reminded him, still curious about his new nanny.

There was a brief pause. "Actually, I think I'll leave it up to her to tell you more about Skelton."

Tyson didn't have high hopes about that. Dakota didn't seem very forthcoming on the subject. "Did she crash into him with her car or something?"

"No." Gabe chuckled softly. "That's my story, remember?"

How could Tyson forget? Gabe had married the woman who'd crippled him, which was almost as shocking as what had happened to him in the first place. "Do you ever find it hard to forgive Hannah?" he asked. He knew he shouldn't pry, but he'd been curious about it ever since Gabe and Hannah had gotten together. A lot of people were.

"No," Gabe responded immediately. "The accident wasn't really her fault. If her ex hadn't taken the boys, she wouldn't have been on the road that night, trying to chase him down. Besides, if she hadn't hit me, I wouldn't have moved home, and I never would've realized that she—and Kenny and Brent—are all I could ever want."

Tyson couldn't imagine the kind of marital bliss Gabe seemed to enjoy. After nearly falling in love with Rachelle, only to learn that she cared more about his money and status and what it could provide than she did him, he wasn't sure he was any better suited to marriage than he was to fatherhood.

"Doesn't Dakota have a sibling or two who can help her with her father?" he asked. "It's gotta be tough to be his sole support."

"She has some relatives in Salt Lake, an aunt and uncle and a few cousins, but as far as I know they don't have any contact. That's it."

"What happened to her mother?"

"She went back to Chile, where she was from."

That explained Dakota's coloring. "Does Dakota ever hear from her?"

"Sometimes. I know Consuela has asked her to visit, but Dakota won't go. She can't leave Skelton for that long."

"How did her mother and father meet?"

"I'm not sure exactly. I know Consuela worked in Boise, where Skelton went to school. But once they were married, she was unhappy."

Tyson sketched a pair of shoulders, complete with pads, and a helmet. "Why didn't she take Dakota with her when she left?"

"She couldn't. Dakota's an American citizen. That was the sacrifice she had to make in order to go home."

Tyson couldn't help feeling sorry for his dark-eyed nanny. It didn't sound as if she'd had many breaks in life. "I guess marriage isn't for everyone."

"Are you talking about yourself?"

"I wasn't, but I might as well be."

"It'd be easier to raise Braden if you had a wife."

Rachelle had forced too many changes on him already. But he knew he and Gabe would disagree, so he veered away from the subject. "Fortunately, I have the help I need now."

"That's all you want?" Gabe asked. "A nanny?"

"That's all I can afford," Tyson said ruefully.

There was a slight pause. "You did the right thing, Tyson. Braden's worth every dime."

Tyson didn't regret the money. Once he'd found out what was going on, he'd had to do something. His sense of responsibility was too strong to allow the child to be neglected. But he still lamented that he'd been fool enough to allow a gold-digger to change the course of his life. "Thanks for stocking the kitchen," he said. "I got in too late last night to hit a grocery store."

"That was Hannah."

"Thank her for me."

"You bet. How's the knee?"

"Healing." *I think.* It wasn't as strong as he'd hoped it'd be, but he had two months to strengthen it. "The equipment you have here will help."

"The whirlpool should be good for it, too. And I'll send the trainer I work with at the high school to meet you. He'll get you on a good therapy program. He's one of the best."

Tyson finished drawing his football player and started on a cowboy. His grandfather had lived a solid, clean life. A simple life. Which seemed damned enviable at this point. "So what's he doing in the mountains of Idaho?"

"He's also the town vet. Loves it here."

Tyson shaded the face of the cowboy he was drawing to reflect the craggy nature of Grandpa Garnier's features. God, he missed the old man. Had his grandfather still been around, Tyson could've taken Braden back to the ranch.

But those days were over. The ranch was now owned by Tyson's uncle, who refused to sell it to him. And Grandpa Garnier lived only in Tyson's memory.

At least in Dundee he had someone to help him with Braden, a trainer to get him ready for the start of the season, top-of-the-line therapy equipment and—best of all—some privacy.

For the moment, that would have to do.

Dakota stared at the light beneath the door in Tyson Garnier's office. He'd been in there since he'd hired her more than five hours earlier. She'd occasionally heard his voice as he talked on the phone, but the cabin had been deathly quiet for at least ninety minutes.

Should she knock? He'd mentioned that she needed to stay four or five hours, which meant she could go home at eight. But it was past eight-thirty and nearly dark, and he hadn't come out to take the baby, make arrangements for tomorrow, anything.

She shifted Braden onto her other hip and double-checked her watch. Sure enough—eight thirty-five. She had to get home before her father headed to the bar. He often grew restless after dark, wanted to go out and join his friends. And he wasn't the same when he was drunk.

"Mr. Garnier?" She knocked softly. He must've fallen asleep, she thought, but he proved her wrong when the door swung open almost immediately.

"Yes?" He towered over her by at least ten inches, appearing even more unkempt than he had before. His brown hair, although short, stood up all over, as if he'd pushed his fingers through it a few hundred times. The shadow of beard on his jaw and chin had darkened. And his eyes were bloodshot.

Except for the hard, flat stomach beneath his T-shirt, he looked like her father after a drinking binge. She couldn't smell any alcohol, but maybe he was on some kind of drug. Who else would promise someone five hundred dollars for a few hours of babysitting?

"It's time for me to go," she said and tried to hand him his son.

He stepped back as quickly as a vampire would from a Christian cross. "It can't be eight o'clock already."

She pulled Braden's hand away from her hair before he could get another fistful. "It's past that. And I really need to go." Or she'd have to track down her father and drag him home. They'd recently taken his driver's license away from him, but that didn't mean he wouldn't try to drive that old clunker truck of his. And if he did get on the road, and the police picked him up, she'd have to bail him out of jail again. They were already so deeply in debt they could barely scrape by.

"Of course," he said but made no move to take the baby. Instead, he gave her the sexy smile she felt certain had garnered him the attention of Hollywood in the first place. "Any chance you could get him... er, Braden...down for the night before you leave?" he asked hopefully. "I'm pretty busy in here."

Dakota would rather have stayed in the elegantly appointed cabin than return to what she called home, but she felt too much pressure. Although her father had once been a kind, responsible, loving man, the pain he suffered from the accident and the alcohol he drank to battle it had changed him. She scarcely recognized him anymore. "I don't think Braden's ready for bed. He had a late nap and could probably use a bath."

"You didn't give him one?"

"I would have," she explained, a bit defensive at his tone, "but I couldn't find the baby shampoo, and I didn't want to disturb you in case you were sleeping."

Tyson also intimidated her. On television, he seemed very cocky—the kind of guy who might stride into an event late and unapologetic, wearing an expensive pair of sunglasses and an "eat your heart out" smile. But he didn't seem very confident right now. "Isn't all shampoo basically the same?"

"Not if it gets in his eyes. You've got to go shopping anyway, so you might as well pick up some."

"Why do I have to go shopping? Hannah already stocked the cupboards."

The muscles in his arms flexed impressively as he shoved his oversized hands into his pockets. She could tell he wasn't *trying* to put on a show, but his well-toned body made Dakota more self-conscious of the twenty pounds she'd gained over the past few months. With her father behaving so badly, she couldn't get out of the house the way she used to. It was difficult leaving him alone long enough to go to work. Now that she'd be putting in longer hours, she'd have to rely even more heavily on Mrs. Duluth. But at least the arrangement was only temporary. She didn't think Mrs. Duluth would mind.

"Hannah did a general stock," she said. "I think she expected you to bring your own baby items."

"Like *shampoo*? That's a baby item?"

"Gentle shampoo, yes—and diapers and formula."

"I have diapers."

"Not anymore, unless they're in your luggage." So far, in addition to the diaper bag in the baby's room, which was empty, she'd only spotted a duffle tossed carelessly at the foot of the bed in the master. But Tyson could have diapers in there, she supposed. Or in whatever vehicle he'd brought. She hadn't checked the detached garage.

"You used them all?"

"There were only three, and I had good reason."

He seemed to grasp that she'd spared him

a few messy changes and backed off. "Right. Okay."

Feeling slightly vindicated, she mentally measured what was left in the can from which she'd made Braden's last bottle. "You also need more formula, or you will in another day or two. And it'd be nice if you could get a teething ring, a couple of baby spoons and a playpen. If you brought that stuff with you, I couldn't find it."

"No, I— Maybe you should make a list," he said.

Dakota's anxiety increased as she imagined her father revving the engine of his old truck, preparing to leave for the Honky Tonk. She'd hidden the keys, but he'd found them before. And Mrs. Duluth wouldn't stop him. She'd be in bed by now. "A list. Sure."

This time he took the baby when she held him out, and she hurried to the desk to find a paper and pen.

"Where can I get those items?" he asked, peering over her shoulder while she wrote.

"Finley's Market is open till ten. But it's a forty-minute drive to town, so you'd better hurry if you plan to go tonight." She ripped off the sheet and handed it to him. "You can follow me, if you leave right away. I drive right past there."

"Thanks. I think I'll do that."

Braden squirmed and reached for her, which made Dakota hesitate. Tyson seemed tense, unsure of himself. And the way he was holding his son—out away from his body instead of cuddling him close—concerned her. What if Tyson really was taking drugs? "Are you on something?" she asked.

Two deep furrows formed between his eyebrows. *"What?"*

She glanced anxiously toward the door but stayed where she was. She couldn't conscionably leave until she knew the baby would be okay. "I'm asking if you've been snorting coke, shooting heroin, swallowing pills…you know."

"Of course not! Do I *look* like I'm on drugs?"

She refused to blanch at his angry response. "Sort of."

His prominent Adam's apple bobbed as he swallowed, and his eyes narrowed. Obviously he wasn't used to hearing the hard truth. But she had a responsibility to the baby. "I'm not," he insisted.

"Not even steroids?" Steroids affected behavior, sometimes caused undue anger, right? She'd read that somewhere.

"Not even steroids."

She wasn't sure he'd admit it to her even if he were. But she didn't dare argue further. Braden was *his* baby. There wasn't anything more she could do. "Good." She headed for the door, her mind now fully focused on getting home to her father, but Tyson intercepted her.

"What time can you be here in the morning?"

"When would you like me?"

"I'll give you a key, so you can let yourself in at dawn."

Dawn? She almost protested. She'd have to get up before five to get back here that early. But the nine thousand dollars she'd earn working for him would stop the bank from taking possession of their home. They were nearly five months behind on their mortgage.

Hopefully, her father would behave so she'd be able to get some sleep tonight.

"Fine." She waited for him to fish an extra key out of the desk. Then she gave Braden an affectionate pat. "If you want to follow me to Finley's, you'll have to keep up," she told Tyson. "I'm in a big hurry."

But it didn't take long to realize he wasn't going to fall behind. While her 1992 rattle-trap Maxima could barely do twenty-five miles an hour on the winding road, Tyson's red Ferrari had no such limitations. His headlights never left her rearview mirror.

Where he'd put Braden's car seat in that sports car, she had no idea. Obviously Tyson Garnier wasn't much of a family man. That Ferrari was as much of a chick magnet as he was.

"You're some father," she muttered. But these days her own father wasn't anything to brag about, and she grew more and more anxious as she drove closer to home.

Chapter 3

*Grandpa Garnier: If you want to forget
all your troubles, take a little walk in
a brand-new pair of high-heeled
riding boots.*

Dakota waved him off at the small super-
market in the middle of town, but Tyson
didn't stop. First he wanted to see where his
new nanny lived. Under her care he hadn't
heard the baby so much as whimper all afternoon; he wasn't about to let her drive off
without at least knowing where to find her.
Two blocks later, she pulled onto the side of
the road. "You missed it," she called when

he came up even with her and lowered his window.

"I know."

"So where are you going?"

"I was…" He couldn't divulge too much, or she'd know how inept he was, and his inability to be a decent father was the last thing he wanted spread across the front page of tomorrow's paper. He deserved a *little* privacy, didn't he? But he knew from experience he had only as much as he could fiercely guard. "…curious to see where you live," he finished.

Her face filled with irritation. *"Why?"*

"Because I'm trying to learn my way around."

Her car rattled and shook as if it was a struggle just to keep idling. "My place is not a landmark. Besides, you don't have time to mess around. You'll miss the store, and you can't survive without diapers, remember?"

"I've got thirty minutes."

"It'll take you that long to do your shopping."

He thought he could get what he needed in fifteen. But whether he had time or not wasn't the real issue. She obviously didn't want him following her any farther. He couldn't imagine what it'd hurt, but she was scowling as though it was out of the question. "Okay."

The tension in her face eased. "You have my phone number. Give me a call if you need anything."

Did she really mean that? "I will."

"Good night," she said pointedly and maneuvered her heap of junk back onto the road.

Tyson nearly turned the Ferrari around. He was being ridiculous. Surely he could make it through eight hours on his own.

But then Braden started to fuss and pull at the harness restraining him, and fear that they'd pass another night like the last one slithered up Tyson's spine. He couldn't do it; he didn't have the patience or the emotional reserves.

Waiting until he could barely see Dakota's taillights, he pulled onto the road and trailed her at a much more discreet distance. She'd said he could call her, but what if she was a deep sleeper and didn't pick up? It wouldn't hurt to see where she lived, just in case.

Initially, he'd expected her to turn into the drive of one of the small brick houses surrounding the high school. It seemed that most folks in these parts lived there. When she passed those neighborhoods, however, he figured she had to live in one of the ranchettes on the outskirts of town. But he was wrong again. Beyond the cemetery, as buildings began to give way to the surrounding countryside, she entered a dusty trailer park that didn't have so much as a patch of grass or a few trees to recommend it.

Tyson crept forward. Cast-off tires, cardboard boxes and wine bottles littered the weed-filled spaces in between twenty or so single-wide trailers. A few cars rested on blocks, and red lava rocks had been used to spruce up those units whose owners had even bothered with landscaping. His mother would've been appalled. If his mother had anything, it was good taste.

"She can't live *here*," he muttered, trying to avoid some of the deeper ruts in the dirt drive.

Tyson knew his car was hardly the kind to blend in. He couldn't follow Dakota any farther without drawing attention, even in the dark. So he parked next to a Dumpster that had apparently been looted by kids or animals—or both. The trash scattered on the ground smelled worse than Braden's dirty diapers, but the Dumpster provided some cover as he stepped out.

Dakota pulled into a lean-to carport attached to what a sign boldly proclaimed was Unit 13. At the far back, it was one of the shabbiest trailers in the park. But someone had hung some cheap wind chimes from one of the beams that supported the carport and planted flowers in front. Tyson could see the flowers in the pool of light coming from the streetlamp right next to her trailer. He was willing to bet they were wilted and badly in need of water—everything here looked wilted and badly in need of something—but Dakota didn't so much as glance at her surroundings as she hurried up the four steps of the landing and let herself in.

The door slammed shut. Then the lights went on.

Tyson rubbed the whiskers on his chin as he listened to those wind chimes tinkling in the evening breeze, a television blaring through an open window of another trailer and a woman in the trailer closest to him ranting at someone, presumably her husband: "Get your ass in here, Willy. How many times do I gotta tell ya to empty your own damn ashtray? You'd think you could get up off that couch at least once a day...."

No wonder Gabe had promised Dakota that

he would triple her pay, Tyson thought. This place was freakin' depressing. He didn't want to stick around. He couldn't, anyway. Braden was crying again, probably tired of being in his car seat. But Tyson wasn't sure taking him out would do any good. Last night, *nothing* had calmed him.

He sighed. The torture was already starting. Eight interminable hours yawned before him, during which he wouldn't know what to do with the little human he'd inadvertently helped to create. But seeing Dakota's home put his own problems in perspective. Life could be worse, right? He could always live *here*.

Settling into the familiar comfort of his leather seat, he turned around and drove to Finley's Market.

Her father's truck was in the drive but he wasn't home.

A sick feeling descended on Dakota as she hurried inside. She hoped he'd gone to bed, but she knew better.

Sure enough, his room was as empty as the rest of the trailer. From the mess in the kitchen, he'd fixed himself dinner, at least, which was good. But there was no note on the fridge, on the counter amid the stacks of bills, or on the cluttered side table that held his glasses, his newspaper, his solitaire deck and, typically, his beer. If he was merely out for a walk or over at Johnny Diddimyer's to play poker, he would've left word. He knew she'd worry.

Covering her face, Dakota tried to steady her nerves. She didn't feel as if she could go through again what she'd been through last week. But she couldn't eat and go to bed. If her dad was already drunk and acting up, the police would put him in jail until he was sober and he wasn't well enough to withstand that. Having to walk with a cane wasn't the worst of his problems. He could have a stroke or a heart attack at any time. He already needed a new liver.

Dakota's stomach growled as she passed the kitchen. She was hungry because she hadn't felt comfortable helping herself to Tyson's food without an invitation—and he hadn't emerged from his office to give her one—but she didn't have time to scrounge through the refrigerator for leftovers. If her father had somehow managed to get to the Honky Tonk, she needed to reach him sooner rather than later. He could get so belligerent, so *violent* when he drank. It had been tough taking care of him since the accident, but it was getting more so as time wore on. He wasn't himself anymore. Sometimes he scared her so badly she didn't know if she'd survive the next few months.

She rubbed the bandage that covered the cut on her arm. She was pretty sure she should've gotten some stitches, but she hadn't dared seek medical care. If anyone found out her father had come at her with a knife, they'd insist she put him in an institution. Most people told her to do that already. But where would she get the money? He received a small check from the state each month but even combined with what Dakota earned, it wasn't enough to pay for institutionalized care. Besides, she couldn't abandon Skelton. It was because of her that he lived in constant pain.

Hesitating at the door, she threw her shoulders back and lifted her head. It'd be okay. She'd find him, and she'd bring him home where she could take care of him. He'd cried— literally broken down and sobbed— when he realized what he'd done last time. Surely he wouldn't hurt her again.

* * *

Tyson didn't know what he was going to do. Braden had fallen asleep during the ride home and had stayed asleep as he was gently transferred into his crib, giving Tyson hope that they'd have an easy night together, after all. But it was only midnight, and the baby was already awake and crying. Tyson had changed his diaper and given him a bottle. He'd even tried the pacifier he'd bought at the store—which he'd boiled just like it said on the package.

Nothing seemed to work.

He considered calling his mother for advice, but he'd tried that last night and it hadn't done any good. Priscilla Garnier, who was single at the moment and living in Phoenix, didn't know what to do with a baby any more than he did. Her suggestion had been to put Braden in his crib and let him cry, and to get some rest, but that answer was completely unacceptable to him. He'd taken Braden away from Rachelle for neglect. He wasn't about to follow in her footsteps.

"What do you want?" he asked the baby, so on edge he felt close to tears himself.

Braden's face turned a deeper shade of red,

and his mouth remained open but no sound came out.

"Breathe!" Tyson said in a panic.

Finally, Braden hauled in a breath and let go of another ear-splitting wail.

That was it, Tyson decided. He had to call Dakota Brown. He hated to do it, especially in the middle of the night. But it looked as if she could use the extra cash, and no price was too high if it'd bring him and this baby some relief. He'd promise her another five hundred dollars, or whatever it'd take, to get her to come back right away. He'd been stupid to let her go in the first place.

He wanted to put Braden in his crib and shut the door, so that he'd be able to hear on the phone, but he didn't dare. What if the monster quit breathing completely? Died of SIDS?

He continued to scream as Tyson carried him to the office. Dakota's number was in a very prominent place—he'd made sure of that—so it wasn't difficult to find. But instead of a sleepy voice on the other end of the line, he got a recorded message.

I'm sorry, this number has been disconnected. If you feel you have reached this recording in error—

What? She'd given him that number just today!

Had he dialed wrong? He thought that might be the case, but when he tried again, he got the same message.

Shit. Now what was he to do? He couldn't keep pacing the floor. Something had to be wrong with Braden—and they were way up in the mountains in an unfamiliar state, completely out of Tyson's element. He didn't even know where to find a hospital if he needed one.

Grabbing the car seat, he strapped the baby inside—which wasn't easy because Braden was straining and kicking so hard—then loaded his demon son in the passenger seat of the Ferrari and drove like a bat out of hell.

By the time Tyson reached the trailer park, Braden had cried himself to sleep. The silence was absolute bliss, but he knew better than to turn around. He wasn't about to fall for the temporary nap trick. Anyway, the peace didn't last long. Tyson could hear shouting the second he opened his car door.

At first he thought it was coming from the trailer next to Dakota's. The light was on there, too. But he soon realized the neighbors were only awake because of the ruckus. He could see an old couple peeking through their blinds, trying to get a look at what was going on next door.

He was wondering himself. He couldn't imagine the father Dakota had mentioned as having "health issues" using the kind of foul language that rang so clearly on the cool night air.

"Make him stop," the old lady called out when she spotted Tyson. "Or I'm calling the cops."

Tyson closed the door of his car before the noise could wake Braden. "What's going on?"

"They're at it again," the woman answered.

"At *what* again?"

"Fighting! Can't you hear?" the man said. "He gets drunk and goes after her every now and then, more often lately than before."

"I swear, he's gonna kill her one of these days," the woman fretted.

Alcoholism was Dakota's father's "health issue"? Tyson nearly groaned aloud. What was he doing here? He was standing at the back of a neglected trailer park in the middle of the night in a town of about 1500 people, which he'd never visited before. And he had a baby with him. *His* baby.

God, how life could unravel. Maybe his grandfather had been right. Maybe he should've stayed in Montana where he belonged.

"Give me the keys!" a male voice roared. "Or so help me, Dakota—"

"Stop it! Dad, listen." She attempted to lower her voice, but Tyson could still hear her. "You're going to wake the neighbors. Then they'll call the police. Again. Do you want to spend the night in jail? You have to calm down—"

"Don't you tell me what to do!"

A scream and a thud reverberated through the air. Then a crash.

"What the hell?" Tyson sprinted for the door and, after flinging it open, found Dakota trying to keep a table between her and her attacker. A vase lay broken on the floor. Several strands of her long black hair clung to her T-shirt, as if her father had gotten hold of a handful and yanked it out. But it was the blood trickling from her mouth that enraged Tyson. Who was this old man to think he could get away with beating up his daughter?

"Sit down!" Tyson shouted.

The man who turned to face him had a yellow cast to his skin and a bulldog's sagging jowls. He also had a mean glint in his eye, and he wasn't pleased to see he had a visitor.

"Who the hell are you? Get out of my house!" He tried to raise the cane he'd been brandishing at Dakota, but Tyson wrested it from his grip. Mr. Brown wasn't all that mobile. His feet were so swollen he could hardly walk. Had Dakota been out where she could run, she would've had no problem getting away.

Tossing the cane out of reach, Tyson grabbed the older man by the shirtfront, dodged a clumsy blow and shoved him onto the couch. "I said sit down."

"Stop! You'll hurt him!" Dakota cried, but Tyson was more concerned with what her father was saying.

"You little prick, I don't even know you! Who do you think you are?"

"I'm your worst nightmare if you don't stay put and shut up," Tyson said. And then, just when Dakota's father looked as if he'd get up and try to take another swing, he blinked and his rage evaporated.

"Hey, you're… *Tyson Garnier? The* Tyson Garnier? What the hell are you doing in my trailer?" he asked, and laughed as though he hadn't been trying to kill his daughter thirty seconds earlier. "Imagine that," he said, sounding awestruck. "Tyson Garnier, right here in my living room."

Tyson's anger didn't dissipate quite so quickly. "My foot's gonna be halfway up your ass if you ever touch her again," he growled.

Mr. Brown seemed befuddled. Then the confusion cleared. "Dakota? Oh, I don't mean her no harm. She's my girl. We have a blow-up every now and then. It's tough having her tell me what to do. But she knows I wouldn't really hurt her."

Dakota avoided Tyson's gaze. Her father had already hurt her. Tyson could see that her lip was swelling, and she had a scratch on her neck.

"Have a seat." Mr. Brown waved magnanimously to an old vinyl recliner. "Dakota, can you get Tyson a beer?"

Dakota stared at her father. "He doesn't want a beer, Daddy."

"What else we got?"

"Nothing. I'm going outside to have a little talk with him."

She stepped out, leaving Tyson standing in the middle of the cramped room, adrenaline still rushing through his blood. He wanted to do something more than he'd done—but he couldn't. It wasn't his place to teach Mr. Brown a lesson. And Dakota's father was obviously a sick man.

Giving him a final glare, Tyson followed Dakota outside and waited through the apology she delivered to the neighbors.

"We're tired of this, Dakota. You need to do something about him," the old man said before he and his wife eventually turned off the lights and went back to bed.

Tyson expected Dakota to ask what he was doing at her house in the middle of the night. He was even prepared for her to be angry. He'd seen that sort of thing on TV, where an abused wife didn't appreciate outside interference. But Dakota didn't bring up what had just happened.

"Where's Braden?" she asked.

"In the car."

"How is he?"

Tyson drew a deep breath. "He's having a hard night." They both were. But after what she'd been through, he didn't feel that he could complain.

"That's why you came?"

"I tried to call. You didn't tell me your phone was disconnected."

A pained expression claimed her face. "It wasn't when I left for the cabin this afternoon."

"Maybe I dialed wrong," he said, reluctant to pile more stress on her.

"No. I noticed it myself just before I went to bed. But... I'll catch up."

He handed her the five hundred dollars he'd withdrawn at Finley's Market. Because the ATM would only allow him to get three hundred dollars in one day, he'd had to take it from two different accounts, but he had several. "This might help."

She said nothing as she slipped the money into her pocket.

"Any chance you'd consider coming back to the cabin with me?" He scratched his neck. "I'm...not very good with babies." After what he'd witnessed, he couldn't leave her behind. But he thought it better to appeal to her sympathy than challenge her pride.

A police siren sounded in the distance. Dakota tilted her head in such a way that he knew she was listening. Then she pressed her fingers to her closed eyelids. "I don't know what to do."

"I'll pay extra."

She touched her lip self-consciously. "And if they see this, they might charge him with assault."

He reached over and plucked the loose hairs off her shirt, being careful not to come too close to her breasts. "Maybe a good long stay behind bars would be the best thing for him."

"No. You saw him. He's not well. He can't sleep lying down, reacts poorly to certain foods, has to have someone keep a close watch on his meds."

"Is that why you stay?" he asked softly.

"That's part of the reason," she replied and went back inside. When she returned, she had a small bag, her purse and her keys. "Let's get out of here."

Chapter 4

Grandpa Garnier: You can just about always stand more than you think you can.

Dakota sat on the veranda of Gabe Holbrook's cabin. Along with her purse and makeup kit, she'd already deposited her small satchel in one of the guest bedrooms, and she'd rocked Braden back to sleep when he woke up after they got home. But she wasn't in any hurry to go to bed herself. She couldn't unwind, couldn't relax. She hoped to sort through her thoughts and emotions while listening to the cicadas and admiring the full moon, which seemed close enough to reach out and touch.

"You okay?"

She hadn't heard the front door open, so Tyson's presence surprised her. She'd assumed he'd retired for the night. "I'm fine," she said, but her lip was numb and swelling from the whack her father had given her with his cane, and she could still taste blood from where her teeth had cut the inside of her cheek. "I'm thinking of going back."

"What?"

She bristled at the incredulity in his voice, but she didn't really have another option. For all she knew, her father was sitting in a jail cell. And, if not for the accident *she'd* caused, he'd be just like he was before—a sober, rational, good man. "I don't expect you to understand."

"According to what your neighbors said, what happened tonight happens fairly often."

"Not so often," she argued.

"Once is too much."

He was right, but there was a lot more to it than what he knew. "It's complicated."

"You want to explain it to me?"

The scent of the surrounding forest—wet earth, evergreen trees, cool wind—filled her nostrils as she hauled in a deep breath. "Not really."

The floorboards creaked as he sat in the chair across from her. "You're more guarded than anyone I've ever met, you know that?"

She laughed aloud. "And you're an open book?"

He shrugged.

"According to *People*, you hide what you really feel behind a megawatt smile and slip out of the limelight at the first opportunity."

"They don't know anything about me."

"I think that was their point. You don't let anyone close enough."

He seemed uncomfortable with that statement, but he didn't argue with it. Getting up again, he moved restlessly around the porch, eventually leaning on the railing. "It's beautiful here."

She let him change the subject. They were employer and employee, and had only met this morning. They had no business getting into each other's personal lives. "Gabe's taken good care of the place." She sank more comfortably into the chair Gabe had built when he was first learning to work with wood after he lost his football career. "He's quite a man.

Have you been to his shop, seen some of the furniture he's building these days?"

The porch light brightened one side of Tyson's face as he turned. Only the subtle hollow beneath his cheekbone bore any shadow. "You mean the store? In town?"

"Yeah. It's across from his wife's photography studio on Main Street."

"I've been there, even bought a few things. It's in a cool building."

"An old one, built in the late 1800s. That used to be Rudy Perez's cabinet shop before he passed away."

"You know a lot about the people in your community." Tyson made that comment as if he'd experienced the exact opposite, as if he didn't know much about anyone. Which made her suspect she'd been right earlier: he didn't let anyone close.

"I've lived here my whole life." Sometimes she thought she'd never escape....

"Have you ever considered moving away?"

"Every day."

Her immediate and unqualified response seemed to surprise him. "You don't like it?"

"Can you blame me? I'm working at the pharmacy making eight bucks an hour. The folks who own it are wonderful, don't get me wrong. They'd pay me more if they could. But that isn't what I always envisioned for my life."

"So what's keeping you?" he asked.

She laughed mirthlessly. "I'll give you one guess."

"That's a pretty big sacrifice for someone who just bloodied your lip."

It was her turn to avoid answering. "I'm going inside. I need to call the police and see what's happened to him."

"I've already talked to them."

His words stopped her before she could reach the door, and she whipped around. "They called here? And you didn't tell me?"

Putting his back to her, he sat on the front steps. "I contacted them."

"Why?"

"I wanted to see what we could work out," he said over his shoulder.

Dakota had never had anyone step between her and her father before. Most people muttered that she was crazy to stick around, or they gave Skelton disgruntled looks for how he sometimes treated her. Which only made her situation worse, because she was always in the middle, trying to defend him. But this was the first time someone had contacted the police for something other than to complain about the noise. "And?" she asked hesitantly.

"We made a deal."

"You didn't think to discuss it with me first?" Anger put an edge to her voice.

He twisted to face her. "I can't imagine you'll have a problem with it. It's the best possible solution, for everyone."

Spoken like a true egotist. *He* thought it was best, so it must be best. But if he really had an answer, she was eager to hear it. She'd been searching for a way out of her current situation for years. "I'm waiting."

"They said they'd overlook what happened tonight if you'd stay away from your father in the future."

"How's that a solution?" she cried. "I'm the one who takes care of him. Half the time he doesn't eat unless I prepare his food. And we can't afford two households."

He stood up, leaned against the pillar that supported the porch and crossed his arms. "I hired the brother of one of the police officers—a Terrance Bennett—to look after him in the evenings and at night when you'd typically be off work."

"You what?"

"I hired some help."

"For how long?"

"For the next two months. That way, you can stay here. If the arrangement works, maybe you can even go back to California with me."

Dakota was speechless, torn between gratitude that this man, who'd only hired her today, would be willing to help her to such a degree, pique that he'd interfered in her situation without consulting her and excitement to think she had the opportunity to go to California. How hard could it be to raise one baby who would never want for anything, while living in a mansion—maybe on the beach—with a professional football player? Think of the places she'd get to see, the people she might meet…

Her mind raced with the possibilities. But she couldn't leave her father. He was her only family. The woman with the heavy Spanish accent who'd called her all of two times in the past ten years didn't count. She was a complete stranger. And what if he died while she was gone?

She massaged her temples, hoping to relieve the headache that had started from the blow she'd sustained to her mouth. She couldn't turn her back on her father now.

She was all he had. "I'm sorry. I can't leave Dundee. I have to stay with him."

"I just told you he'll have someone looking after him."

"It won't be the same. No one else really cares about him."

Tyson moved close and tipped up her chin, making a point of studying her fat lip. "You have *nothing* here."

She jerked away. "I have my self-respect. If I turned my back on the one person who really needs me, I wouldn't even have that."

She started into the house, but he caught her elbow. "If you go back, they'll put him in jail. They've had it, Dakota. I spoke to Chief Clanahan myself."

"They can't. I'm fine, so there's no need. And he's sick."

"That doesn't mean they'll keep putting up with his behavior. He could really hurt you, and then they'd be partially to blame because they didn't stop him when they had the chance."

Her head was pounding too hard to make such a difficult decision. "So what do I do?" she asked. She wasn't really talking to him— it was more of a rhetorical question to herself—but he answered.

"Stay here for a couple weeks. You can go into town every afternoon if you want—check in on him, make sure the new guy is doing a good job, cook his dinner, whatever. The fact that you're not living with him should mollify the police and your neighbors. Then…we'll see where things go from there."

The warmth of his fingers sank through the thin sleeve of her blouse, but she doubted he even knew he was still holding on to her. "Is this really about helping *me?*" she asked skeptically.

He glanced at the house. "I need you and you need me," he said simply and let go.

He was talking about Braden. She could tell he wanted to leave it right there, but she couldn't. Lowering her voice, she asked, "If you didn't really want him, why'd you take him?"

He stared at some mysterious point over her shoulder for so long she thought he wasn't going to answer. Finally he spoke. "I had no choice."

"You could've left him with his mother."

"Then I would've lost my self-respect," he said and went inside.

A knock at the door woke Tyson early. He scowled, but then something became apparent to him that quickly countered his irritation at being disturbed before he was ready. He couldn't hear any crying. Not one cursed peep.

He opened his eyes and lay still for a moment, holding his breath.

Yep, no crying.

"God that feels good." Rolling over, he started drifting off to sleep again when a second knock reminded him that someone was at his door.

"Come in." His voice was muffled by a pillow, but Dakota must've heard him because the door opened, and she poked her head in. "You have a phone call."

He sat up and rubbed his eyes. "I do?"

"It's Greg Higgins."

His agent. "Oh." He fell back onto the bed. "Tell him I'll call him later."

"I already told him you weren't up yet. He said it's important."

With Greg, "important" was always relative. He might be calling simply to pass along a compliment the owner of the Stingrays had paid him. Or it could have to do with Rachelle. When Tyson forked over the one mil in exchange for her signature on the custody papers, she'd agreed not to disclose the terms of their agreement—and it made Greg even madder than Tyson that she'd flagrantly disregarded that stipulation. They couldn't fix it now, but maybe something else had happened. Or maybe she was trying to renege on their deal.

"Fine." He reached for the telephone next to the bed, but Dakota spoke as his hand closed around the receiver.

"He called on line two, which I finally figured out is only in the office."

"How'd he get that number?" Tyson asked.

"It must be the one you gave him."

Which meant it had originally come from Gabe. Tyson hadn't expected two lines. This was supposed to be a *remote* cabin.

When he started to get up, the door closed so fast Tyson startled, then realized he'd fallen into bed in just his briefs last night. When he'd thrown off the covers, he hadn't even considered that his near nudity might offend Dakota. He'd lost all sensitivity to modesty after spending the past decade dressing and undressing in a locker room that allowed female reporters to wander through at will. But he found it interesting that Dakota had beat such a quick retreat.

He grinned at the memory as he pulled

on a pair of sweatpants and headed down the hall to the office. And that was when he caught the scent of bacon, eggs and…waffles? There was coffee, too. This was certainly a better morning than the one he'd spent yesterday. He couldn't wait to gorge himself. He hadn't had a solid meal since he'd picked up Braden.

The receiver was resting on the ink blotter next to the football player he'd drawn yesterday. He brought it to his ear and said hello, then realized that someone had added a number to the jersey on the paper. *His* number. Imagine that. Dakota had never mentioned football, and yet she knew his number.

"We've got problems," Greg said.

Pasty-skinned and habitually nervous, with what he called a "power haircut" and football tattoos on both forearms that looked like a failed attempt to fit in rather than an extension of his own personality, Greg worried about *everything,* which drove Tyson crazy. But it was also one of the reasons Tyson kept him around. Tyson viewed life as one big picture; Greg minded the minutiae.

"What kind of problems?" Tyson wasn't nervous. Buying the wrong kind of toilet paper could be a serious problem for Greg.

"That bitch went on *Montel Williams* yesterday."

"That bitch" was, of course, Rachelle. "She already disclosed the terms of our agreement," he said, wondering why Greg had to wake him up for this. "No use getting our jocks in a knot over that."

"But that's not all," his agent went on. "She hinted that you took advantage of her when she was down on her luck."

Tyson sat up straighter. *Now* he was worried. "*I* took advantage of *her?*"

"Yeah. She led everyone to believe…" Greg hesitated.

"What?" Tyson snapped.

"You're not going to like it."

"Say it anyway."

"That you forced her to have sex with you."

The image of Rachelle climbing into his bed filled Tyson's mind. Sleeping together had been her idea. He hadn't demanded, or even asked, for anything.

He rubbed his left temple. "Shit."

"I contacted her, told her you'd sue her for libel if she ever said that again."

"Good. I will."

"It doesn't end there."

Why not? It should. He'd fulfilled his end

of the bargain, and now he was trying to live with the fallout. "What's that supposed to mean?"

"She…she said she was thinking of going to the police and telling them the same story."

"*That I raped her?* The only thing I forced her to do was get the hell out of my house!" He drummed his fingers on the desktop. This couldn't be happening.

"It's her word against yours."

"Then I'll take a lie detector test."

"No, you won't. Those things aren't completely reliable. They depend on the interpretation of the technician. If, for some strange reason, the tech happens to screw up and we get a false positive, we'd be done for. That's a risk we can't take."

There had to be *something* they could do. "I know if we check her background, we'll find she's no virtuous saint."

"Doesn't matter. Just the claim will drag your reputation through the mud. You'll lose your endorsements. Strive Athletic Equipment is already acting funny after that newspaper article. I had to send Howard the private investigator's report that made you decide to take Braden in the first place."

"What'd he say?"

"That he wasn't happy. And he told me what we already know—with endorsements, the truth doesn't really matter. It's the public's perception of an athlete, that's all. You can't be perceived as a womanizer or a jerk or a man who has no kindness for the mother of his baby, no *feelings*."

Just because he refused to wear them on his sleeve didn't mean he didn't have them. Rachelle had cut him to the quick. Even Greg didn't understand how betrayed Tyson felt. "So what's the bottom line?"

"We've got to stop her."

"How? I don't even know why she's doing this!"

"You're kidding me, right?"

Tyson jumped to his feet. "She got the money she wanted."

"But she didn't reach her true objective; she wasn't admitted to your world."

Tyson knew Greg would understand that. The man had been trying to fit in since he started agenting. "She expected me to marry her?"

"I'll bet that was her fondest dream. Now that she knows she's not going to get it, she wants the money *and* the baby."

Turning the slats of the wooden blinds to

protect his eyes from the glare, Tyson began to pace. "She's not getting the baby. That's bullshit."

"You're committed to 'no'?"

"To the tune of $1,000,000, remember?"

"This could cost you your career, Tyson. And that's worth a lot more than a measly one mil."

He gripped the phone that much tighter. *"You're telling me to give the baby back?"*

"Having you step in scared her. She knows we're watching now. Maybe she'll take better care of him."

Tyson didn't believe it for a minute. He'd never met anyone more self-serving than Rachelle Rochester, no one more coldly calculating. That she came off so sweet and innocent made her all the more dangerous.

Even if she took better care of Braden's physical needs, how would it be to have her for a mother? Tyson had always thought his own mother was too consumed with building her title and escrow company to be a good parent. He'd become nothing more than a painful reminder of the only man she'd ever really loved. This would be worse. Braden would fall second to mere vanity and greed.

And Rachelle would use him shamelessly until he turned eighteen.

Tyson wouldn't allow it. "Tell her she can go to hell."

There was a long pause. Obviously his agent wasn't happy with his response. "Tyson, with your knee the way it is…"

"What are you saying, Greg? What does my knee have to do with this?"

"I'm saying you need to be cautious. You're not as young as you used to be. I don't know if you can afford this kind of fight. Maybe it's better to concede this round."

Concede? To a crook and a phony? *Never*. If there was one thing his mother *had* taught him, it was to fight when he felt he had to. "Whose side are you on?" he asked and slammed down the phone.

There was a rattle of plates, and he turned in time to see Dakota hurrying away from the open doorway. She'd obviously been bringing him breakfast—but had changed her mind when she heard him screaming into the receiver.

Damn. She'd caught him at a vulnerable moment.

He considered calling her back so he could smooth over his temperamental display. He didn't want her whispering about him to the locals. Who knew what might leak out? The press would follow him here eventually. The last thing he needed was to do anything that could be interpreted as supporting the terrible things Rachelle was saying about him.

But he was too angry to pretend he wasn't. Besides, he no longer felt like eating.

Chapter 5

*Grandpa Garnier: Never kick a
cow chip on a hot day.*

After Tyson's phone call, the house fell silent, except for the television, which was tuned to *Good Morning America,* and an occasional squeal from Braden as he crawled around the living room. While Dakota did the dishes, she wondered what kind of news the man Greg Higgins had delivered to Tyson. Clearly, her employer wasn't pleased with whatever he'd heard.

A few minutes later, a creak on the stairs alerted her that he was coming. Then he appeared wearing basketball shorts, a Stingrays T-shirt and tennis shoes.

He still hadn't shaved. Maybe he was trying to make himself less recognizable. He obviously didn't want to draw any attention, or he wouldn't be staying by himself in a friend's cabin way out in the boonies.

"Hungry?" she asked, trying to pretend she hadn't just tried to bring him a tray.

"No." He jerked his head toward the baby. "How's he doing?"

"Good. He ate some cereal and mashed banana for breakfast, with a bottle of juice."

Braden gave his father a beaming smile. But Tyson, who was already wearing a scowl, didn't acknowledge it or respond.

"And what about you?" he asked.

Dakota had been doing her best to keep her face averted when possible. She knew her lip and the bruise on her cheek looked worse than they would if she'd had the chance to shower and use the cover-up that came in handy when she needed to hide the remnants of her and her father's fights. "Better," she said, rinsing off another dish.

"Let's see."

She kept working. "There's nothing to see."

"Look at me. How bad is it?"

Again she tried to shrug him off. "It's fine."

He didn't respond, but he stood in the center of the room watching her—she could feel his attention—so she finally relented and turned.

His eyes zeroed in on her lip. "Damn, he clipped you pretty good."

"It'll be better tomorrow."

"And that bruise on your cheek?"

"I've got something I can put on it. You won't be able to see it."

"Just because you can't see it doesn't mean it isn't there."

What could she say? She was getting used to hiding the worst of her injuries. The cut on her arm still hadn't healed. She was afraid it was getting infected.

"I'm going out for a jog," he said and took a water bottle from the cupboard above the fridge.

Dakota put another plate in the dishwasher. "It's about to rain. You might want to run inside. Gabe's got two different treadmills back there." The workout room took up as much square footage as the living room, dining room and kitchen combined, and was better equipped than most professional spas. Dakota had already wandered through it, admiring the expensive equipment and imagining how she could look if she had access to that every day.

"I don't care about a little rain. Running in place has never made much sense to me."

The door slammed shut, leaving Dakota alone with Braden. "Don't worry about him," she told the baby. "He's just in a bad mood."

Braden sat on his diapered behind and jabbered as he played with her keys, which she'd given him because he didn't seem to have any toys.

"I'll get you some blocks when I go to town today," she promised.

Finished drying the last pan, she scooped the baby into her arms and laughed as he planted a wet kiss on her chin. She knew the behavior had more to do with teething than affection, but it felt good all the same. "You're something else, you know that?" she told him, tickling him under the chin.

He giggled and buried his face in her neck, and she hugged him close. He felt so solid and round and soft. He was going to be big, just like his daddy.

She could get used to this job, she decided.

She already liked it more than anything else she'd done.

"If your father's not going to use the gym, maybe I will," she said. "Then you and I will go outside and see what needs to be done to plant a garden."

As long as she'd be at the cabin so much, she figured she might as well take advantage of all the amenities. The cupboards in the kitchen, and the freezer in the mudroom, were so well stocked maybe she'd even do some cooking. She'd found steaks, shrimp, crab, even a couple of lobster tails—and Tyson acted as if he didn't care what she did as long as she kept the baby happy.

She thought of the magazines piled in her bedroom in the trailer—mostly fan magazines because they were quick reads, but there were plenty of food and wine magazines, too. Mr. and Mrs. Cottle at the pharmacy gave her the outdated ones they pulled from the shelves. When she was young, she'd dreamed of becoming a gourmet cook and had spent a lot of time since then studying food preparation and experimenting with various menus.

Later today, she'd pick up a few recipes she wanted to try. She needed to check on her father anyway. But she didn't really want to see him. His irrational and violent behavior wasn't easy to forget. After he cut her last time, he'd promised he would never raise a hand to her again.

She ran her tongue over her sore lip. Since he'd started drinking, he was no longer the man she'd once known and loved.

She wouldn't visit today. Nor would she call, she decided. Mrs. Duluth would alert her if there was anything serious going on. Feeling better, she hurried to exercise before Tyson came home.

Tyson forced himself to run uphill so fast he felt as if his lungs might burst. With so many personal problems and so much competition on the field, he had to be better, stronger, faster. *Mind over matter*, he reminded himself, and kept going even when he was convinced he'd drop if he didn't quit. His knee was starting to hurt—he knew a trainer would tell him to take it easy—but he was tired of giving in to the weakness. He wasn't ready to leave the NFL. He still had five good years in him.

If only his body would cooperate.

As long as he could play, the endorsements

wouldn't matter, he told himself. He'd still be gainfully employed. And if he played well, he could outlast the scandal over Rachelle's accusations and, eventually, maybe he'd win a few of them back.

But that wasn't very realistic, and he knew it. By then, he'd be older and that much closer to retirement. It was the young guys the big names wanted—the ones with a perfect reputation.

"Damn her," he said aloud. Then, unaccustomed to the altitude, he finally stopped and bent over to suck some cool, mountain air into his burning lungs.

He had to go back to California, he realized, had to meet with Rachelle. Maybe he could talk some sense into her. He knew it wasn't likely. She had no conscience or she wouldn't have done what she'd done in the first place. But what other option did he have? He wouldn't relinquish Braden. He was convinced taking the baby had been the best thing to do. How else could he be sure his son would be raised right?

But he couldn't stand by and let her destroy his reputation and possibly his career.

"I can be back tomorrow," he promised himself and headed for the cabin.

* * *

Tyson's visit to California didn't turn out to be the quick trip he'd intended. He couldn't get a flight out of Boise until the following morning, and when he reached L.A., Rachelle wouldn't respond to his attempts to contact her. After three days, he finally showed up at her place unannounced, only to be confronted by a man who claimed to be her bodyguard.

"I'm afraid I'm going to have to ask you to leave, Mr. Garnier." The giant Samoan left the security chain in place and spoke through the crack. "You can get in a lot of trouble for being here."

Garnier wasn't intimidated by the hulky bodyguard. He faced men who weighed one and a half times his weight for a living. "Why? All I want to do is talk to her."

"I'm sorry, but you're violating a restraining order."

"A *what?*" Tyson cried in confusion. Restraining orders were for dangerous, violent men. He'd never struck a woman in his life.

The man shoved some papers through the crack. "Consider yourself served."

Tyson stared down at the official-looking paperwork.

"You can't come within two city blocks of Ms. Rochester or you could be arrested," the bodyguard informed him. "The hearing is in six days."

Disbelieving, Tyson scanned the fine print. It was true. Rachelle had filed for a restraining order. "Wait!" Tyson put a hand on the door so the Samoan couldn't close it. "The only thing I should be arrested for is being stupid enough to get mixed up with her in the first place," he nearly shouted.

The man glanced nervously at Tyson's hand. "The cops are already on their way."

Tyson's muscles bunched in impotent rage. "This is nuts!"

"Just because you're a famous football player doesn't mean you have the right to harass women."

"*Harass* them!" This time Tyson did shout. "When have I done *anything* to her? She's a freakin' parasite, that's what she is. It's *my* money that's paying your salary!"

At Tyson's sudden burst of temper, the Samoan stepped back. "You're losing your cool," he said. "Please leave before the police have to drag you away."

No, this was too unfair! "Look." Rolling up the papers, he shoved them in his pocket and forced himself to lower his voice. There was no need for a hearing, no need for this to get out of hand. All he wanted was for Rachelle to live up to the agreement she'd made. "You can stay in the room if you want. Or bring her to the door so we can talk through the crack. I'm not going to touch her. I swear." He lifted his hands to convince the man of his honesty. "I just want to speak to her. I need to know what's going on."

A female voice said something in the background that led Tyson to believe Rachelle was close by, but the bodyguard shut the door before Tyson could address her directly. A moment later, the Samoan opened it again, but only as far as the security chain would allow. "Sorry. Ms. Rochester feels she'd be unsafe."

A tic began in Tyson's cheek. "In what way?"

"She says you're not stable."

Until that moment, Tyson had never seriously considered hurting anyone. "Rachelle, what the hell are you doing?" he yelled. "We had a deal. You got every penny you asked for. What more do you want?"

"I want my baby back," he heard her say. Then the door closed again.

Tyson banged on the wooden panel. He

even went around back to see if he could get Rachelle's attention through the windows. He hoped the police were really on their way— maybe they'd help him sort this out. But, evidently, she'd called the media, too. Because it was a reporter who showed up first—and snapped a picture of him climbing over her fence, the set of his jaw so rigid that, when it was published in the paper the following day, he looked ready to kill.

Tyson had been gone for ten days when Dakota spotted his picture on the cover of one of the tabloids. She was in Finley's Market, picking up more baby food, and had Braden in the shopping cart. Tired of being strapped in, the baby kept holding his arms out for her to pick him up, but she was too mesmerized by what she saw.

Football Star Stalking Ex-Lover

What a headline! Her heart raced as she grabbed the paper and began to read:

Tyson Garnier, five-time all-pro wide receiver for the Los Angeles Stingrays, was caught Sunday trying to force his way into the home of twenty-four-year-old onetime waitress Rachelle Rochester.

Although the pair have a nine-month-old baby together, friends of Ms. Rochester say they've never been a couple. One woman, who agreed to speak only upon condition of anonymity, says Garnier became obsessed with Rochester after spotting her at the restaurant where she worked, going so far as to follow her home and insist she accompany him to his place. She was gone nearly three weeks, during which time her roommate filed a missing persons report.

Ming Lee is the owner of the restaurant where Rochester worked. "She just disappeared," Lee said of her waitress. "When she came back, I asked her, 'Where'd you go?' And she said she was kidnapped."

Another friend adds, "When Rach finally resurfaced, she told me a bizarre tale about how this professional football player had kept her locked up as a sex slave, and forced her to do all kinds of kinky things."

If that were true, why didn't Ms. Rochester go to the police? Dakota wondered. Or had she tried? Did Tyson have connections that would enable him to clean up his mess without any penalty?

As if in direct answer to her question, the article continued:

When asked why Ms. Rochester never filed a police report on the incident, her roommate, Adrienne LeFever said, "She told me it was because no one would believe her. Tyson Garnier's a star athlete. Everyone loves him. She's a lowly waitress who barely graduated with a GED, poor thing. My guess is he paid her off."

"It's not true."

The voice cut through Dakota's concentration. Lowering the paper, she found Gabriel Holbrook sitting in his wheelchair next to the newsstand. His black hair was wet, suggesting he was fresh from a shower, and she was pretty sure he'd just shaved, because there was a tiny nick in his cleft chin. With his dark coloring, vivid blue eyes, massive shoulders and disarming grin, he was as handsome as ever.

"They're looking to sell papers," he explained.

The story was gripping, she had to give them that. And a little frightening, if it was true.

"Of course." She quickly put the paper away. Tyson was her employer. Thanks to him, she'd be able to make the back payments on her mortgage and catch up on most of her other bills. Besides, Braden was so sweet and loveable she couldn't imagine him coming from anyone as twisted as that article implied.

In any case, she had no complaints against Tyson personally. Everything he'd said and done where she was concerned had been normal enough. He'd called to check on Braden every night since he'd been gone, and had been polite, if slightly aloof. Before he'd left, he hired Terrance Bennett to look after her dad, just as he'd promised, which seemed to be working out okay despite her father's displeasure at having "a babysitter." Tyson had told her to go ahead and enjoy any food she found in the house, and when she'd expressed an interest in gardening, he'd gotten permission from Gabe for her to plant what she wanted.

Then again, she wasn't the type of woman to inspire obsession, especially from someone as handsome and famous as Tyson. Her only boyfriend had broken up with her when he realized she wouldn't leave her father and go with him to the oil fields of Colorado.

"Where's Hannah?" she asked.

"At the studio. She has a couple shoots today."

"I should have her take Braden's picture."

"Sounds like the job's working out."

"I love it."

"You're not getting lonely up there all by yourself?"

"No. Not yet, anyway." She'd never been to an expensive resort, but she couldn't imagine it being any more enjoyable than Gabe's cabin. She'd been able to work out and lift weights, use the Jacuzzi tub, build a fire in the fireplace when the air grew brisk at night, take Braden on hikes through the forest by putting him in the baby carrier she'd bought with the money Tyson had left for her to use. She'd put in an entire spring garden, as well, complete with tomatoes, zucchini, squash, corn, carrots, peas and string beans. And she'd been driving Tyson's Ferrari. Hannah had watched Braden while Dakota went to the airport with Tyson so she could bring the car home. For the first time, she'd been glad that her own car had a manual transmission.

Otherwise, she wouldn't have known how to drive the Ferrari.

The only blight on the whole week was the way her father behaved whenever she went home to check on him. He treated her as if it was a personal betrayal that she'd involved Terrance in their lives. "They feedin' ya enough caviar over there?" he'd taunted her yesterday.

"I think I'm getting spoiled," she told Gabe with a laugh. "I've been meaning to tell you that you don't have to hire the housekeeper that came on Wednesday. I'd be happy to keep the place clean while I'm there."

"I appreciate it, but I can't do that to Rosalee. I think she really counts on the income."

"See that? I don't have to clean. And now I don't even have to feel guilty about it. It's like staying at Club Med."

"You deserve the break, Dakota." Gabe was a little too serious, serious enough to make her uncomfortable. She didn't want him to pity her. She hated that.

"Tyson will probably be back soon," she said, trying to keep the conversation on the light side.

"He never should've left."

There were several gawkers gathering a few feet away. Like Tyson, Gabe attracted stares. It was inspiring just to see him get around so capably. But he was also a local hero. Everyone was eager to get some face time with him, so they could talk about next year's high school football season, if nothing else. High school football was The Town Event.

"Why did he?" she asked, lowering her voice so she wouldn't be overheard. It was none of her business and she knew it, but she was hoping to hear something that would bolster her faith in Braden's father.

She glanced at the photo of Tyson scaling Rachelle Rochester's fence. With that glint in his eye, most *men* would scramble to get out of his way.

"He keeps his personal business to himself. But if I had to venture a guess, I'd say Braden's mother is causing some trouble."

Was it him—or her? "That's too bad."

Gabe looked her over. "You losing weight?"

She smiled, suddenly shy. "A little. I've got a lot more to go."

"Not a lot. You look fantastic."

She felt herself flush. "Thanks."

"Are you enjoying the baby?"

Dakota took Braden, who was starting to cry, from the cart. "Very much!"

The babe quieted immediately. "Ba...ba... ba...ba," he cooed and nearly broke her nose with his eagerness to give her another wet kiss.

Gabe laughed at the collision. "That kid keeps growing, he'll be a lineman someday."

Dakota hugged Braden close. She loved his chubby body, especially the soft rolls at his thighs and the place where he would one day grow a wrist. "He's in the ninety-ninth percentile for height and the eighty-seventh percentile for weight. I looked it up on the Internet."

"Sounds like Paul Bunyan's kid to me."

She brushed her lips across Braden's temple, enjoying the scent of his shampoo. "It's not as if his father is small. Tyson's at least six-four, isn't he?"

"Around there."

"And Braden's going to be every bit as handsome."

An odd expression flitted across Gabe's face. Or maybe it was her imagination.

"Is something wrong?" she asked.

He seemed slightly hesitant, as though he was unsure whether or not to speak his mind.

She shifted the baby, so her hip could help support his weight. "What is it?"

"I hope I did the right thing."

"What do you mean?"

"Nothing." He smiled again, but it wasn't quite as genuine as before. Now it was tempered with a hint of worry.

"Gabe?"

A furrow formed between his eyebrows. "I don't want to see you get hurt, Dakota. I envisioned this as a great opportunity for you, but—"

She waved her free hand in an unconcerned motion. "I'm not going to get hurt."

"I hope not. Lord knows you deserve a lot better than what you've had. I'd like to see you get it. But…"

"Tyson would never go for a plain girl like me?" Dakota's chest constricted. It was one thing to know the truth in her heart and another to have someone she admired as much as Gabe point it out to her. But she added a scoffing laugh so he wouldn't know he'd hurt her. "Come on, Gabe. I know he's way out of my league."

Gabe's eyes fell to Braden. "I wasn't talking about Tyson."

Chapter 6

*Grandpa Garnier: Don't let so much
reality into your life that there's
no room for dreamin'.*

It was late, yet most of the lights were on in
the cabin. Was Braden back on the rampage
and keeping Dakota up?

Tyson sort of hoped so. She'd stepped in
and taken over as if caring for a baby was the
easiest thing in the world. Which made him
feel like an absolute idiot.

He thought of their phone conversations
over the past week: *He's such a good baby...
Slept all night, even though I'm pretty sure*

he's cutting another tooth... He's napping right now...

From the sounds of it, Braden had been nothing but sheer joy.

"Anything else I can do for you, Mr. Garnier?"

Tyson realized he was still sitting in the back of the cab, staring at the house. "No, thanks."

He paid the man, then waited as the cabby pulled his suitcase out of the trunk. The plane ride from Los Angeles to Boise hadn't been that long, but Tyson still felt cramped, rumpled and exhausted. Probably because the days he'd spent in California had been a nightmare. When he appeared in court after being served, Rachelle had presented the picture of him scaling her fence and claimed he'd been calling her night and day and had nearly broken down her door in an attempt to "get to her." With her bodyguard there to give witness, the judge had granted the restraining order. Tyson had requested a meeting so they could come to some sort of agreement, but Rachelle refused to talk to him unless he was willing to hand over the baby.

What really upset him was that she wasn't acting out of regret for having given up her child. Regret he could understand, maybe even forgive. Regret was what a normal mother would be feeling. But Rachelle still cared more about the money than Braden. She hadn't offered Tyson a dime of his money back. Instead, she'd been spotted all over Beverly Hills, laughing and shopping with her best friend.

"It'll be a cold day in hell when I give in to her," he muttered.

"Excuse me?" the cabby said. The squat, fifty-something-year-old had a hold of his luggage and was prepared to bring it to the house.

"I've got this." Tyson gave him a hefty tip and took the suitcase.

"All right, then. Have a good night, Mr. Garnier. It was a pleasure driving you. You call me any time you need a cab, you hear? I'll come from Boise if you want. Just like tonight. No problem."

"I appreciate that."

"Okay. You be careful with that knee now," the cabby called after him. "I can't wait till next season. I'm a big Stingrays fan. Purple and silver. Those are my colors, too. To me, those are as American as red, white and blue. But you've got some work yet to do.

Jerry Rice still holds a few of those receiving records."

"That he does." Tyson threw the words over his shoulder, but he knew, unless his knee healed up better than it was, he wasn't going to be a threat to Jerry Rice or anyone else.

Finally the driver got back in the cab and drove off in a cloud of exhaust, a last remnant of the big city Tyson had left behind. The pollution smelled completely foreign among the fresh air and pine trees and, for a moment, he felt just as out of place. There was a woman inside the cabin who was caring for his baby. He didn't know her or the baby, not really. He'd never even imagined finding himself in such a situation.

"A man's got to do what a man's got to do," he mumbled, repeating what his grandfather would've said. He had to face the consequences of his actions, shoulder the responsibility for his mistakes and move on, right? What other choice did he have? None that would allow him to hold up his head.

Taking a deep breath, he went inside.

The music that greeted him came as a surprise. It wasn't western, which was what most folks around here listened to. It was classical, and it was loud.

"Dakota?" he called.

She didn't answer but she was obviously around. A single glass of wine sat on the counter and a fire crackled in the fireplace. The scent of oregano and garlic permeated an immaculate kitchen that seemed far homier than when he'd left it. Fresh fruits and vegetables filled a basket on the countertop; a loaf of bread—homemade from the looks of it—was wrapped in plastic next to the fruit.

Taking his bag upstairs with him, he poked his head into the baby's room. The light was on, but the crib was empty. He noticed the subtle scent of baby powder, reluctantly recognized the life Braden and Dakota were breathing into this cabin, which had felt so vacant when he arrived, and moved on to Dakota's bedroom. It was empty, too. Only it didn't smell like baby powder. Dakota's room smelled like spaghetti sauce and homemade bread, and a light kind of fragrance that could come only from a woman.

It certainly wasn't the expensive "business" scent he associated with his mother. It wasn't reminiscent of anything he'd experienced on Grandpa Garnier's ranch. And it wasn't even close to the musky perfumes used by the women he'd dated in the past. Yet he liked it. Enough to linger for a moment.

The low hum of a television finally drew him around the bend in the hall, where he encountered a light peeking through a partially closed door—the door to his bedroom.

Swinging it open, Tyson saw that his bed was still made. Dakota held the baby in a rocking chair she must've dragged in from the nursery so she could watch TV. She didn't stir as he came in. She and Braden were both asleep.

Tyson put his bag on the bed before walking around to wake her. But what he saw stopped him cold. She was wearing an old football sweatshirt of his, along with his *briefs*. The drawers she'd taken them from were still hanging open.

His eyebrows shot up. What was this all about? "So you're a cross-dresser?" he said.

She jumped at the sound of his voice, and he took the baby, who stirred but didn't wake, before she could accidentally dump him onto the carpet.

"Tyson!" Blinking rapidly, she glanced around the room. When she recognized that it wasn't her own, she flushed deeply. "I'm sorry. This…this isn't as strange as it might seem."

He was more than a little curious to hear her explanation. "Because…"

"I don't usually come in here or get into your stuff. After I put Braden to bed, I wanted to shower, but—" she rubbed a hand over her face, still struggling to rid her mind of the cobwebs "—the pipes in the hall squeak so badly I was afraid it'd wake him. So I used yours."

"And the clothes?"

"Braden started crying as I was getting out of the shower. Since I'd already shoved what I'd been wearing down the laundry chute, I had to grab something else—fast."

"And that was my briefs."

"Your pants would never have stayed up." She bit her lip self-consciously. "I'm sorry."

"Don't be," he said with a shrug. "I'd steal your underwear if I was in a hurry."

She eyed him as if she wasn't sure he was joking, and he grinned to let her know he was. Now that he was fairly confident she wasn't acting like some obsessed fan, he didn't care that she was wearing his clothes. He was distracted by the mental image her explanation had created, and wondering what it might've been like to come home and find her *naked* in his room.

His body reacted immediately. She was soft and curvy, with damn pretty legs, and for some reason, she suddenly seemed far more enticing than a woman who was model thin.

Only because she was different, he told himself. It was the "I would never take advantage of you" sentiment she'd expressed the day he'd hired her that tempted him. Or maybe it was even more basic than that. Maybe it was the scent of baby powder, spaghetti sauce and flowers that clung to her. None of it screamed sex kitten. She seemed… *safe.*

He had the sudden impulse to bury his nose in her neck and feel the solace her soft skin could provide—the solace that had been missing in his life for eighteen months. Until she stood. Then her breasts swayed against the cotton fabric of his sweatshirt and his desires centered on touching other parts of her body. He'd spoken to her on the phone every night for ten days, but she was still largely a stranger, naked inside *his* clothes. He found that incredibly erotic.

Okay, maybe he did want sex. Eighteen months of celibacy was beginning to wear on him. But not hot sex. Not porn movie kind of sex. He wanted *comfort* sex. And that scared him more than anything because it suggested that he was getting old and tired, losing his edge. He was in the NFL, for crying out loud. He was supposed to be interested in Playboy Bunnies, not average, everyday women who were a little on the plump side.

Scowling so she'd never guess his thoughts, he tore his focus away from her breasts. But when he met her eyes, he knew she'd noticed exactly what had caught his attention.

"I'll put Braden to bed," she muttered, almost breathlessly. Then she took the baby and left the room.

After Dakota settled Braden in his bed, she went straight to her room and changed out of Tyson's clothes. She brought them downstairs to the laundry, where she dropped the sweatshirt on top of a pile of colors and put his underwear into the washing machine with the whites. The whole time, she tried not to think about the hunger she'd seen in his face a few minutes earlier. She hadn't witnessed that kind of expression very often, but she knew she hadn't mistaken the appreciation in his eyes.

Or maybe she *had* mistaken it. Why would he look at her that way? He could have any woman. It wasn't as though she was all that pretty.

But she was convenient, and professional athletes weren't known for discriminating. Because of Rachelle, Tyson had a worse reputation than most. So why was she so flattered—and excited? She'd be stupid to get mixed up with him. It would be a blatant use on his part. And, other than limited groping with her high school boyfriend, she didn't have the experience to handle it. Her father had watched her far too closely when she was young, and after graduation all viable candidates either married or moved on. She hadn't even dated in over a year. The last time she'd gone out it was on a blind date set up by her employers at the pharmacy. The guy made funny sounds when he ate and couldn't get over the fact that she wasn't willing to put her father in a facility, even though she'd tried to explain how miserable he would be in such a place.

Tyson's eyes flashed in her mind—and again she felt that strange tingle that had coursed through her in his bedroom. Evidently those latent sexual urges were building. When she'd been standing before him, every nerve had quivered with the desire to be touched.

"Don't be stupid," she muttered.

"Excuse me?"

Whirling around, Dakota spotted Tyson in the doorway. "Sorry, just thinking aloud."

"You don't have to wash those." He indicated the clothes she'd borrowed. "You couldn't have been wearing them for more than an hour."

"It's no problem. I'll have them back in your room by morning. I feel so silly. I didn't expect you home tonight. But I should've considered the possibility, since you didn't call." She had postponed her nightly workout, waiting to talk to him. She'd grown accustomed to his calls, had started anticipating those brief few minutes when she told him about Braden and all she'd done in the day.

"Go ahead and go to bed. We can worry about laundry tomorrow."

"I'm just getting a load started."

When he came into the room, the dimensions seemed to magically shrink to Lilliputian proportions. Probably because she was still so embarrassed and would rather avoid him.

"How's your father doing?"

"Fine. Good." Or maybe not so good, considering Skelton would scarcely talk to her. Even though Mrs. Duluth and Terrance Bennett both told her his condition seemed relatively unchanged, he'd been complaining more than ever about his health. Was he trying to make her feel guilty for leaving him?

"I'm glad." He peered at her a little more closely. "Looks like the bruising is gone."

"It didn't last long."

"He hasn't acted up again, has he?"

"A couple days ago he got drunk before Terrance arrived and tried to bar Terrance from coming in, at which point he stumbled and knocked over a lamp. But Terrance seemed to gain control of the situation okay. Dad was sleeping off his bender when I checked on him the next morning. He wasn't hurt."

When Tyson didn't respond, she looked up to see why. He didn't seem to be paying attention. He was frowning at the pile of laundry where she'd thrown his sweatshirt. "Would you rather I wash that first?" she asked, uncertain of his expression.

Crossing the room, he picked it up. "Is this *blood?*"

He indicated a large red spot on the inside sleeve, and Dakota's stomach lurched as she realized it was from the knife wound on her arm. She'd taken off the bandage before her shower, and when she pulled on Tyson's sweatshirt, she'd been in too big a hurry to remember how inflamed and infected it was getting. "I'm *so* sorry," she said, mortified. "I can get it off. Here, give it to me. I'll use a laundry stick and—"

"What's it from?" he interrupted.

She didn't want to say. She couldn't believe she'd helped herself to his clothing, then soiled it with something most people would be afraid to touch for fear of acquiring an infectious disease. What had she been thinking? She *hadn't* been thinking. She'd grown too comfortable here in the cabin while he was gone, living as if it was all hers. "My arm. I…scratched it out-outside and didn't know it was bleeding when I put on your shirt. But I can get the blood out," she repeated.

"When did it happen?"

"This morning."

"That's a deep scratch if it's still bleeding in the middle of the night."

She couldn't tell if he was suspicious or simply stating the obvious. "It's nothing."

"Then you won't mind if I take a look at it."

She kept her focus on what she was doing. "Not right now. It's too hard to reach."

"You're wearing a T-shirt under that sweat-shirt, aren't you?"

If she continued to protest, he'd know something was up. Hoping the injury didn't appear as angry now that she'd had a shower, she peeled back the zip-up sweatshirt, re-moved the bandage and flashed the wound at him. She tried to cover it up again right away—but he caught the hand that held the bandage and dragged her into better light.

"Son of a bitch," he muttered when he saw it and, for some inexplicable reason, a lump rose in Dakota's throat. Her father had done this to her. The man who'd raised her. The man she was trying so desperately to stand by.

"It might be a little infected," she managed to say, wishing her heart would stop its crazy pounding. Or that Tyson's face would clear and he'd simply take her word for it. Or that he'd realize it was stupid for him to care. He was a short-timer here. What did it matter to him if she had a cut on her arm?

"That's deep, all right. Especially for a scratch," he said. "How'd you get it again?"

She couldn't meet his eyes, was afraid he'd read the truth if she did. "On a—a tree branch."

"Pretty clean cut for a jagged tree branch."

That was definitely suspicion. And he was watching her too closely. For the first time since she'd come to the cabin, she wished she was in her room at home, where she didn't have to worry about anyone prying. The situation with her father was humiliating, and she felt foolish—even childish—for lying. But the truth would get her father into more trouble than she could get him out of. And he hadn't meant to do it. Not really. "Looks different now. Wasn't much to start with."

"That so."

It wasn't a question. "Yes, of course." She managed to jerk her arm away. "I'll get your clothes clean. Don't worry about that, okay? Good night." She tried to slip past him, but he inserted himself between her and the doorway.

"Dakota, that scratch is more like a cut."

She said nothing.

"And it looks like it's been there awhile," he said softly.

She hated the sympathy in his voice. *You have your own problems. Quit poking through mine.* "I've been putting antiseptic on it."

"That isn't enough. You should see a doctor."

She was tempted to argue. It was nothing; it'd heal. But she knew contradicting him would only push him into taking a stronger stand, and she certainly didn't want him getting involved.

So she capitulated, thinking he might forget about it if she did. "If it doesn't improve by tomorrow morning, I will. Get some sleep, okay?" The brief smile she offered him seemed to struggle against more gravity than normal, but this time he let her go.

Tyson paced his room for almost an hour, then went downstairs to see if Dakota was still up. They were forty minutes from the closest town—he had no idea where a doctor was beyond that—but he didn't want to wait until morning to see something done about that cut. There were red streaks going up her arm, which meant the infection was spreading. He was afraid she'd end up with blood poisoning if they didn't act soon. But he doubted she'd listen to him, even if he offered to drive her to a hospital. She hadn't been very receptive before. And when he ventured into the hall to talk to her, he found the music off, the place dark. She was already in bed.

He hesitated at her closed door, tempted to wake her. Then he retreated. No doubt she had her own reasons for not seeking help. He suspected he knew what those reasons were and was torn as to whether or not to support them. Regardless of her love for the old man, her father had to be stopped. But then, as long as he was around to keep an eye on her, Tyson supposed he could let the Skelton situation slide. For now. He'd have to make a more permanent arrangement when it came time for him to leave.

Meanwhile, maybe he could call in a few favors and get her the help—along with the privacy—she needed.

The sound of Tyson's voice, coming from downstairs, woke Dakota the next morning. For a minute, she thought she'd overslept, that Tyson was talking to Braden, but she could hear the baby playing in his crib across the hall. He'd shriek every now and then because he was getting restless, but he hadn't yet broken into a full "come get me *now*" cry.

Tyson didn't have the baby, which meant her employer was probably on the phone. It was going to be strange living in such close proximity, Dakota decided. Especially after having the place to herself for more than a week. It felt like he was moving into her house, instead of the other way around.

Getting up, she started across the hall, then remembered what she'd gone to bed thinking about—what had happened in Tyson's room last night—and paused in front of the mirror. Tyson had wanted her sexually. Just for a brief second. But he'd wanted her.

This morning, with her hair mussed, and the pattern of her blanket imprinted on her cheek, she could easily believe that the incident had been more fantasy than reality. But her breasts weren't bad. And she was almost positive he'd been looking there.

She lifted her shirt to take a candid peek at herself. It had been a long time since she'd evaluated her own sex appeal. She'd let the years when a young woman usually experimented and dated slip by unfulfilled. Now she felt middle-aged—probably because most of the people in her life were a generation older.

But she hadn't felt old last night. Standing

in Tyson's room with him staring at her like he was two seconds away from carrying her off to bed made her feel young and vibrant and very much alive.

"Dakota?"

Letting out a startled yelp, she pulled down her shirt. Tyson was at her door. Her heart pounded at the thought that he might've poked his head in, expecting her to be in bed, and spotted her gawking at her bare chest. It was bad enough that she'd embarrassed herself last night by being caught in his underwear.

"Yes?" she said, struggling to keep her voice level.

"Get up. We're going into town."

"We?"

"You want to check on your father, don't you?"

She did and she didn't. But whether she wanted to or not didn't matter. She'd do it anyway. "Yes."

"Great. I'll take you."

"In the Ferrari?"

"Why not?"

"Where will we put Braden?"

There was a slight hesitation, as if he'd

forgotten his son. "I guess we'll have to take your car," he said at last.

She couldn't imagine Tyson Garnier in *the Bomber*. Was it even clean? She doubted it. It didn't look any better when she washed and waxed it, so she rarely bothered, and it was usually only she and her father who ever saw the inside. "What about Braden's breakfast?"

"We'll eat out."

"Do I have time for a shower?" *Say yes, please!*

"What time does the pharmacy open?"

The *pharmacy?* "Ten. Why?"

"It's a quarter after eight right now. We'll leave in an hour."

"Why are we going to the pharmacy?" she called, but he'd already walked away.

Hearing his footsteps recede, she lifted her tank top again and turned from one side to the other. Not bad, she decided. Some women would pay big bucks to have breasts like hers. But…she studied the rest of her body. The four pounds she'd lost wasn't enough. She needed to keep working out.

Chapter 7

*Grandpa Garnier: If you get to thinking
you're a person of some influence,
try ordering someone else's dog around.*

Dakota tried not to feel self-conscious about
the way her car shimmied whenever they
came to a stop. She'd managed to hurry out
of the cabin ahead of Tyson and throw away
all the trash she'd collected in the back seat—
mostly wrappers from Arctic Flyer, where
she often went for lunch. But there was nothing she could do about the smell. One window didn't close all the way, so if it rained
unexpectedly while she was at work, water

rolled in and soaked the seats and carpet. She always did her best to air it out afterward, but the scent of mildew lingered.

At least the radio worked—or would when they cleared the mountains and could get a signal. For now they rode in silence, except for the Maxima's overloud motor and the occasional squeal or gurgle from Braden, who sat in the back seat playing with his teething ring. She'd given him a bottle to tide him over until they reached the restaurant, but she knew he'd be getting hungry soon.

"When's the last time you had your oil changed?" Tyson asked.

Dakota had no idea. Oil was way down her list of priorities. She was generally more worried about scraping money together for gas. "I'm not sure."

"Maybe we should drop off the car while we're having breakfast. Is there a Quick Lube or something in town?"

"No."

"There has to be someplace to get the oil changed. I can't imagine everyone in Dundee drives to Boise for that kind of thing."

"They don't. They go to Booker Robinson. He owns the only repair shop."

"We'll swing by there, then."

She glanced at him. An oil change cost $24.95, and she didn't have the money. She'd put all the money he'd already paid her toward overdue bills. But she didn't want to admit she was *that* broke, especially to a man who owned a Ferrari. "Come to think of it, I'm pretty sure I just did it," she said.

He slung an arm over the steering wheel. "In the past few months?"

She stared at the scenery flying past her window. "Yeah."

Either he didn't believe her or he didn't care because as soon as they arrived in Dundee, he spotted Booker T & Son's Automobile Repair on Main Street and turned in.

"What are you doing?" she asked.

He whipped the Maxima into a narrow parking space between a van and the police chief's Blazer. "Having the oil changed."

She lifted her chin. "But I don't want to have the oil changed."

"Why not? This old thing is going to give out on you if you don't do a little maintenance, Dakota. That pinging in the engine isn't good."

How could he hear the pinging above every other harbinger of a potential breakdown? "I'll do it later."

He leaned in front of her, as if determined to claim her undivided attention. "There's no reason to refuse. In case you're worried about the expense, *I'm* planning to pay for it. I won't even take it out of next week's wages."

"I don't want you to pay for it," she said.

"It's twenty-five bucks. Not even enough to argue about."

She spotted one of Booker's repairmen making his way over to them. "It's my car, and I want to go. Now."

"But—"

"Now!" she snapped.

He mumbled something about her being too stubborn for her own good, but he finally waved off the repairman and backed out of the space. "I don't know what your problem is," he said.

Of course he didn't. There'd probably never been a time when he didn't have twenty-five bucks in his pocket. And she wasn't about to explain what the experience was like. "What do you want from the pharmacy?" she asked instead.

"I'm picking up a prescription."

Steroids? She hated the thought of that. He was too healthy, too fit to take anything that could eventually destroy his body. But what could she do? She was merely the hired help. "It's one block down, across the street from the Arctic Flyer."

He followed her directions and parked in the back lot. "Stay with Braden. I'll only be a minute."

He returned before Braden could get too impatient about being left in his car seat and tossed a brown bag in her lap.

"What's this?" she asked.

"Antibiotics," he replied as he climbed back behind the wheel.

"For what?"

"For you."

"Me?"

"Who else is suffering from an infection that's turning into blood poisoning?"

She rolled her eyes. "You don't know that it's turning into anything."

He put on his seat belt. "I know if it doesn't clear up within three days, you're seeing a doctor whether you like it or not."

She cocked an eyebrow at him. "Says who?"

His expression told her he knew he was perfectly capable of enforcing his words. "Says me."

Dakota could've kept fighting. Tyson had

no right to force her to do anything. But deep down it felt sort of good—maybe even *very* good—to have someone looking out for her for a change. To cover the fact that such a small gesture, made by a temporary employer who'd be part of her life for maybe two months, could affect her to the point that her throat suddenly clogged with unshed tears, she kept her face averted and grumbled, "You can be a real pain, you know that?"

He shrugged. "I'm your boss. That's what I'm here for." And with that the transmission gave a loud *clung* as he shifted into Reverse. It probably did that whenever *she* moved the gearshift, too, but every noise, lurch or shudder seemed so much worse with Tyson in the car. "This baby needs some major work," he muttered.

She focused on the medicine as she battled that brief, unexpected welling of emotion. "How'd you get this without a prescription?"

Another *clung* signaled their arrival into first gear. "I *did* have a prescription."

"How?"

He brought the Maxima to a grinding stop at the exit and waited for traffic. "I know an M.D. who's…shall we say…*friendly* to professional athletes."

Which would explain why Tyson's name was on the package even though the medication was meant for her. "You mean he dispenses performance-enhancing drugs."

He angled the car onto Main Street and headed toward the diner. "For a rather large fee."

"You told me you're not on steroids."

Impatience etched lines on his forehead. "Criminy, Dakota, you're almost as bad as the press. I'm not on steroids, okay?"

"Because they're illegal—or because they can cause birth defects?"

"I'm not planning on having children."

She felt a hard lump somewhere in her midsection. "You mean *more* children."

He glanced into the back seat, and she imagined him thinking, *Yep, still there.* "Right."

"So it's the legality. You're afraid of what might happen if you get caught." Jerry's Diner came up on their left. She pointed to make sure he'd seen it.

"Of course. I don't want to disillusion all the kids out there who are buying and wearing my jersey, and the only sure way to avoid destroying my image is to steer clear of steroids entirely."

She thought of his most recent picture in the paper, and the interviews and articles that portrayed him as a callous womanizer. Surely those rumors and interviews with Rachelle didn't set him up as an ideal role model. But she wasn't about to point that out. So far, he'd been pretty decent to her. He'd even cared about the infection in her arm enough to contact a black market steroid dispenser, acquire an illegal prescription and bring her to town to pick it up. Heck, he'd even paid for it. The pharmacy had charged him seventy bucks, she saw. Who knows how much he'd had to promise the doctor?

"If you don't typically buy from this doctor, how do you know him?" she asked.

"I have some friends who don't mind the risks as much as I do. Mostly linemen."

"Why didn't your doctor friend put the prescription in my name?"

"I thought you might not want anyone at the pharmacy asking questions. There's got to be a reason you're trying so hard to hide that thing, right?"

His sensitivity and protection nearly brought tears to her eyes again. What was wrong with her? Had that much time passed since she'd had a friend? Rita Campbell, who'd been like a sister to her all through high school, had married and moved away nearly four years ago, and Dakota hadn't been close to anyone since. She'd been too busy dealing with her father and making ends meet.

Today those four years felt like forty. "That was sweet," she said.

He tossed her a grin. "I have my moments."

"What'd you tell him?"

"Who?"

"The doctor."

"That I had a cut on my arm." He parked next to two handicapped spaces. It was getting late for breakfast, so the lot was mostly empty. The ranchers in Dundee hit the diner early, then headed off to work. "I didn't want him to prescribe the wrong antibiotic."

The sack crackled as Dakota read the instructions: *Take two pills each day, one in the morning, and one at night.* "What about the dosage? Is this geared for someone of your weight?"

He turned off the engine. "No."

"How'd you manage that?"

"I told him I'd lost about a hundred pounds."

One *hundred?* Surprise and relief flashed

through Dakota. Did that mean he somehow hadn't noticed the extra pounds she was battling? "How much do you weigh?" she asked.

He started to answer as he got out, then laughed and shook his head. "So you can figure out how much I think *you* weigh? Sorry, I'm not starting that."

She got out, too, and took Braden from his car seat. "I'm only trying to see if you think I'm *sort* of fat or *really* fat."

"Nope, not getting me that way, either," he said resolutely. "I won't be drawn into any conversation regarding a woman's weight."

"Why? It's a simple question. I haven't dated in a while, and I'm just now starting to…you know, think about it." She carried Braden as they crossed the blacktop to the sidewalk. "I'm planning on losing some weight, but I haven't decided exactly how much. Should I shoot for ten pounds? Fifteen?"

"I didn't say you needed to lose any."

"No, but that's obvious…er…isn't it?"

"Do whatever you want to do."

"But you think I need to do *something,* right?"

As they drew closer to the entrance, the scent of pancakes and bacon seemed to radiate from the entire building. "That question has no good answer," he said.

"No's a good answer."

"But you wouldn't believe me even if I said it."

She shot him a glance. "Not unless you were sincere."

"Stop it," he said in mock irritation.

Braden buried his face in her neck, and she kissed his fuzzy head. "If you're not trying to hide your true opinion, why don't you want to talk about it?"

He groaned in exasperation. "What is it with women? I think you're…" his eyes slid over her but did little to reveal his true opinion "…curvy, okay? Curvy's good, right?"

"Unless 'curvy' is another name for fat," she mumbled.

"See?" He threw out his hands. "I can't win!"

"I was just asking your opinion."

They reached the front door, but he didn't open it. "You want my opinion?"

"I wouldn't have asked if I didn't."

"You have a great pair of legs, okay? Is that good enough?"

She checked out the part of her legs that could be seen beneath her blue jean skirt, which hit at midthigh. It was the high heels. No matter how poor she got she always managed to buy at least one pair of attractive, strappy sandals to herald the advent of spring. This pair had only cost eighteen bucks, but she liked the shape they gave to her legs. "I guess they're not bad," she admitted. "And I have nice skin and teeth. And a few other things."

Her offhand comment seemed to render him momentarily incapable of movement.

"What's wrong?"

"I can't help picturing what those other things might be."

She smiled and reached for the door handle—then paused. She was already this far into it.... "One more question."

"I can hardly wait," he said dryly, but she could tell he was preoccupied with fighting the urge to let his gaze wander lower, to see if she'd been talking about her breasts.

"Do you think what I've got is enough to… you know…revive my love life?" His eyes widened but she didn't give him a chance to respond before she corrected herself. "Well, not *revive* so much. More like *get* a love life?"

He focused on her mouth—but the change

did little to slow her galloping heart rate. "Uh—"

"I mean, supposing you were an average guy from around here, a cowboy or something," she quickly added. "Do you think you'd ever be interested?" Dakota knew the question put him on the spot, but she really wanted to know, and she figured Tyson was the perfect man to ask. She couldn't imagine anyone had met more women than he had. And he was only staying for eight weeks. He'd be here and then gone. She'd probably never see him again.

"Do you have a particular cowboy in mind?" he asked.

She nibbled on her bottom lip. This was an odd conversation to be having with her employer, but until the past few days, she hadn't realized how terribly lonely she'd become. "I don't know. Eddie Garwin's always nice when he visits the pharmacy. He brought me a specialty coffee two weeks ago and had them add whipped cream because he knows I like it that way. But there's a bit of an age gap." She imagined kissing Eddie, with his wet, slack lips and shuddered. "I don't think I could touch him in a romantic sense."

"How old is he?"

"He's got to be thirty-five."

"That's too old for you." Tyson's answer sounded like a final, irrevocable edict. "Anyone else?"

She sorted through the short list of possibilities. "Not yet. When you live in such a small town, you don't have a lot of options."

"I think I would've figured out a way to solve that problem by now."

"You're a guy. You're used to being the aggressor. And I've had other priorities."

"What's changed?"

She was fairly certain that jittery feeling that had coursed through her last night had something to do with her awakening. "I'm not getting any younger."

He rubbed his chin. "We'll have to see what's available, assess all potential candidates."

She peered more closely at him. "Are you serious or—" Spotting the devilment in his eye, she felt her hopes plummet. "You think this is funny."

"A little," he admitted with a lopsided grin.

"Thanks a lot," she said in disgust. But she couldn't blame him. Her lack of a social life wasn't his problem.

Shifting Braden to her other arm, she

tried to enter the diner, but he held the door closed. When she looked up to see why, she found him wearing a more serious expression. "Don't sell yourself short, Dakota. You have a lot more going for you than a pair of nice legs," he said. Then a blast of air-conditioning hit her as he swung the door wide.

Chapter 8

Grandpa Garnier: Never miss a good chance to shut up.

As they ate breakfast, Tyson couldn't help viewing his nanny in a completely different light. When he'd first met her, he'd thought he could never be romantically attracted to her. But that wasn't proving entirely true. She had…something. He wasn't sure what it was, but it was definitely appealing.

Maybe it was innocence. He hadn't encountered that very often. He and the men he associated with were pretty jaded when it came to relationships. Most of the women were just as bad. But Dakota was different. She deserved more than this backwoods town was giving her.

"What?" she asked, a forkful of pancake midway to her mouth. "Why are you staring at me?"

Besides the avid curiosity some of her comments had engendered? "I'm thinking," he said.

It had to be that the situation with her father scared men away, because there was nothing wrong with Dakota's personality— or her appearance. Maybe, through the eyes of a man who'd nearly been blinded by all the glitz and glamour Tyson had seen, she could come off kind of plain. At first. But a woman could do worse than having all that golden brown skin. Just looking at it made Tyson long to touch it. He was afraid he was quickly becoming fascinated with the idea.

"What are you thinking about?" she asked, watching him skeptically.

"Helping you."

Her fork slowly lowered. "You've already helped me. I just took some of the antibiotics you got me."

"I'm not talking about that kind of help."

"Then what?"

"You want to meet guys, right? I could introduce you to a few friends." Why not? He didn't have anything to lose. It'd give him something to focus on while he performed the therapy necessary to recover full use of his knee and waited for the media roar over Rachelle to die down—as much as it would ever die down while he was still playing football.

"How are you going to arrange that?" From the flatness in her voice, she wasn't too thrilled with the idea.

"I could get Gabe's permission to throw a party, you know, a big barbecue. I'm sure he wouldn't care. He knows I'm good for it if anything gets damaged." He pushed his coffee cup to the edge of the table so the waitress would refill it when she made her rounds. "What kind of man do you like?"

"Do you have any friends who aren't professional athletes?"

"None who could afford to fly here just for a barbecue. Besides, what's wrong with professional athletes?" he asked, slightly offended. "You told me you wanted to spice up your love life, didn't you? They can definitely do that."

She glanced around to be sure he hadn't

drawn any attention with that statement. "But I'm not interested in a quick lay," she whispered. "I wouldn't be what they'd want, anyway."

"How do you know?"

"I just wouldn't be, okay?"

He couldn't see why not. *He* wanted her, didn't he? "Give me one reason."

"I'm not the kind of woman who hangs around that type of man. As we've already discussed, I'm a little overweight right now."

He swallowed the egg he'd put in his mouth. "So? Some of these players are *a lot* overweight. They pride themselves on their size." He grinned. "And I'm talking about their whole body. Anyway, not everyone wants a woman who looks like a toothpick."

"I was envisioning a Barbie doll."

He saluted her with his orange juice. "The fact that you're not plastic is a good thing, trust me."

"But—"

"What?" he prompted when she stopped abruptly.

"At my age, they'd expect me to…you know…have a bit more experience."

Perplexed by her hesitancy, he put his orange juice back on the table. "You don't have to let it get physical if you don't want to."

"But isn't sex part of the fun of having a love life?"

"*I* think so, but I was making an allowance in case you're a prude." He smiled to let her know he was teasing her again, but she remained serious.

"I'm not a prude. I'm—" her face beamed bright red "—sort of new at that kind of thing."

Where was she going with this? "How new?"

"More than sort of," she admitted.

He suddenly lost interest in his food. "As in…complete virginity?"

She leaned closer. "Is there any other kind?"

"Actually, there are probably degrees. But for our intents and purposes, you're saying you've never made love, right?"

"If you have to spell it out," she said flatly.

"Wow." He shook his head.

She frowned as she poured more syrup on her pancakes. "That expression suggests you've just discovered the last great wonder of the world, which is making me feel like a total loser. I hope you know that."

"My thoughts were running more toward your being deprived." He scooped up another bite of egg but didn't bring it to his mouth. "To be honest, I was also thinking that if you're not looking to get laid, you should be."

"Boy, aren't I glad I told you."

He finished his eggs, then added Tabasco sauce and ketchup to what was left of his hash browns. "Sorry if I'm a little surprised, okay? But you've got to be twenty-five years old."

"Twenty-six."

"I don't think there are many *eighteen*-year-old virgins in America these days."

She shoved the extra butter on her plate farther to one side. "I sincerely hope you're wrong about that."

"Why?"

"Eighteen? That's *so* young. Sex is supposed to mean something."

He took another drink of his orange juice while considering the sizable libido of most of the men he knew—the men he'd been considering for Dakota just a few minutes earlier. "Your attitude might prove to be a problem, after all."

"My *attitude?*"

"Some people think sex between mutually

consenting adults doesn't have to work like a permanent tether."

She arched her eyebrows at him. "People like you and your friends?"

He gave her a sheepish grin, and they both waited as the waitress filled his coffee cup.

"At least now you see my point," she went on when the waitress was gone. "I wouldn't blend in so well with a crowd of professional football players. I'd be way out of my league."

He added cream to his coffee. "Can I ask you a question?"

She hesitated but finally relented. "I guess."

"How do you get to be your age without ever having sex?"

"Enough already," she said, waving him off.

Braden squealed and slammed his hands on the top of his tray. Tyson gave him a cracker, too interested in the conversation to allow Dakota to be distracted. "I'm serious."

"You live with an overprotective father who has special needs, that's how. It keeps you cloistered more surely than a convent."

No kidding. Tyson was quite certain he'd never met a twenty-six-year-old virgin—at least not one as attractive as Dakota. "Isn't it about time you do something about the situation?"

"What? I'd like to let go and experience life, meet someone I want to sleep with so badly I'm ready to tear his clothes off…"

Tyson shifted in his seat, wondering if he could volunteer for that position—until she continued.

"…but I don't want to have sex with just anyone. I want to fall in love, make babies and grow old with the father of my children."

"Right." In other words, she wanted the whole package—love, marriage and the baby carriage, just like in the song.

He wasn't even open to that. But then he thought of Quentin Worrack. He was a really good guy, and he *was* ready to settle down. Last fall, Quentin had freely admitted finding his current life too empty, had said he wanted a family. "I think I know someone who might be perfect for you."

She seemed to perk up. "Who?"

"He's on my team, but he's tired of livin' *la vida loca*."

"Okay, but how can we have a relationship if I live here and he lives somewhere else?"

Tyson cradled his coffee cup. The diner didn't serve the best coffee he'd ever tasted, but he was enjoying it. Or maybe it was the company. "Long-distance relationships spring up all the time. We have the Internet now, remember? Besides, Quentin can afford to fly up here whenever he wants. He's one of the best tailbacks in the league."

"How will we get to know each other?"

"I'll introduce you, then we'll see where it goes." His cup clinked as he returned it to its saucer so he could add yet another spoonful of sugar. "Maybe it'll work, maybe it won't. But it's worth a shot, right? You're not going to meet anyone working at an isolated cabin. We have to take aggressive action or you could go another decade without—"

"Shh!" She angled her head toward a man in the far corner who sat with his own breakfast but was watching them intently.

"That's the guy who asked for my autograph when we first walked in. He's not listening to us," Tyson assured her. "So—" he lowered his voice anyway "—are you interested?"

"I'm thinking about it."

"Don't think about it. Do it. You're too conservative. You need to take a chance. Meet new people."

"Da-da-da!" Braden cooed, pulling at the crackers he'd smashed in his hair. He was a damn cute kid, Tyson realized, but he refused to forgive the chubby little tyke that easily. Braden was only being good because Tyson had reinforcements.

Dakota dipped her napkin in her ice water to clean up the cracker mess. "Okay. I guess. But give me a couple weeks to lose some more weight."

"You're fine the way you are," he argued.

"No, I need to feel confident, and I won't be confident unless I'm where I should be on the scale."

"If that's what it's going to take," he said with a shrug. "Maybe I can even help you."

"How?" She pushed her plate away, which was the signal he'd been waiting for so he could finish her pancakes.

"I'll put together a workout regimen for you. I may not have much experience with diets—" the fact that he was eating her breakfast as well as his own served as proof "—but I've made a career out of exercise."

"That'd be great." She smiled and nudged the syrup closer to him.

The waitress slipped the check onto the table as Tyson took his last bite. "Time to visit your dad," he said, taking his credit card from his wallet.

Her enthusiasm visibly dimmed, but she

nodded. "If you have something you could do in town for half an hour or so, I could run over there myself. I can't imagine you have any interest in returning to my house."

She was wrong. "I don't mind."

"But my father may not be very friendly now that—" she hesitated, obviously searching for the right words as she removed Braden from the confines of his high chair "—now that I'm gone so much."

"Why does he care? You're working. Bringing in money. Isn't that good?"

She carried the baby as they made their way over to the cashier. "He's not real happy to have Terrance over so much. It's definitely cramping his style."

"That's what Terrance is supposed to do."

"And he's feeling a little neglected by me."

Skelton Brown deserved to be neglected. He deserved to be *abandoned*. But Tyson knew it'd only upset Dakota if he said so. On some level, she had to know it already, and yet she remained in that trailer, in Dundee. For the life of him, Tyson couldn't understand why. In his opinion, the way Skelton treated her dissolved any obligation she had as his daughter. Maybe that was because Tyson's mother was so practical. Priscilla had always expected him to find his own way out of trouble. When he'd called to tell her he was taking custody of his son, she'd said she was sure he'd do a fine job, and that was that. No offer of help or support. No particular interest in meeting her grandson.

Dakota was waiting for his response, so he said, "Sorry, but I can't allow you to be alone with him."

"Who gave you any say in the matter?" she asked.

He tossed his credit card on the counter. "You're not safe." He'd seen that cut, knew from the way she acted about it—and where it was located so far up on her arm—that it had probably come from Skelton. Tyson wasn't about to give the old man an opportunity to hurt her again.

"Don't get involved," she said resolutely.

"I'm already involved." How could he turn a blind eye to what he'd seen? Maybe everyone else in Dundee could stand back and let Skelton beat her, but he had no tolerance for that, regardless of the familial relationship. His mother's second husband had sent her to the hospital once when Tyson was only eight years old. They'd separated immediately afterward, and divorced, but hearing the fight=

ing that night and being the one to call the cops had left a lasting impression on him.

Dakota looked ready to argue—but she didn't. Instead, she gave him a mutinous frown as he paid the bill, then followed him out.

"Dad?" Dakota called above the sound of the television, which drifted out the open windows of the trailer. She would've walked in, as usual, but she had Tyson along and didn't want her father to embarrass her any more than he had already. After a bender, Skelton almost always slept until late in the day, and he couldn't lie flat because he had trouble breathing. Half the time she found him passed out in his recliner wearing whatever he'd found comfortable the moment he sat down—and that could be as little as a pair of boxers.

"Dad? We've got company. Tyson and Braden are here with me."

When she caught his eye, Tyson raised his eyebrows, probably wondering what the heck they were doing yelling from the landing, but she quickly glanced away. Sending up a silent prayer that her dad would be dressed and behave himself, she gave the door a sharp rap and poked her head inside.

Skelton was in his recliner, as she'd expected. He was dressed in a tank top and coveralls—thank God—and he was awake.

"Why didn't you answer me?" she asked as she carried Braden inside and held the door for Tyson to come in behind her.

Her father shot Tyson a disgruntled look, pulled out a cigarette and lit it—all before he bothered to respond. His mouth twisted as he exhaled. "You think I should get all excited just because you've brought that hotshot over here?"

This wasn't going to be good. Dakota could tell already. But instead of asking Tyson to wait outside, as she should have, she tried to improve the situation by cajoling her father. "You were pretty excited last time he was here."

"That was before he stuck his big nose in my business."

Tyson's nose wasn't big at all. It was as close to perfect as Dakota had ever seen. But that was beside the point. "You were out of control, and he stepped in. That's all. Let it go, okay?"

"I'm not gonna let it go. He had no right. I wasn't gonna hurt you. You know that."

She didn't know that.

A muscle flexed in Tyson's cheek at her father's words, but to his credit, he took the baby from her and remained silent.

"I brought Braden," she said, hoping to distract Skelton from his bad mood. He loved babies and had asked about Braden before, so many times that she'd finally had to tell him about Tyson's stipulation that she leave Braden at the photography studio with Hannah when she came by.

"I thought you said Braden couldn't come over here." He breathed smoke through his nostrils as he spoke. "I'm not safe, remember?"

"Tyson didn't want me to bring the baby while he was out of town. Which is understandable. He barely knows you and you didn't do much to impress him the night you first met. But he's back now, and the baby's right here. See? Isn't he cute?"

Skelton wouldn't even look at Braden. "I'm not interested."

Dakota swallowed a sigh. "Fine. We'll get you some lunch, then. It'll only take a minute," she added for Tyson's benefit, but that proved to be a mistake.

"A minute?" her father echoed. "What's the hurry? You don't have time for your old man now that you're hanging out with a football star?"

"Dad, I *work* for Tyson." She accentuated the words she considered most important. "Tyson's *paying* me to watch Braden, and that's a good thing for *us,* right?"

"If he's only your employer, why's he here? Does he think I can't handle myself alone with my own daughter?"

"We brought one car to town and—"

"We?" he interrupted.

Dakota didn't know what to say, but she felt as if she had to say something before the situation could unravel any farther. "Yeah, *we.* Is there anything wrong with that?"

"He didn't need to come here. You're the only one who has any reason to visit me."

When Tyson cut in, Dakota knew he'd finally been goaded beyond his ability to resist. "Are you going to force me to spell out the obvious?" he asked.

"Tyson, I'll take care of his." Instinctively, Dakota put one hand on his arm to hold him where he was. "Dad, he's just responding to past problems. Cut him some slack."

Skelton stuck his cigarette in his mouth and hefted himself out of the recliner. "Why should I cut *him* some slack? He's not cutting *me* any slack. Sending Terrance Bennett over here to keep an eye on me. Your man's a legend in his own mind, you ask me."

Tyson tried to pass her the baby, but she wouldn't take him. She couldn't let this erupt into a fight. "That's not fair," Dakota protested, but her father wasn't listening.

Grabbing his cane and using it to help him maneuver closer to Tyson, he shoved a belligerent finger in Tyson's chest. "Why'd you bother to come to Dundee in the first place, huh? You don't belong here. Take that baby back to his mother. Dakota said you don't want him, anyway."

Dakota gasped and felt her cheeks flush hot. When she'd confided that juicy tidbit to her father, she'd been trying to get on common ground with him again, to revive the better aspects of their old relationship. The way her father worshipped NFL and NBA players, she knew he'd be interested in a little gossip that no one else, not even the tabloids, could provide. But that was right after Tyson had left for California, before her father had had a chance to realize that Terrance Bennett wasn't going away.

"You don't know anything about me." Tyson held Braden off to one side as he knocked her father's finger away from his chest.

"He... Fatherhood's new to him," Dakota said, getting between them.

Skelton tossed his cigarette on the floor and ground it into the carpet. "He should go back to California where he belongs."

Dakota was so worried the butt would start a fire, she immediately knelt to pick it up.

"Next time I need advice on how to care for my child, remind me to look you up," Tyson said. "You're a textbook example."

"At least I wanted my own kid! You won't even touch your son if you can help it."

"I'm touching him now, aren't I?" Tyson growled. But after shooting Dakota a glance that said he'd been a fool to trust her, he walked out.

The slamming of the door rattled the whole trailer. Dakota did find Tyson's behavior toward Braden strange, but she also felt a great deal more loyalty toward him today than she had ten days ago and fervently wished she'd kept her mouth shut. "Thanks a lot," she muttered.

"Let him go. You don't need him. *We* don't need him."

That wasn't true. Not only were they desperate for the money Tyson was paying her, Dakota longed for the peace and quiet and safety the cabin provided. She craved the hope and good feelings Tyson had created simply by making her feel desirable in that instant after she awoke in his bedroom last night, was excited about his plan to help her meet other men. But mostly, she needed a friend. And she felt as if she'd just betrayed the only person, unlikely candidate though he was, to reach out to her in a long while.

Her father leaned on his cane as he grabbed for his pack of cigarettes. "Tell him to take his lousy job and shove it—and to have Terrance Bennett leave me the hell alone."

As he lit up and she breathed in the acrid scent, the walls seemed to close in on Dakota. Would she spend another decade, maybe more, here? Choking on that same cigarette smoke?

She gazed at the filthy kitchen, which was piled high with dishes she hadn't been around to wash. She doubted her father had bothered to do any laundry, wondered if he'd showered or brushed his teeth in the past few days and, suddenly, knew she couldn't take it anymore. Maybe her father had hurt himself trying to save her, but right now, she had to get away.

"I'm not going to tell Tyson any such thing," she said. "If he doesn't fire me over how you've treated him, I'm going to apologize and make sure I don't tell you anything I'd rather not have repeated."

"Screw you," Skelton said. "You're more worried about him than you are me."

There it was. The real reason for her father's anger. He was so afraid of losing her, just as he had her mother, that he chased her away at every opportunity.

Struggling with her emotions, Dakota shook her head in disgust. Sometimes she wanted to run away and not look back. But then what? She couldn't run far enough to outdistance the guilt that would close in right behind her. She'd once been close to her father.

"I was going to clean up around here and get some food in the fridge," she said. "But you can fend for yourself today."

This time, her father managed to stub out his cigarette in the overflowing ashtray.

"Fine, then leave. That's what you want to do anyway!" Using his cane to cross the room, he threw the door open and let it bang against the outside wall. "Go! I don't have any way to keep you. Not when you could be with someone like him."

Dakota hesitated only a second. "You're your own worst enemy, you know that?" she said. Then she walked out.

Braden was in his car seat, crying. Tyson sat in the passenger seat, his jaw set as he stared straight ahead. Although they were in *her* Maxima, Dakota was tempted to pass right by and keep going, to walk out of Dundee with only the clothes on her back. But at the moment, Tyson seemed to need her as badly as her father did. He tried to cover it with plenty of bravado and indifference, but it was growing more apparent by the day.

Why had he taken Braden from his mother? He indicated that he had no choice, but surely there were other options.

Regardless, as difficult as it was for him, he was determined to keep his son. Which meant Tyson was as shackled as she was.

Chapter 9

Grandpa Garnier: Always be a bit nicer than is called for, but don't take too much guff.

Tyson's mother had her shortcomings, but he'd been grateful to her for sending him to Montana whenever school let out. There, he'd learned to rope and ride, to cook and clean, to appreciate the outdoors and respect wildlife. And maybe he didn't always live up to it, but he'd also been given a good example of when to bite his tongue and hold his temper, and when to let his anger drive him to immediate action. His grandfather had made a huge impact on his life simply with an occasional disapproving look, a nod that indicated Tyson should get up and try again, or a few terse statements—most of which Tyson could remember by heart: *Always be a bit nicer than is called for, but don't take too much guff.*

With a sigh, Tyson replayed the message his agent had left on his voice mail. He was taking a lot of guff right now. But fighting back only made the situation worse. The more he tried to defend himself against Rachelle's accusations, the more guilty and hardhearted he appeared.

The police would be calling him....

God. He raked his fingers through his hair as he wondered what Grandpa Garnier would have had to say about that. When the old man first learned of Braden's existence, he shook his head and clicked his tongue. Tyson could almost hear his thoughts: *You've fallen into it this time.* But in almost every conversation they'd had after that, his grandfather ignored the fact that Rachelle had custody of Braden and asked, "How's that babe of yours?"

The question was obviously meant to encourage him to get involved, but Tyson would always mutter, "Fine," and refuse to entertain the possibility that it might not be true. Then he'd go on to talk about subjects he wasn't trying so hard to avoid.

Too bad his grandfather wasn't here to see that he'd finally stepped in.

He played Greg's message over: *Tyson, come on. You've got to give the baby back before Rachelle destroys you. Do it now, so this whole thing will blow over before next season. She's promising to take good care of him. She—*

Hitting the Delete button on his phone, he hung up. She'd take good care of him? Like before?

He didn't believe it. Besides, Braden was doing fine here. No one could take better care of him than Dakota. She adored that baby. As soon as they'd returned from town, Tyson had gone directly to the office and closed the door, but he could still hear her, playing with Braden in the room down the hall.

"Funny boy. Look at you. Aren't you perfect? That's it. Peek-a-boo…"

The phone rang. Tyson grabbed it to block out her voice, which was so full of enjoyment that it made him feel as if he was missing something magical. "Hello?"

"There you are. Why aren't you returning my messages?"

His mother. Just the person he wanted to talk to during the biggest crisis of his life. "I've been busy."

"I can see that. Your attempt to break into Rachelle's house is in all the papers."

"I wasn't breaking in."

"What were you doing?"

"Trying to talk to her."

"Not the best way to go about it."

"Thanks for pointing out the obvious."

"How's fatherhood?"

"Good," he lied.

"You're adjusting, then?"

"As well as can be expected. I've hired a woman to help me out." But even that wasn't as simple as it should've been. He was a fool to allow himself to be drawn into Dakota's life. He'd made the same mistake with Rachelle, hadn't he?

"Will she take care of the baby while you travel with the team?"

If she stayed with him that long. Although Tyson had toyed with the idea of getting Dakota away from her father by taking her to California, he was no longer sure he wanted her constant company. He was beginning to feel too conflicted about her. He sympathized with her situation, but didn't want to be taken in again. He was beginning to feel the stirring of sexual awareness and attraction, but couldn't imagine why. And after what she'd told her father about him, he felt betrayed. It was weird.

"Maybe."

"Who is she?"

"Someone Gabe recommended to me."

"Is she pretty?"

"Yes," he said, then caught himself. "I mean no," he corrected.

"Yes *and* no?"

"She's the type who gets a lot prettier as you get to know her."

"I've never heard you describe a woman in that way."

"She's a good nanny." He hurried to change the subject. "How's your business?"

His mother's voice warmed as she launched into the incredible volume of closings her escrow agents had going this month. But Tyson tuned her out to listen to Dakota's laugh. Maybe his nanny didn't have a business or a successful career like he and his mother did, but when she was with Braden, she seemed a hell of a lot more content—

"Tyson? You still there?"

"Yeah, I'm here. Listen, I'm glad business

is booming, but I've got to go. I haven't done any weight training today, and I don't have long to get this knee back in shape."

"No problem. My next appointment should be here, anyway."

He almost said goodbye and left it at that. Instead, he succumbed to a weak moment. "Mom?"

"Yes?"

Tyson jiggled his knee to siphon off some of his nervous energy. "When do you think you might come see the baby?"

"You want me to visit you in Dundee?" she asked in surprise.

"Why not? It's nice here. And it'd be good for you to take some time off."

"I take time off. I come to at least half your games. And we spend Christmas in New York together every year."

Along with Grandpa Garnier. Tyson felt the omission like a gaping hole in his chest. "This is different."

"How?"

"In a lot of ways." For one, it wasn't an elegant dinner at some expensive restaurant, where they talked and laughed, then went their separate ways. He was stepping into a whole new world, a world that no longer included Grandpa Garnier, and he was trying to figure out how to navigate it. He didn't want to do it alone. "You've never seen your grandson," he pointed out.

"It's not as if he was born yesterday, Tyson. He's nine months old. *You* hadn't even seen him until a month ago. And now we're tickled over the baby some woman used to extort a million dollars from you?"

Not tickled. Scared. But admitting that made Tyson feel like a baby himself. "What Rachelle did isn't Braden's fault."

"I understand that. And I'm happy to meet him, but it'll have to wait. This is my busiest time of the year."

"Sorry I asked," he muttered.

"Tyson?"

He tossed away the pen he'd been using to embellish his blotter drawing and rocked back in his chair. "What?"

"Is something wrong?"

Of course! He resented Braden even more than his mother did, and the guilt he felt for resenting a baby—*his* baby—only exacerbated the problem. But Priscilla wouldn't want to hear any of that. She wasn't one to talk about anything very deep. It made her uncomfortable. "No."

"Good. I'll call you later, then."

Tyson allowed himself a wry smile at the relief in her voice. She preferred to ignore unpleasant feelings, in herself and others, and simply hope the cause went away. But Tyson wasn't sure this situation could be resolved quite so unobtrusively. Regardless of what Rachelle said or did, Braden was here to stay.

At least, that was how he felt until the police called.

Dakota hovered near the glass doors that opened onto the cabin's expansive deck. She had an apology prepared for Tyson, and was eager to deliver it so she could relieve the strain that had sprung up between them since the incident at her father's trailer. But by the time she'd worked up the nerve to approach the subject, they'd arrived at the cabin and she hadn't had the opportunity. After closeting himself away in the office for hours, Tyson lifted weights, then went outside, presumably to the Jacuzzi, where he'd been for the past hour or more—the whole time she'd been bathing Braden and putting him to bed.

Dakota was beginning to worry that maybe Tyson had fallen asleep and drowned. Or that he would drown if she didn't rouse him. But she was hesitant to interrupt his solitude. His black mood, which seemed to permeate the whole cabin, told her he'd rather not be bothered.

As if to emphasize that point, he hadn't turned on any lights. He was sitting out there alone in the dark....

Taking a deep breath, she decided to go out in spite of all that. She couldn't retire until he came in. She wouldn't be able to sleep, anyway.

The door didn't make any sound when she stepped outside, but the deck creaked. If Tyson was awake, she thought he might hear her coming and say something. But he didn't speak. She found him slouched low in the water, a bottle of wine and an empty glass beside him.

"You've been out here a long time," she said, shivering because the wind had come up.

He watched her dispassionately as she drew closer. "Does the Jacuzzi close at ten or something?"

The heavy sarcasm told Dakota his mood hadn't improved. It probably didn't help that he was drinking. Alcohol certainly never had a positive impact on her father. "I can't imagine it's safe to drink out here all alone," she said.

One muscular, water-slicked shoulder lifted in a shrug. "I'm a big boy."

Dakota wanted to voice the apology she'd been mulling over, but she knew she couldn't talk to Tyson when he was like this. "Suit yourself," she said and turned back to the house.

"Dakota."

She faced him again.

"Should I give him back?"

The question took her off guard. "I'm not sure what you mean."

"Braden. His mother wants him back."

Dakota could sense Tyson's turmoil, but she didn't know enough about him or Rachelle to give advice on such a serious issue. She didn't want to lose the happiness Braden brought her, or the income, but she couldn't be selfish enough to base her judgments on what *she'd* lose over the next several weeks. What would be best for the baby? And for that baby's father?

"You're the only one who can make that decision, Ty," she said softly. Only after she'd already spoken did she realize she'd shortened his name. It was a reflection of the affinity she was beginning to feel for him. He wasn't *the* Tyson Garnier to her anymore. He

was a decent man wrestling with inner de-
mons she didn't understand.

Fortunately, he didn't seem to notice the
name thing. He was too distracted by whatever was eating away at him. "You said yourself I'm not good with Braden."

She winced at the reminder, because this
time she understood that all the publicity and
censure he'd endured was taking its toll. "I
told my father what he repeated to you today
before I figured out that…"

He toyed with his wineglass as if he felt
uncomfortable looking at her.

"…you deserve more credit than you're
getting."

When his gaze lifted, he seemed more vulnerable than she would've thought he could
be. Maybe that was why he hid his inner self
from the public. His macho, "I have it all"
image concealed a sensitivity he was afraid
others might exploit.

"A detective from California is flying up
to meet with me tomorrow," he said, pouring
himself more wine.

"Why?" she asked.

He hesitated, downed his drink, then set
the glass on the sidewalk. "Rachelle is claiming I raped her." Before Dakota could re-

spond, he gave a bitter laugh. "Evidently, I'm pretty dangerous. Maybe you should think twice about working for me."

Dakota didn't believe it for a second. She supposed anyone, even a football star, could let certain situations get out of hand. But her instincts told her Tyson would never force a woman. "What really happened?" she asked, moving closer.

"Nothing. That's why this is so damn… *frustrating.* I've never harmed a woman in my life." His hair stood on end as he ran his wet fingers through it.

"So she's lying?"

"Of course she's lying. That's all she ever does. But once a woman makes that kind of claim, a guy has no way to defend himself. How can I prove I didn't do anything wrong? It's more sensational to think I'm some sort of predator, so once the press gets hold of it, my reputation will be completely destroyed. I can't even point to all the things she did before she met me without coming off like I'm claiming she deserved it."

"What types of things did she do?"

"Let's just say a woman doesn't get that self-serving overnight." He glowered at his wineglass. "And even if I manage to convince some people of my innocence, there'll always be those who will wonder."

Dakota remembered him talking about the little boys who were buying his jersey. Being accused of rape was much worse than being accused of using steroids. No wonder Tyson was so upset. "What does she get out of doing this to you?"

"She's trying to pressure me into returning Braden to her."

"Why'd she give him up in the first place, then?"

"I didn't leave her much choice."

Dakota crouched down to let her fingers dangle in the water. "If the police ask the same question, I wouldn't give that answer."

"I did what I had to do," he said. "She wasn't taking care of him. I kept getting reports that she was leaving him unattended and going out till all hours of the night. The day I showed up, I found him sitting in a soggy diaper in his crib, hoarse from crying, and the only other person in the apartment was the seven-year-old daughter of one of Rachelle's friends. The kid was fixated on the TV and had simply turned up the volume to cover the noise. And the place was filthy."

So *that* was the story. Knowing Tyson, it

made sense. He didn't necessarily want to raise Braden, but he'd felt obligated to step in. And now Rachelle was making trouble. Just because she wasn't the best mother in the world didn't mean she had *no* love for her baby. "If she's that greedy, won't she be loath to part with the million you gave her?"

"I'm sure she doesn't expect to part with it. No doubt she's already spent a sizable portion. Besides, in her crazy, mixed-up logic, she feels entitled to that money."

The cold was beginning to seep into Dakota's bones. Shivering, she crouched closer to the warm steam rising from the water. "So what do you think this detective will have to say?"

Tyson didn't immediately answer. Her movements had obviously distracted him and when he spoke, she knew why. "Get in. You're freezing."

"I don't have my suit."

"Do you really need it?"

Dakota didn't know how to answer that. Of course she needed it—not that she was anxious to be seen in a swimsuit at this point.

"You don't have anything to worry about," he explained. "Without the light on, the water's dark as ink." He hooked his arms over the edge of the Jacuzzi. "I'll look away when you undress, and I won't touch you. I promise."

When she hesitated, he gave a bitter laugh. "Never mind. I don't blame you for being scared."

"I'm not afraid of you." If he wanted to force himself on her, he'd had plenty of opportunity. They were completely alone in the mountains. He could even do so now, whether she got in the Jacuzzi with him or not. It was those unwanted pounds that paralyzed her. That and the fact that she didn't know how much he'd had to drink. "Are you drunk?"

He scowled. "Hell, no. I don't get drunk. Especially on wine." He considered his empty glass. "But that doesn't stop me from trying every now and then."

"Are *you* wearing anything?"

"Why do you think the light's off?"

"Right." They'd be naked together. Somehow that made it worse...but the idea of skinny-dipping with Tyson Garnier had its merits, too. The sudden whirlwind of butterflies in her stomach was making her almost light-headed. She couldn't remember ever feeling quite so breathless and excited. Besides, this wasn't really about skinny-dipping. He was testing her to see if she trusted him enough to leave herself so vulnerable.

"Okay." She forced a smile, trying to act as nonchalant as possible—but acting nonchalant was tough when her heart was making such a racket against her ribs.

Dakota eyed the stack of fresh towels she'd put out yesterday. She thought Tyson would say something else to encourage her, but he didn't. He simply pushed the wine and his glass farther away and averted his face.

He won't see anything.... Taking a deep breath, she pulled her shirt over her head.

Chapter 10

*Grandpa Garnier: A woman with an edgy
smile is like a dog with a wagging tail:
she's not happy, she's nervous.*

Somehow Tyson was feeling better. Even
with his agent nagging him to give Braden
up. Even with a detective coming to question him about his relationship with Rachelle.
Even with Rachelle doing her level best to
destroy him.

Amazing what one naked woman could do.
He couldn't even see anything—but having
Dakota in the Jacuzzi sitting opposite him
had accomplished what several glasses of

wine could not: he was beginning to let go of some of the anger that had kept him fuming ever since he'd heard from Detective Donaldson of the LAPD. The natural surge in hormones probably contributed, but it was more than that. Dakota had to believe him, or she never would've taken off her clothes. A twenty-six-year-old virgin didn't slip naked into a Jacuzzi with a man she didn't trust. And he was just tired and beleaguered enough that the vote of confidence felt damn good.

"I say you hang on to Braden," Dakota said, speaking for the first time since she'd sunk in to the swirling water.

He shifted to allow one of the jets better access to his spine. "I thought you'd say that."

"That's why you asked me, isn't it?"

She was right. He wasn't really considering giving Braden back. He knew what he had to do even without his grandfather around to give him the resolute nod that would mean, "Sometimes you gotta dig in your heels, son." Heaven and earth couldn't shake Reed Garnier when he made up his mind, and Tyson knew he'd inherited that stubborn streak. He was simply mourning what it'd cost him— and he didn't mean in terms of money. He'd go from being viewed as a sports icon to being viewed as a man who used his fame and fortune to harm innocent women, which was even worse than the basic, garden-variety scumbag.

"You're too nice for your own good, you know that?" he said.

She pulled her wet hair over one shoulder. "What makes you say so?"

"Have you ever been skinny-dipping before?"

"No."

"Are you nervous?"

"Isn't it apparent?"

He chuckled. "A little. But you're still here."

She gave him a sly smile. "I'm trying to make up for what happened at the trailer."

He wanted to ask if he could get a bit more mileage out of that. He was thinking about comfort sex again and the solace he could find with her in his bed. But he refused to reward her trust with that kind of solicitation. It had to be the wine messing with his head for him to even be tempted. He didn't want to alienate Dakota. She seemed like the only person on his side.

"You don't owe me anything," he said.

"Then it's working?"

"Maybe a little too well."

"What's that supposed to mean?"

"Nothing—but unless you want to see more of me than you've bargained for, I suggest you turn away. I think it's time I went inside."

She blinked in surprise. "So soon?"

Not soon enough. He'd tested her, she'd risen to the occasion, and now he'd be plagued with unfulfilled desire for the rest of the night.

"I'm getting tired," he lied. Then he climbed out and reached for a towel, but when he glanced back, he saw that Dakota hadn't covered her eyes or ducked her head as he'd expected. She was watching him openly, her expression filled with curiosity and unmasked admiration.

"Dakota?" His hand clenched the towel he had yet to bring to his body. A lot of women had seen him—from the female reporters he encountered in various locker rooms to the lovers he'd taken over the past decade. But no one had ever looked at him quite like that.

"You left it up to me, didn't you?" she replied.

He *had* left it up to her. What happened next was also up to her. "And?"

"You're *beautiful*."

Tyson's muscles tensed as blood shot immediately to his groin. It was all he could do not to get in the water and show her what she was asking for. But he managed to deny the impulse—because he wasn't sure she knew she was asking for anything. She was too different from the other women he'd dated for him to tell. Besides, he'd never been with a virgin.

His conscience warned him not to say what came next to his lips, but he couldn't seem to help himself. "I could teach you a few things, if you want."

"About…"

He let his gaze lower for the first time to where the water bubbled around the soft swell of her breasts. "Use your imagination."

Her mouth closed and her throat worked as she swallowed. "Maybe when I lose a few more pounds."

He didn't give a rat's ass about her weight. What he was feeling had to do with more than finding a perfect female body. He was attracted by the whole package that made Dakota Brown who she was, wanted her sweet innocence to soothe the scar Rachelle had left behind and wash away some of his disillusionment and bitterness.

But he didn't feel good about pushing her. Gabe had recommended her to him. Besides, Tyson had other considerations. Like whether or not it'd be smart to let their relationship go to that level. Chances were good she'd take sex too seriously and it wouldn't end well, and he didn't want to make her as cynical about relationships as he was.

"You know where to find me," he said and went inside.

Dakota stayed in the Jacuzzi for another thirty minutes. It took that long to slow her pulse. Just when she'd thought she was forever doomed to a life of obligation and poverty in a small town that contained no one of particular romantic interest, she was thrust into a situation where she was staying at a cabin with one of the sexiest men in America—who was also a pretty nice guy.

And he'd just propositioned her.

Scooting over, she claimed Tyson's wine bottle and used his glass to drink the rest of it. Maybe he was attractive, and maybe he was a lot better person than the tabloids acknowledged, but there was no way she'd ever let him see her the way she was now. Not after she'd seen *his* body. Jeez, he didn't have an *ounce* of fat.

She had another glass of wine. On the other hand, maybe this was her one chance to experience something she'd never forget. It wasn't as if he'd look at her all that closely. He was merely taking advantage of what was available. He'd probably spend a quick fifteen or twenty minutes showing her what she'd been missing and that would be that. Even people in Dundee had an occasional one-night stand.

Of course, gossip being what it was around here, their reputations were ruined afterward. But there wasn't anyone within miles of her and Tyson. No one would know, so no one would tell. They had absolute privacy.

She wanted another glass of wine. The more she drank the more she thought she could overcome her nervousness. But the bottle was empty. Sweat rolled down her scalp because the water had brought her body temperature up, and the pads of her fingers were wrinkled to an uncomfortable degree. She needed to go in.

But Tyson was there. Even if he'd gone to

his room, she'd feel his presence everywhere. What was she going to do?

Take a chance, a voice in her head whispered. *Let yourself live.*

She was fairly sure that was the wine talking, but it presented a good case. Why not? What could it hurt? Her life was notoriously dull. Regardless of what happened, an encounter with Tyson would be interesting. Then, after her two months were over, she could go back home with a renewed sense of purpose. Every woman was entitled to at least one romantic affair.

Why not let hers be with the best wide receiver in the NFL?

Tyson had pulled on a pair of jeans, turned on the television and spent the past half hour pacing. He'd told himself to go to bed, but at the moment, sleep wasn't a realistic possibility. What had he been thinking? He couldn't touch Dakota. It was too risky. She could become attached and get hurt when he moved on. She could get angry, decide he'd taken advantage of her and jump on Rachelle's bandwagon—at which point he wouldn't have a prayer of convincing anyone that he was any better than a cockroach. She could poison Gabe against him, and then he'd lose his good friend. She could even get *pregnant*. He doubted she was on any birth control. What would a virgin need with the pill? And the only thing he had was a couple of condoms. As far as he was concerned, after Rachelle, a condom wasn't enough. A million different things could happen and, other than the immediate satisfaction of getting what he wanted, none of them good.

Sex was what had started the worst of his problems. He doubted it was a good idea now.

Telling himself to relax, he rubbed his eyes. He was worrying for nothing. Dakota was too self-conscious about that weight she'd mentioned to come anywhere close to his bed—

A soft knock interrupted. Pivoting, he faced the door, feeling the same surge of desire he'd had in the Jacuzzi. All the logic in the world couldn't erase it, he decided. Desire was a force to be reckoned with. But he couldn't let it get the best of him.

"Tyson?"

The sound of Dakota's voice—a little hesitant and unsure—scared the hell out of him. What was he doing getting involved with someone like her? He needed a worldly woman, a woman who could take a sexual encounter in stride and move on.

Like Rachelle? another voice whispered.

No, not like Rachelle. Nothing like Rachelle.

"You asleep?" she asked.

Hoping she was here for something completely unrelated to his offer, he crossed the room and opened the door. Dakota was standing in the hall, wearing a fluffy white robe and carrying a fresh bottle of wine with two glasses. As if the wine and the glasses weren't enough to tell him what she wanted, he was pretty certain she didn't have anything on underneath.

Oh, boy...

He pretended not to notice the wine. "What can I do for you?" he asked, his tone as brisk and businesslike as he could make it.

She stepped back and put the wine and glasses behind her back. "I was just..."

He scowled as though impatient to hear the rest. "Yes?"

Her eyebrows knitted in confusion, but she finally lifted the wine. "I thought you might want a drink."

He didn't want a drink. He wanted to slip his hand inside her robe and cup her breast, lay it open to his view. But he'd already decided he couldn't touch her. He'd had lots of good reasons, too. He just couldn't remember what they were when she was standing there, naked in her robe. "I think I've had enough," he said.

He watched a blush creep up her neck and felt horrible. He'd offered, she'd tried to accept, and then he'd rejected her. He was a total jerk, and he knew it. But a jerk was better than what he'd be if he capitalized on this moment, right? At least he was putting a decisive end to the chemistry between them. After this, she'd never approach him, or let him approach her, again.

"Right," she said. "Sorry to have disturbed you."

Her words were barely audible, as if he'd just knocked the wind out of her. He knew how difficult it must've been for her to gather the nerve to come to his room. But he couldn't tell her why he'd changed his mind, or she might promise him he was worried about nothing. Then he'd believe her, because he *wanted* to believe her.

"Good night," he said, and shut the door before he could pull her inside with him.

* * *

In T-shirt and shorts, Dakota ran on the treadmill for over an hour the following morning. She also lifted weights until her arms and legs ached. Then she did two hundred stomach crunches.

"I'm going to…get this weight off…if it kills me," she said between breaths, talking to Braden, who was playing with toys in his playpen. She never wanted to put herself in the same kind of position she'd been in last night at Tyson's bedroom door—feeling awkward and unworthy, a fool for showing up. No, she'd look so good even a man like him wouldn't be able to resist her.

A door closed somewhere in the house. Braden squealed, and she grimaced. "Yeah, he's here," she muttered. "Not that I want to see him."

Don't think about last night. He offered! It's not like you propositioned him.

But she *had* approached him in a robe with a bottle of wine. And he'd acted as if he'd sooner eat worms than touch her.

Distracted, she didn't get her hand out of the way as she adjusted the weights on one of the Nautilus machines and managed to pinch her finger. "Ouch," she cried.

"What's wrong?"

Tyson had just come into the room. Dakota heard the concern in his voice, but quickly disregarded it. She obviously didn't know how to read him.

"Nothing," she said, doing little to hide the grumpiness in her voice, and stuck the offended finger in her mouth.

He came into the room wearing a T-shirt, jogging shorts and tennis shoes. As soon as Braden saw him, he stood, clutching one side of the playpen, and began to jump up and down, but Tyson ignored him completely. "You hurt?"

"No." Shaking her hand, she put it behind her back.

"Let me see." He moved forward, but she backed up step for step, keeping the same amount of distance between them.

"It's fine."

He stopped several feet away. "Speaking of injuries, how's that cut on your arm?"

Lines around his mouth and eyes suggested he hadn't slept well. Dakota couldn't have been happier. She'd had a miserable night. It wasn't easy to drift off while kicking herself for being so gullible. "It's fine."

"Right. In one day."

She shrugged. "Antibiotics are amazing."

"Let me see for myself," he said skeptically.

"I'm taking care of it. There's no need."

Darting forward so fast she didn't have time to react, he caught her wrist. She tried to jerk free but only managed to bang her other elbow on a different machine. "Ow!"

"Take it easy," he said. "I just want to check it."

"Don't touch me. I'm all sweaty." She glowered at him. But he wasn't looking at her face. And he didn't seem to care about the sweat. He was already removing the bandage.

"It's not much better," he said with a scowl.

She wrenched her arm away from him. "The antibiotics haven't had a chance to work."

"How do you know?"

"Because it takes a few days."

They stared at each other, and she lifted her chin.

"Don't you want me to take you to a doctor?" he asked. "That's gotta hurt."

It did hurt. Especially when the sweat ran into it. But she didn't want to go anywhere with Tyson, couldn't visit the local doctor without having a good explanation, and doubted her car could make it to Boise. With her luck, she'd get stranded along the way. Besides, the antibiotics Tyson had bought her would take care of the problem eventually. It was a simple infection.

"It'll heal," she said again. "Give it some time."

He seemed uncertain. "Maybe you're resistant to the medication."

"We'll find out soon enough." She gingerly pressed the bandage back over the wound. "Anyway, you've got your *own* problems. Detective Donaldson called this morning. He said to tell you that he's taking the early plane and will be here by three."

She hadn't meant to sound so smug about it. But after some of the fantasies she'd spun in the Jacuzzi last night, having him touch her had left her a little rattled. She didn't feel as if her legs were firmly underneath her anymore.

"Da...da...da!" Braden slapped the netting with his hands, but Tyson continued to stare at Dakota. Finally he turned and left.

She heard the front door slam a few minutes later and knew he'd gone out for a jog. "Good, you're gone," she said. But she wasn't happy about it at all. And neither was Braden. The slamming door startled him so badly he puckered up and began to cry.

Chapter 11

Grandpa Garnier: It's best to keep your troubles pretty much to yourself, because half the people you tell them to won't give a damn, and the other half will be glad to hear you've got them.

Short and stocky, with a military-style crew cut, Detective Donaldson had definitely spent some time in the weight room. He took off his sports jacket almost as soon as Dakota let him in, then laid it carefully across the arm of the couch and pulled a pad and a pen from his shirt pocket.

Now that she was coming to know him,

Dakota could tell that Tyson was nervous. She believed the truth would eventually win out, couldn't imagine he'd actually go to prison just because this Rachelle woman was so vindictive. But she understood he had a lot to lose even if the accusations didn't go that far.

"I'm sorry to bother you, Mr. Garnier," Donaldson said. "I realize this can't be a pleasant experience for you."

To Dakota, he didn't *sound* sorry, or even slightly regretful, but Tyson accepted the hand he extended. "No problem."

"Can I get you a cup of coffee or something else to drink?" Dakota asked. Her first instinct was to slip away and give them some privacy. This didn't concern her. But Tyson had asked her to stay as a witness. He also wanted her to record the conversation.

Detective Donaldson shook his head. "I just had a soda in the car."

"Detective, this is Dakota Brown, my nanny," Tyson said.

"Nice to meet you," Donaldson mumbled, but clearly more interested in studying Tyson, he scarcely acknowledged her.

Dakota decided she didn't care for the detective's manner. She wondered if Tyson should've had a lawyer join them. She'd overheard him on the phone with his agent earlier, talking about postponing the interview until he could arrange for one. But the detective hadn't given him much time, and Dakota knew he'd had to weigh the advantages of legal protection against appearing uncooperative. Tyson didn't want the detective to get the impression that he was already building some kind of legal fortress. If the police had it out for him, the situation could get much worse.

The two men sat opposite each other. "I've asked Dakota to stay and record the conversation, if you don't mind," Tyson said.

Dakota knew it was small protection, but at least he'd have an accurate copy of everything that was said, which he could share with an attorney if it ever became necessary that he hire one.

"*I* don't have a problem with it," the detective said and Tyson gave her the signal to start, and she clicked the recorder as she took a seat at the bar.

"You're acquainted with Ms. Rachelle Rochester, most recently of Beverly Hills, California, correct?" Detective Donaldson began.

"Yes."

"Can you tell me the nature of your relationship?"

"I have a nine-month-old son by her."

"Where is your son?"

"Upstairs, taking a nap."

"Were you and Ms. Rochester ever…committed?"

"No. I wasn't even sure Braden was mine until I had a lab do a paternity test."

"Didn't she tell you the baby was yours?"

"Yes, but she and I were intimate for a very brief time. She's been involved with a lot of men, and I wanted to be sure."

His pencil scratched as he made several notes. "How many men would be a lot?"

"Excuse me?" Tyson responded.

"Would you say she's slept with more men than you've slept with women?"

"What does that have to do with anything?"

The detective's lips curved into a smile that looked far from sincere. "I'm just saying you've probably been with more than your fair share, right? Being a famous athlete and all."

Dakota's nails curved into her palms. At first she'd tried to convince herself that the detective was a Stingrays fan and was feeling a little starstruck at meeting one of football's finest, but that wasn't proving to be the case. He was obviously hoping to spot some kind of arrogance or deceit.

"Not as many as you might think."

"Can you give me a number?"

"No. I've never counted. And, as I mentioned, I don't see how this is relevant."

"I'm trying to establish patterns of behavior. Certainly you don't expect Ms. Rochester to act any more, shall we say, *virtuous* than you do yourself."

"I never said I did."

Dakota grew more nervous. This wasn't a good beginning.

"Then how can you claim she's slept with a lot of men as if that somehow makes her less reliable than she would otherwise be?"

Tyson's eyes narrowed. "If she told you she was carrying your baby, wouldn't you find that an important detail?"

Dakota thought Tyson had made a salient point, but the detective merely glanced at his notes.

"So how many would you say she's been with?"

"I have no idea."

"Do you have any proof that she's been with an unusually high number?"

"I haven't purposely collected eyewitness reports, if that's what you mean. It's just general knowledge among her friends and acquaintances. I've even met a few of her boyfriends."

"Does that mean you've continued to socialize with her?"

"I wouldn't call it socializing. Occasionally she brought someone with her when she met me."

"Met you for what?"

"To pick up her child support check."

"And this someone was usually a man?"

"I wouldn't have mentioned it if it was a woman."

The detective stopped writing. "There's no need to get sarcastic, Mr. Garnier."

Folding his arms, Tyson studied the detective as if seeing him across some scrimmage line. "I have to admit, I'm having trouble with your attitude."

Donaldson cocked his head. "Then you understand how I feel about yours."

Tyson said nothing, but his mouth formed a grim line.

"Why did she bring other men with her?" Donaldson asked, moving on.

"I have no idea."

"Because she was afraid of you?"

"Hell, no. If anything, she was—" he lowered his voice as if he was slightly embarrassed "—I don't know, showing off."

"What makes you think that?"

Tyson shifted uncomfortably, stretched his neck. "Some of these guys brought footballs and stuff for me to sign."

Donaldson seemed to ignore the allusion to his fame. "She brought them to your house?"

"No, we usually met at the team offices."

"Why?"

The furrow between Tyson's eyebrows deepened. "Because I didn't want her constantly invading my privacy."

"She claims that *she* was the one who asked to meet in public places."

"I know what you're getting at, but it's not true. She wasn't afraid of me."

"She's hired a bodyguard. You know that, don't you?"

Tyson briefly pinched the bridge of his nose. "Don't you get it?" he said, looking up at the detective again. "It's all for show. She's enjoying the attention this is bringing her."

"How do you know?" he countered.

"Because *I* was the one who dictated where we would meet. You have to understand, she was always calling me, asking for money, could never wait until it was time for me to make my next payment. Sometimes I'd give in and let her pick up a check so she could have it early."

"Because you're such a nice guy."

Tyson was teetering on the edge of action without thought, Dakota could tell. Donaldson was purposely antagonizing him, bullying him to see how much he'd take before his temper snapped, seeing if he could get more information when he was off his emotional center.

Don't let him do it....

A cold smile curved Tyson's lips. At least, Dakota thought, he recognized what was happening. "Whatever you think, Rachelle was the one who climbed into my bed."

"Of course. You're such a big star, who can resist you?" the detective said with a chuckle.

Tyson's smile remained, but the warning in his eyes was difficult to miss.

No, Ty...

"It's the truth. I didn't know her from Adam, I was exhausted from having played that day, and I didn't want to take advantage of a woman who was so down on her luck. I made no sexual advances. She approached me, and as the situation grew more—" he glanced over at Dakota as if he'd rather she not be around for the next part "—intimate, I voiced a concern about birth control, and she assured me she was on the pill. Then shortly after I broke off the relationship, she called to tell me she was pregnant with my child. That's how it happened. There wasn't any force involved."

"I see. And after that?"

"I couldn't allow her to show up at the house, or she'd come by at all hours, stoned or drunk and demanding money. I told her I'd pay her as long as she stopped doing drugs and took good care of Braden."

The skepticism in Donaldson's manner increased. "You were that worried about a son you never saw?"

A muscle began to flex in Tyson's cheek. Dakota held her breath, praying he'd be able to contain his anger. "I didn't want him harmed or abused."

"But you never made any attempt to see him."

"No."

Dakota wanted Tyson to provide a sympathetic explanation for his not taking a more active role in parenting—he was traveling, Rachelle made visitation difficult, *something*—but now that his attempts to explain had been met with so much doubt, even derision, he was beginning to clam up.

"*None?*" the detective pressed.

"Isn't that what no means?"

The detective gave a bark of laughter. "Yes, sir, it does. I just find it a little hard to believe. Or is that kind of indifference common in your circle?"

Tyson's Adam's apple bobbed as he struggled to retain control. "Is there a meaningful question in there somewhere?"

Detective Donaldson spoke slowly, as if Tyson was such a stupid jock he had to spell it out. "I guess the question would be, why didn't you have any contact with your son?"

"Because I didn't want any."

Dakota nearly groaned aloud.

"How many other illegitimate children do you have, Mr. Garnier?"

Tempted to intervene, Dakota opened her mouth, then told herself to stay out of it.

"None," Tyson said.

"That you know of, right?"

The muscle in Tyson's cheek flexed again, making his jaw look hewn from stone. "Braden's the only one," he reiterated, his voice deceivingly calm for all Dakota sensed happening below the surface.

"And yet you still weren't interested in him."

"No."

"That would've changed," Dakota interrupted, unable to keep silent another second. "It *has* changed. As Tyson said earlier, Braden's upstairs. Tyson was just…upset at first, you know? Anybody would be upset."

Both men turned to stare at her, and Dakota realized she should've listened to the voice in her head that had been warning her to keep her mouth shut. But the detective was prejudiced against Tyson before he'd even started questioning him, and Tyson didn't seem very good at defending himself.

"Well, it's true," she said when they didn't immediately return to their interview.

"How long have you known Mr. Garnier?" the detective asked, smiling in a patronizing way.

Dakota wiped her damp palms on her jeans. "A couple of weeks."

"A couple of weeks," he repeated. "But I'm sure you know who he is."

"I'm starting to figure that out. From what I can tell so far, he's a good man. A very good man."

"I'm talking about his public persona. You know he's a professional football player, don't you?"

Tyson got up and moved between them. "Leave her out of this, okay?"

Dakota merely stepped around him. "Of course."

"And that doesn't influence your opinion in any way? Make you give him a little extra leeway?"

"No. I'm not some stupid groupie who—"

"I'll keep that in mind." Donaldson cut her off as he waved for Tyson to sit down again. "Can we finish?"

Tyson seemed hesitant. When he caught Dakota's eye, his face was unreadable, but he finally sat on the edge of the couch. "I didn't rape Rachelle. That's all that really matters, isn't it?"

"I'm afraid it's not that clear-cut."

"What else do you need to know?"

"What made you decide to take custody of

your son? You've admitted that, initially, you didn't want to see him."

"Rachelle wasn't a good mother. She only wanted the baby as a way to get more money out of me. So I offered her a settlement."

"One million dollars."

"Yes," Tyson said with a sigh.

"Where did you first meet Ms. Rochester?"

"She was working at a restaurant where I went to eat with some of my buddies."

"She was the hostess, the cook, the server?"

"The server."

"Could you tell me how the relationship evolved from there?"

After a small hesitation, Tyson finally started talking again, but in a steel-edged monotone. "After we ate that night, I went to the restroom to wash my hands. When I came out, I found her huddled in a corner of the hallway, beyond the pay phone, crying. I recognized her as our waitress, so I went over to see if she was okay."

"And?"

His chest lifted as if he'd taken a deep breath. "Her girlfriend had just called to tell her that all of her belongings were sitting on the curb of the house where she'd been living with her boyfriend."

"Why were they on the curb?"

"Who knows? At this point, I'm wondering if that call was part of the con."

"I don't need any editorial," Donaldson said. "Just give me the facts."

The anger apparent in Tyson had Dakota sitting on the edge of her own seat. "There aren't any facts in this part of the story. Just lies, the lies she told to manipulate me."

Donaldson studied him. "Which were…"

"According to her, she and her boyfriend had broken up a few weeks earlier and he'd kicked her out. Originally, he'd agreed to let her stay until she could make other arrangements. But she claimed she was having trouble doing that because she didn't have enough money. She told me there was a spot opening up in a girlfriend's apartment and that she needed a stopgap."

"What happened from there?"

Tyson jammed a hand through his hair. "Like an idiot, I offered to pick her up when she got off work and give her a place to stay for a few days. I didn't think there was any danger in helping her."

"And she accepted."

"Immediately."

The detective took a few seconds to write some more notes. "How long did she stay with you?"

"Three weeks."

"You're sure it was that long?"

"Positive." Tyson leaned forward. "Don't you think it was odd that, if she didn't want to be there, she stayed so long?"

Donaldson's eyebrows went up and he continued in that "I'm going to slow this down so you can grasp it" tone. "She claims she took you at your word that you'd help her out. She didn't know she'd have to pay for your help by having sex with you. When she refused, you eventually forced the issue." He tapped his pad of paper with the back of his pen. "That's just as plausible, isn't it? That's why she moved out."

"That's not true," Tyson argued. "I kicked her out. I had to. I finally realized that she wasn't making any other arrangements."

"*According to you*, when did the relationship turn romantic?"

"Right away. During the first two weeks we were hot and heavy. But the more time I spent with her the more I could tell she wasn't anyone I wanted to get involved with and began to pull away."

"What made you decide she wasn't what you wanted?"

"She was so lazy she wouldn't even pick up after herself." Tyson spoke as if his words were futile, but Dakota found them interesting. She knew he'd never go into so much detail if he didn't have to. "Beyond that, she was materialistic and flirted outrageously with every guy who came to the house. And I was beginning to catch her in little lies."

"Like…"

"The second day she was at my place, she told me she'd been fired because she couldn't pull herself together after that upsetting call. I later found out it wasn't true."

"How?"

"I checked."

"Did you confront her?"

"Yes. She said she lied because she couldn't face working at that restaurant another day."

Donaldson turned to a fresh page and continued to write. "So you asked her to move out?"

"Not right away. I knew she didn't have the money. She hadn't been working. I was leaving for a few days. I told her she could stay at my house while I was gone—and that I'd help her get her own place when I got back."

"Did that cause a fight?"

"No. She suddenly calmed down and started acting normal again, and I began to make excuses for her earlier behavior. We hadn't been together sexually for almost a week, but when she came to my room that night I didn't turn her away. She told me she wanted to take advantage of our last chance to be together. Little did I know she was trying to increase her odds of creating a permanent bond between us."

"When did she notify you of the pregnancy?"

"As soon as she could show me a blood test. I think she thought I'd let her move in again."

"You didn't?"

"No way. It'd been too hard to get rid of her the first time."

"So you…"

"Sent her some money."

The detective scratched his head in what appeared to be Columbo-like feigned confusion. "Why did you give her money if there wasn't even a baby yet?"

"It was easier than fielding her incessant

calls. When she couldn't reach me, she'd start calling my friends. I just wanted her to stop."

"Why didn't you contact the police?"

"And tell them what?"

"That someone was harassing you."

"The media harasses me all the time, and no one does anything about it. I didn't even think about going to the police. I felt responsible for the mess I was in because *I* was the one who was dumb enough to invite her to my house in the first place."

"I see," Donaldson said, but Dakota didn't think he did. He seemed to be picking out words like *responsible* and putting more weight in them than he should.

"Did you see her during the pregnancy?" he asked.

"She showed up a few times, tried to kiss up to me. She even—" he glanced over at Dakota again "—never mind. I asked her to leave. Then when the baby was born, she called from the hospital. She wanted to establish paternity right away so she could start receiving support."

Donaldson watched Tyson from under his thick eyebrows. "You make her sound pretty bad."

"I've never met anyone like her," Tyson said.

The detective folded his notepad and found his feet. "Well, I think that's it for now. I'll call you if I have any more questions."

Tyson followed him to the door. "Will you be honest with me about something?"

Donaldson paused. "I'm always honest."

Dakota barely refrained from making a face.

Tyson seemed too intent on his question to react. "Am I going to need a lawyer?"

"That'll depend on the district attorney."

"But I didn't do anything."

"Sorry," the detective said with a shrug.

"Yeah, you sound sorry," Tyson muttered.

The detective pivoted. "You expect me to pity a guy like you?"

"What's that supposed to mean?"

"It's my job to look out for the little guy."

"The *little* guy?" Tyson snapped. "It's your job to investigate and find the truth."

Donaldson moved out onto the porch, where Dakota could see only a slice of him through the crack in the door. "Don't lecture me, Mr. Garnier. I know how to do my job. And just because you're famous doesn't make your word worth any more than hers."

"This has nothing to do with fame or anything else. Rachelle's a known liar!"

"She's a woman who's had some rough breaks."

"Rough breaks?"

The detective motioned toward the exterior of the cabin. "She's not as rich as you, now, is she?"

"Neither are you," Tyson replied. "And I'm beginning to wonder if that isn't the real issue here. What, did you get cut from your high school football team or something?"

"Tyson!" Dakota cried, but it was too late.

"That temper's already landed you in a lot of hot water, Mr. Garnier," Donaldson said. "I suggest you don't make it worse by insulting me." The detective stood toe to toe with Tyson, but at five-eight, he fell well below Tyson's six-four and Tyson didn't seem the least intimidated.

"I told you, *I never did anything to her.* She's better off now than she was before she met me. She's a million dollars richer, isn't she? How can you feel sorry for someone like that?"

"That depends."

"On what?" Tyson cried.

"On whether you were paying her to keep her mouth shut about what you did to her."

Tyson's jaw dropped. "What, is she sleeping with *you* now?"

"You're not helping yourself, buddy. I hope you know that," the detective said and stepped off the porch.

When Tyson started after him, Dakota jumped to her feet and intercepted him. "Tyson, no!" Shoving him back, she shut the door. "What are you trying to do? Land yourself in prison?"

"That guy's an idiot! Did you hear what he said? How could he listen to everything I just told him and still think Rachelle's some kind of victim?"

"Let him go. He's jealous."

"Of what?"

"Of you!"

Tyson didn't seem to care. Ignoring her, he reached for the door handle, but she knocked his hand away and spread her arms and legs across the entrance. "I'm not letting you go out there."

"I've got to…do…*something* before I explode!" he said.

"I know. But whatever you do, do it in here."

He grabbed her by the waist, as if he'd set her aside, but the moment he touched her, she grasped his chin in her hands and forced him to look at her. "Listen to me," she whispered. "Calm down, okay? Just calm down."

Wearing a tortured expression, he remained resistant for a second. Then he scooped her into his arms and buried his face in her neck.

"It'll be okay," she promised, and breathed a huge sigh of relief as she heard the detective's car turn out of the drive.

Chapter 12

Grandpa Garnier: When a cowboy gives you the key to his truck, you know you're close to winning the key to his heart.

The anger and adrenaline coursing through Tyson's body at first made it almost impossible to relax. He wanted to chase down the detective and wipe that smug expression off his face. The man was *enjoying* his misery. It was almost as if he'd come here merely to taunt him.

But as the seconds passed, Tyson began to breathe in the scent that lingered on Dakota's smooth skin and feel her hands rubbing his back. She was telling him that everything would be okay, which he sincerely doubted. But when he closed his eyes and simply abandoned himself to her ministrations, nothing else seemed to matter.

"My grandfather would've liked you," he said. He wasn't sure why he volunteered that information, but it somehow seemed important.

The hand moving over his back stilled, then started up again. "Would have?"

"He's gone now." He breathed deeper, trying to capture a portion of Dakota's essence and pull it inside himself. Her touch suddenly seemed so healing, so vital.

"Were you and your grandpa close?" she asked.

A familiar pain twisted in his gut. "Yeah."

"What happened to him?"

Suddenly tired, Tyson held her closer. "He had a heart attack and died. Last month."

"I'm sorry," she whispered soothingly.

Her sympathy sounded so sincere that Tyson's throat tightened, even hurt, but he knew the unshed tears would never come. As a child he'd grown too adept at burying his emotions, couldn't give in to tears now even if he wanted to. Which he didn't. "I lived on his ranch every summer."

Her fingers brushed against the bare skin at his nape, found his hair and began to comb through it. "What about your parents?"

He couldn't resist pressing his lips to the soft skin of her neck. "My dad died when I was two. I don't remember him."

"And your mother?"

"She's a force to be reckoned with, a strong woman."

"Do you see each other very often?" Her voice faltered slightly—he was pretty sure it was because his touch had changed. He was kissing her neck, climbing toward her ear.

"Only when her business slows down and she can break away."

She arched her neck, and he palmed the back of her head, threading his fingers through the silky mass of her hair.

"So you get along?" she breathed.

Completely different emotions were overtaking the outrage and upset of only seconds earlier. Tyson welcomed them, embraced them. He hadn't felt half this good in months. "We have a cordial relationship."

"Cordial?" She pulled back a few inches to look questioningly into his face, and he

immediately regretted starting this conversation.

"She has difficulty expressing herself," he explained.

"But you know she loves you."

"She probably does." He wanted Dakota back in his arms. "In her own way."

Confusion drew Dakota's eyebrows together. "You said 'probably.'"

"Right." He gazed down at her mouth. She was still close enough that, with a slight dip of his head, he could kiss her. But he was afraid that might break the tenuous hold he had on his restraint, so he forced himself to step away. "I've got to go back to California," he said.

"Why?"

"I need to get an attorney." He knew he could handle that from here—his agent could certainly be trusted to get a good lawyer— but if he stayed in Dundee much longer, he'd soon find himself in bed with his nanny.

"I see." There was a heartbeat of silence, then she said, "That's probably a good idea."

"You'll be okay here with Braden while I'm gone?"

She started getting food items out of the

pantry for lunch. He was quickly discovering that she was one hell of a cook. "Of course."

He hesitated at the periphery of the room. "Don't go to your father's alone. Make sure Terrance is there, or take Gabe with you."

"There's nothing to worry about. I'll leave Braden with Hannah, like before."

"That keeps *him* safe."

"Exactly the point."

"I'm asking about *you*."

"I'll be okay."

Pulling his wallet from his back pocket, he moved into the room and tossed several hundred dollars on the counter. "Here's something for gas and groceries. And...get yourself some new clothes. The ones you have are getting baggy."

She glanced at the money but didn't pick it up. "It's not your responsibility to buy me new clothes."

"You'll need something for the party."

"What party?"

"The barbecue we're going to have when I get back."

She delved into the refrigerator and came up with an onion. "Oh, right. I'm excited about that." She didn't sound like it, but Tyson knew he had to do something to put her out of reach. He was in too much trouble to get involved with someone who'd never even slept with a man. Especially when sex was the only thing he had to offer.

"Good." He started toward the office so he could make arrangements for his trip, but turned back as a new thought occurred to him. "Maybe you should see a doctor while I'm gone."

She set a frying pan on the stove. "I'm not going to a doctor. I told you, my arm will heal."

"To get some birth control," he clarified.

Her eyes widened. "You're kidding, right? The only doctor in this town goes to my church!"

"You said you wanted to get a love life."

"I want to meet people. That doesn't necessarily mean I plan on sleeping with them. I'm...open to the possibility, not set on it."

"Open means you should be prepared. You're going to like Quentin Worrack."

She put some butter in the pan and began peeling the onion she'd taken from the fridge. "When will you be back?"

"I have no idea. But you have my cell number if you need me. And I'll keep in touch."

He stared at her for a moment, wondering

when exactly she'd gotten so pretty. She'd lost a few pounds, but not enough to drastically change her overall appearance.

"What?" she said when she met his eye.

"Quentin's going to like you, too."

Braden was beginning to fuss. Tyson heard him as he was packing for his trip early the next morning. He expected Dakota to go to him. She was generally quick about it, and he knew she was awake—he'd heard her moving around the house, smelled the coffee when he'd poked his head into the hall just after his own alarm had gone off. But she didn't get him.

Chances were she was out in the garden, trying to put in an hour of work before Braden woke up. Or she was exercising in the gym with the fans on. At her request, Tyson had outlined a fairly rigorous workout schedule, and she was being incredibly diligent about following it. He couldn't imagine she wouldn't see some success, especially because she was watching her diet, too. Last night she'd made the most delicious salad for their dinner—with candied pecans, crumbled gorgonzola cheese and sliced chicken breast—but she refused to eat her own dessert. So Tyson had compensated by having two. He'd never tried homemade carrot cake before, hadn't had homemade anything since his summers at the ranch, and didn't want to leave something that good sitting on the counter going to waste while he was gone.

"Da…da… DA… DA…" Braden's babbling was beginning to turn into disgruntled yelling. The kid was probably hungry and standing in a wet diaper. Tyson wished Dakota would hurry, so he wouldn't have to be faced with all the emotions he experienced whenever he looked at his son but—

He listened for her tread on the stairs.

Nothing.

He didn't want to go downstairs to get her. He knew she wouldn't understand why he didn't just bring the baby to her. He didn't understand himself. He only knew he was overcome with a deep, almost sickening resentment whenever he encountered his son.

But this was starting to look like one encounter he couldn't avoid. His conscience wouldn't allow him to let a child stay in there and cry.…

Finally, he went to Braden's room and opened the door. He was going to leave it ajar, to make it easier for Dakota to hear him.

But the moment Braden spotted him, he quit fussing, plopped onto his chubby bottom and offered Tyson a smile.

They stared at each other from opposite sides of the crib slats. At last Tyson went inside and grabbed a diaper. "Okay. I'd hate to be so dependent on others, so I'll make you a little more comfortable. But don't think this makes us friends," he grumbled.

Amazingly, Braden didn't fuss when Tyson laid him down. He clapped his hands, munched on his fingers and began to babble. Tyson figured he must be getting used to the cabin or the routine or both. Or maybe he was just happier all the way around. Dakota had his bottom so smeared with diaper rash ointment Tyson thought the kid could spend the day in a bucket of water and not feel the wetness. But it seemed to be working. There wasn't a speck of diaper rash—nothing like the terrible sores Tyson had seen when he first got Braden.

"She takes good care of you, doesn't she?" he asked as he fastened the diaper tabs. "She takes good care of both of us." He was thinking of that carrot cake, which was almost as good as sex. Sex with someone else would come in second. Not sex with her.

The memory of kissing Dakota's neck rose to his consciousness, but that created a different kind of happiness.

Braden cooed at the mobile hanging over his head, and Tyson figured he might as well dress the baby now that he had him in a dry diaper. Digging a pair of mini-jeans and a T-shirt from the dresser, he held them up. "This okay?"

Braden didn't seem to have a preference.

"Good. I like that about you," he said. "See? We're making progress."

Braden obviously agreed because he was holding out his arms, wanting to be lifted out of his crib.

"Now you're pushing your luck," Tyson told him. He gave his son the evil eye. "But then I'm done."

Evidently, Braden didn't know the evil eye was a bad thing, because his smile widened. But that didn't make it any easier for Tyson to touch him, which only made Tyson feel worse. The kid was being good and he still didn't want anything to do with him. He kept seeing Rachelle in the baby's features, imagined her laughing at how easily she'd forced his hand and disrupted his whole life.

What happened has happened. There's

no way to change it, he reminded himself and, fighting his own resistance, carried the baby downstairs. But he wasn't able to pass Braden off as quickly as he'd hoped. Dakota wasn't gardening or working out. She was in the shower. And the second he tried to put Braden in his walker so he could get some breakfast for the both of them, the baby twisted in his arms and clung to him.

"Way to make this easy," he said. But he managed to make a bottle one-handed. Then he used the bottle to encourage Braden's co-operation, and when the kid was finally pushing his walker around the floor, he poured himself a cup of coffee. "Hey," he said. "I did it."

A few minutes later, when he was sitting at the breakfast bar reading an old issue of *Time*, which he'd found in a stack of gardening and cooking magazines near the couch, Dakota called to him from the top of the stairs. "Tyson?"

He handed Braden the crust of the toast he'd just buttered—because he'd seen Dakota do the same thing once before and knew it was okay. "What?"

"Where's the baby?"

"Down here," he said. "With me."

* * *

Dakota felt very conspicuous in Tyson's Ferrari. But he'd told her to use it. He didn't want the Bomber to strand her and Braden up in the mountains while he was out of town, and she didn't want to run that risk, either—not after he'd specifically warned her against it.

"That's some car," Booker Robinson had hollered from the open window of his truck as they both sat at the same intersection.

"Girl, you're livin' *large*," her old friend Tawny Cutter had exclaimed when they saw each other in the parking lot of Finley's Market. "And you're losing weight, too. Look at you!"

Dakota had never felt better. She was cooking and gardening and playing with Braden, which encompassed most of her favorite pastimes. She'd already dropped into a smaller pant size and was beginning to feel attractive again. Then there were the fantasies about Tyson, which were a completely new diversion but more exciting than anything she'd ever experienced. Almost in the blink of an eye, her life had changed from the drudgery and constant worry she'd known before to beauty and peace and romantic interest, as if she'd somehow stepped into one of her pretty magazines. She found herself smiling all the time.

Except when she remembered her father, of course. Then guilt for being so happy without him dogged every footstep. He'd saved her life and nearly lost his own in the process. Where was her gratitude? Her determination to take care of him?

It was there somewhere. And yet, when she thought of going home, she experienced such terrible dread. Before living at the cabin, she hadn't realized just how dreary their trailer was or the trailers around it or the hard-packed weed-filled yards or the broken-down Chevy Impala with the cracked seats that never moved from the neighbor's driveway. She'd grown too accustomed to those sights, had quit seeing them. Now that her eyes had been opened, however, her heart felt as heavy as lead every time she approached the park, beginning with the moment she dropped Braden off at Hannah's. And today was no different.

"Wow, Tyson's letting you use his Ferrari?"

Gabe's wife smiled in appreciation as she held open the door to her photography studio so that Dakota could get both Braden and his car seat through. "Yeah. Can you believe it?"

With long, thick brown hair and green eyes, Hannah was attractive in a wholesome way. Dakota had long admired her, but more for her poise than her looks. "What does he do, call you daily to make sure you haven't wrecked it?" she asked with a laugh.

Dakota smiled at the memory of her last conversation with Ty. "He checks on it every now and then, but not obsessively." Probably because he had worse things to worry about. Although Dakota had yet to see anything about it in Dundee, he'd told her last night that the story of his supposed crime was starting to leak out to the press. According to Tyson's agent, an L.A. paper had already printed something about it.

"How's the baby?" Hannah reached for Braden, but he scowled and leaned away from her. Now that he was becoming so attached to Dakota, he didn't like it when she left him.

"Hey, buddy, I won't be gone long, remember?" Dakota gave Hannah a baggie filled with Cheerios to encourage him to go to her. Braden loved being able to dig into the bag and feed himself.

"Are you enjoying the cabin?" Hannah asked.

"I love it. Someday I hope to own one just like it. You should see how fast the garden's growing."

Overcome with the temptation of the bribe, Braden succumbed to Hannah's outstretched arms. "What have you planted?"

Dakota wanted to slip out while Braden was preoccupied with his Cheerios, but she paused at the door long enough to give Hannah a quick list. "Carrots, tomatoes, zucchini, peas, squash. And there'll be pumpkins for Halloween."

"Halloween?"

"Even after Tyson's gone, I plan on going up there every few days to weed and harvest, if that's okay with you and Gabe," she explained. And to spend a little time at the place she'd come to love. But she didn't add that. It was silly to be so attached to the cabin.

"Of course it's okay, if you think it's worth the drive."

"It's worth the drive. I'll bring you some of the produce when it's ripe." Unable to remember where she'd stuck her keys in the colossal amount of effort it required to carry Braden and all his paraphernalia from place to place, she dug through the pockets of her jeans before realizing she'd dropped them in her purse. "Thanks for your help," she said as her fingers closed around the minifootball at the end of Tyson's keychain.

"No problem."

With a final goodbye, Dakota ducked out, climbed back into Tyson's car and headed to the trailer.

Almost everyone she passed gawked at the shiny red sports car, then honked and waved, as if they enjoyed seeing her drive it almost as much as she enjoyed driving it. She waved in return, her smile broad—until she reached the trailer park. Then, as she pulled into the rutted driveway of her father's home, the sun dipped behind the clouds and her smile slipped away.

"That was awesome!" Greg said. "Rachelle's going down. It's just a matter of time."

Tyson couldn't help but grimace. He and his agent had just come out of his attorney's office, which was located above one of the expensive boutiques in the shopping district of Beverly Hills. Harry Andrews had talked pretty tough, and Greg was following suit. Greg wanted to keep going over their strategy, to recap the session and reassure each other of ultimate victory. But Tyson had had a hard time sitting through the meeting in the first place. He could take no pleasure in fighting a woman, even on paper. Thanks to Grandpa Garnier, treating the fairer sex differently, as something to shield and protect, was too ingrained in him.

Which is what had gotten him into trouble in the first place, he supposed. Anyway, in this case, fighting had become a necessary evil. He couldn't allow Rachelle to destroy his life, and she was attempting to do just that.

"We'll do what we have to," he muttered, shoving a pair of sunglasses on his face with the hope that, along with the goatee he'd grown eight days ago, he wouldn't be recognized.

"We'll sue her for defamation of character, that's what we'll do. You heard Andrews. If she's not careful, she'll lose whatever she's got left of that million, even what she bought with it. Then she'll be sorry, huh? You'll have the money *and* the baby."

"No one wins in this kind of thing."

Greg frowned. "I thought Andrews was

encouraging, didn't you? That meeting was absolutely cathartic."

"Cathartic?"

"Emotionally cleansing."

"I know what it means." Tyson palmed the keys to his black Mercedes. "Let's go," he said, but then he caught sight of something that promised to be a much more positive diversion than dealing with his hyped-up agent and his past mistakes.

"Where are you going?" Greg demanded when Tyson started for one of the fancy shops facing the street.

"I want to look at something." He pulled his ball cap a little lower as he entered the store.

Reluctantly following at his elbow, Greg rose up on his toes to see over racks that were nearly as tall as he was. "Are you crazy?" he whispered. "If someone happens to snap a picture of you in here, it'll be plastered all over the papers, right next to Rachelle's allegations."

"This won't take long."

"But *everyone* has a camera on their cell phone these days. Especially in Beverly Hills."

"I said I'll only be a minute. If I don't do

this she won't have anything to wear. She's not the type to buy it for herself."

"She? Are you seeing someone I don't know about?"

Greg nearly stepped on the back of Tyson's heel as Tyson turned to respond. "No. I'm setting a friend up with Quentin Worrack."

"And you're buying this friend *lingerie?*"

"Just a bra and a pair of pretty panties." He started thumbing through the racks. "There's nothing kinky about that."

"You don't think sexy lingerie is an odd gift, Ty?"

"No, and you wouldn't, either, if you could see where this woman lives. I can't imagine she owns anything remotely like this." Especially because, from the sounds of it, there had never been anyone in her life to appreciate it. But Tyson was about to change all that. If he found Dakota a good husband, he wouldn't have to worry about the cut on her arm or leaving her behind when he started the season.

"How do you know her size?"

"I have a good eye."

Greg toyed nervously with the goatee he'd been trying to grow ever since Tyson started his. "Can't you give her the money and tell her to go out and buy her own?" he asked.

Tyson remembered the response Dakota had given him when he'd suggested she get birth control. "I told you, I don't think she'd have the nerve to buy it. Even if she did, I doubt they have anything this nice in Dundee. I'd have to drive her to Boise." And she'd be there to argue with him. This kind of purchase was too sexual for her to buy before she'd even met someone, but Tyson wanted to cover every contingency. By the time he returned to the cabin, he'd have only five weeks. Five weeks wasn't a lot of time to work with.

"Then drive her to Boise," Greg said. "At least you'd have a woman with you when you went shopping for panties. You're killing me here."

"There's not much time. The party's the weekend after I get home."

I've already contacted everyone, he'd told her on the phone last night.

Your friends? Can't we wait one more week? Why?

I've lost six more pounds, which puts me at twelve, total. He smiled at the pride he'd heard in her voice. *But I have another eight or so to go before I'm really ready to meet anyone.*

You're fine the way you are. How's that cut on your arm?

Gone.

The antibiotics came through?

Thanks to you.

Greg snapped his fingers, yanking Tyson out of the memory. "Hey, I don't want to be a pain in the ass or anything, but can you possibly hurry so we could get the hell out of here?"

Tyson hated that he couldn't be caught in a lingerie store, even a classy one like this, without it serving as some kind of proof that he was a lecher. He hadn't done anything wrong—other than getting involved with a cheat and a liar. "I won't let Rachelle dictate what stores I can frequent," he said. "I won't let anyone do that."

Greg rolled his eyes, muttering something about not knowing what was good for him.

Tyson didn't ask him to repeat it. Ignoring his agent's discomfort, he picked out a sheer black bra and panty set. "What about this? It's really *hot* but classy." He nodded in approval. "I could see Dakota wearing something like this."

Greg's eyebrows shot up almost to his receding hairline. "I thought you were setting this girl up with someone else."

"I am," he retorted. "I'm just saying that this looks like something she'd choose."

"You said you could *see* her in it. There's a difference." The bell jingled over the door and Greg sent a nervous glance toward the entrance, relaxing only slightly when the woman who entered didn't seem particularly interested in them. "Who is it we're talking about, anyway?" he asked, lowering his voice again. "Who is this Dakota?"

"Braden's nanny."

"Nanny?" Greg smacked his forehead with the heel of his hand. "We're in over our heads already! Please tell me that she's over eighteen and—"

Grabbing him by the shirtfront, Tyson nearly lifted him off his feet. "Are you *trying* to make me punch you? Of course, she's over eighteen. Since when have I ever touched a woman who's under age?"

Greg squirmed out of Tyson's grasp, then made a big show of brushing himself off. "I thought you weren't going to touch *this* woman," he said sullenly.

"I'm not."

"Yet you're buying her underwear. That's not something a guy typically does for a friend."

Tyson refused to hear the logic in his argument. "This is an unusual situation. She needs my help."

"Your *help*? Come on, Ty. You must want to get into her pants to be so interested in this. And it's scaring the hell out of me that you're so damn preoccupied with panties when your whole career's at stake."

"Thinking about panties beats the hell out of thinking about prison," Tyson muttered. "Besides, I don't want her the way you're accusing me of wanting her."

"Yes, you do. Why not admit it?"

"I'm not talking to you anymore," Tyson said, turning away.

"That's good," Greg responded. "Because you're not making sense."

Tyson fingered a beige garment that was, as far as he could tell, supposed to push a woman's breasts up so far they were all but spilling out the top. "I'm merely doing her a favor, okay?"

"How about doing *me* a favor?" Greg replied. "Stop trying to rescue every unfortunate woman you find. It always leads to trouble."

"Dakota isn't anything like Rachelle—"

"*Every* woman is like Rachelle. They want your money. What don't you get about that? When are you going to start protecting yourself?"

Tyson shook his head. "Man, I'm glad I don't have your view of life."

"Just give me those panties so I can buy them. And take a walk outside while I do it, okay? Before that bell rings over the door again and gives me a freakin' heart attack."

Tyson laughed in exasperation. "You're one cynical son of a bitch, you know that?"

"I accept the way things are. You? You try to fix everything."

"Whatever." After handing the item over, Tyson went out and sauntered down the street, burning time until his agent could join him. But in the window of a store half a block away, he spotted something else of interest.

"Can I help you?" the clerk asked as soon as she noticed that he'd come in and was standing near the display.

Before he could answer, he saw recognition dawn on her face. "Hey, you're Tyson Garnier!"

"No, I just look like him." He used his thumb to turn his Super Bowl ring around before she could catch sight of it.

"The resemblance is striking," she marveled. "If he had a goatee, you could be his twin brother. Except I think he's a little bigger."

"He's got me by at least two inches." Tyson pointed at the display. "How much is that?"

"Five hundred and eighty dollars."

"Do you ship?"

"Anywhere in the United States," she said proudly.

"Great. I want it sent to Idaho."

"Would you like it gift-wrapped?"

"I guess."

"What about a message?"

Tyson considered the question but eventually shook his head. "No message."

Chapter 13

*Grandpa Garnier: Never squat
on your spurs.*

"Think you're too good for your old dad,
now? Is that it?"

Dakota hesitated, grocery sack in hand, as
her father stood in the doorway of their trailer
and gazed out at the Ferrari.

"He's only letting me drive it while he's gone,
for practical reasons," she said. "He's afraid I'll
get stranded somewhere with the Bomber."

"A cell phone could've solved that problem."

"There's no service in the mountains, and
you know it."

"I know that's an eighty-thousand-dollar car, which makes it worth four times as much as our trailer."

"It's the only one Tyson has at the cabin."

"Your own car isn't broken down yet." Her father whistled as he admired the Ferrari. "He's sure treatin' you like you're somethin' special."

Her father was getting at something, but she didn't want to consider what it might be. "Ty's a nice guy," she said simply.

"Ty." Squinting against the brightness of the June sun, her father lowered his voice. "He hopin' to have a little fun while he's here?"

"I don't know what you mean."

"I'm asking if he's trying to get in your pants."

"Stop it." Keeping her eyes averted so he couldn't see any evidence that she might actually welcome such an advance, Dakota forced her feet to start moving again. She needed to stock the fridge, clean up the place and get some dinner made, and she needed to do it right away so she could get back to Braden in a reasonable amount of time.

"He must want *somethin'* pretty bad," her

father added in the same "I've got his number" tone.

She brushed past him, then held her breath as she entered the trailer. It smelled old and stale, as stale as her life had been before she'd started working for Tyson. "What have you been doing?" she called over her shoulder. "Chain-smoking? You should air this place out once in a while, you know. All you have to do is open the windows."

"What's the matter? Is home sweet home a little too humble for you now that you have such fancy friends?" he called back.

She had to clear a spot on the counter to put the groceries. Maybe Terrance kept a good eye on her father, but he certainly didn't do much of anything else, except help himself to the beer and cigarettes.

"What time is Terrance coming today?"

"Who the hell cares? I don't want him here."

Her father had been baiting her all week, but so far she'd managed to avoid an all-out argument. She hoped to do that today, as well. "He's not so bad."

"You're not the one who has to spend every evening with him."

"I thought I'd make some chicken marsala for dinner," she said, changing the subject.

Skelton followed her inside and stood near the breakfast bar, leaning on his cane. With his skin a jaundiced yellow and his dark hair dirty and standing up on one side, he looked even worse than usual. Obviously he'd had a bad night. Remembering how long she'd curled up in her bed talking to Tyson on the phone last night made the guilt Dakota already carried even heavier. She'd enjoyed every minute of that conversation, had even dreamed of Tyson afterward—while her father was probably up, sick again.

"Chicken *what*?" Skelton said in the same tone he might use if she'd told him she was making dog food for dinner.

"Marsala," she replied, struggling to keep a lift in her voice. "It's Italian. I tried it last week for the first time. Turned out great."

"I want the kind of meat and potatoes you used to make before you ran off to kiss Mr. Wide Receiver's rich ass."

Taking a steadying breath, Dakota tried not to let her father get the better of her. She was in a good mood, right? Her arm was almost completely healed and looked as if it would leave only a small, thin scar. She was getting to know a side of Tyson he showed to very few people, which meant he trusted her. And she was out and about on a glorious summer day, driving his Ferrari. But the fact that she cared more about feeling close to Tyson than she did about having the use of such a luxury item told her a lot about the crush she'd developed on him.

She returned her focus to the food. "What would you rather have?" she asked. "Meat loaf and potatoes?"

He didn't answer right away. He seemed surprised, almost disappointed, that she wasn't willing to give him the fight he was spoiling for. "Meat loaf's fine," he grumbled at last.

"No problem. Meat loaf it is."

To discourage further conversation, she avoided eye contact, and Skelton eventually shuffled over to his recliner and sat in front of the television.

After a few minutes, he hit the mute button and spoke again. "You know he's only using you. Women are a dime a dozen to men like him."

"He's not what you think."

"Oh, yeah? Don't you read the papers?"

"I don't believe them anymore."

"Don't be naive. Look at what he did to Braden's mother. Is that what you want to have happen to you?"

Knowing it wouldn't do any good to continue to defend Tyson, Dakota bit her lip.

"Well?" her father prompted.

"That's not going to happen."

"It could if you give him what he wants."

She opened her mouth to tell her father the truth—that she'd all but asked Tyson to sleep with her and he'd refused. But that little detail was better kept to herself. For the sake of peace, she simply needed to acknowledge her father's concerns and move on. He was ill and afraid for them both. "Consider me warned," she said as she washed the lettuce she was using to make a salad. "And for your information, I'm not sleeping with him. He hasn't even kissed me."

He leaned around his chair. "Well, he's not letting you drive his car because he's afraid you'll get stranded, I can tell you that much."

Allowing herself a wry smile, Dakota went on with her work. Her father was worried about Tyson's motives, but *hers* were the ones he should concern himself with. She couldn't count the number of times she'd imagined Tyson coming home early to find her in the shower. In those fantasies, she'd already lost every extra pound of excess weight and looked incredible, of course. It was a dream, after all. But Tyson didn't apologize and leave.

"He'll drive away when it's time to go and never think of you again. Remember that."

Her father's words finally succeeded in leaching away the last of the good feelings she'd had when she left the cabin. "I know it's not as if he would ever fall in love with me, okay?" she said softly. "But stop with the dire warnings. Can't you give me a couple of months, just *a couple of months,* to be happy, Dad?"

He turned to stare at her.

"I'll still be here when he goes. That's all that matters, right?"

The volume went up on the television. But it wasn't long before her father yelled over it. "Whatever you do don't get yourself knocked up. It ain't easy raisin' a kid by yourself."

"I get that," she said.

"Maybe it'd be different if I was going to be around to help you," he added. "But you can't always count on me...."

Tears burned the back of Dakota's eyes as his words fell off. She'd been feeling so hard done by, having to take care of him. But he'd been there for her when she was growing up. He'd supported her alone all those years before the accident, and in the many years after they'd struggled to get by together. If not for her disregard of his cautions that day, things would've been different. She knew that. It was part of the reason she stuck around.

Crossing to his chair, she laid a hand on his shoulder. "I'll be careful, okay, Dad?"

He covered her hand with his and gave it an awkward pat. "How's Braden?"

"Good."

"You still enjoying babysitting?"

"More than ever."

"I would never hurt a baby, you know." He craned his head to look up at her. "I never hurt you when you were little, did I?"

He was as appalled by what he had become as she was, she realized. "No. You were a good dad," she said and managed a smile.

The telephone rang just as Dakota finished working out for the second time that night. With Tyson coming home in only four more days, she'd stepped up her exercise routine. She didn't have enough time to lose *all* the rest of her weight, but she was hoping to get rid of four or five more pounds before the night of the big party.

"Hello?" She held the cordless phone to her ear with her shoulder as she used a towel to wipe the perspiration running from her temple.

"Who's this?" came a not-so-friendly response.

Dakota sat on the edge of the treadmill she'd been using. Because it was getting late, she'd expected the call to be from Tyson. But the voice on the other end of the line belonged to a woman.

"Dakota."

"Who are you?"

Was this a wrong number or something? "Who are *you?*" she countered.

"I'm Braden's mother."

Rachelle Rochester? Dakota's nails dug into her palms. "How did you get this number?"

"I did a favor for a friend."

"Well, you wasted your time and energy. Tyson's not here right now."

"Where is he?"

"I'm sorry, but I wouldn't tell you even if I knew."

There was a long pause. "Do I detect a bit of misplaced loyalty?"

"That depends on your definition of misplaced."

"He must have you convinced he can walk on water, like he did me."

"He's a good man."

Rachelle laughed bitterly. "You'll learn soon enough."

"Learn what?"

"That he's not what he seems to be."

"He didn't rape you, I know that much," Dakota argued.

Rachelle's voice turned hard. "Yeah, well, maybe you gave it up too soon."

"He hasn't even touched me."

"Then you're too fat, too old or too ugly, because a man like Tyson likes to use what he's got between his legs."

Dakota winced at the reminder of her own shortcomings. She'd never be a blond bombshell like Rachelle. But sometimes it seemed as if Tyson cared about her. They were certainly spending more time on the phone than it took him to ask after Braden…

"If you're not his girlfriend, who are you?" Rachelle asked.

Suddenly exhausted, Dakota wiped the sweat from her arms. "Your son's nanny."

There was another long silence. "How *is* Braden?" Rachelle asked at length.

"He's fine."

"So he's in Idaho somewhere?"

"Somewhere. What is it you want?"

"To see my baby."

"How bad? Bad enough to give back the money?" Dakota challenged.

"Go to hell," Rachelle said and hung up.

Apparently not. Dakota stared at the phone, wondering if she had to worry about Rachelle trying to steal Braden, and finally called Tyson on his cell.

"Rachelle just called," she said as soon as he answered.

"*What?* How'd she get that number?"

Dakota got up to wander through the house, checking to make sure the doors and windows were locked. "She said she did one of your friends a favor."

"But why? She has my cell."

"She said she wants to see her son."

"If she really wanted to see him, she'd contact *me*," Tyson muttered.

"I know."

"She's just poking around, checking out the possibilities," he added.

Maybe she was even having a moment of remorse. But it didn't seem to last long.

A peek in Braden's room showed he was sleeping peacefully. Dakota had known that was the case, but she still felt a certain measure of relief. "I think she was also trying to check up on you, see what you were doing, who you were with." She whispered until she could get far enough away from the baby's door that her voice wouldn't wake him.

"Then she hasn't changed much. She used to drive by my house a dozen times a night. Did she say anything else?"

You're too fat, too old or too ugly....

"She asked if I was your new girlfriend."

There was a long silence. "What'd you tell her?"

"That I'm Braden's nanny."

"Okay. Go ahead and get some sleep. There's nothing to worry about."

"You don't think she'd ever try to kidnap Braden, do you?"

"No, having him would only hamper her ability to go out and stay out," he said.

But when Dakota took Braden for her daily hike the following morning, she realized that *someone* knew where they were. A man had parked his car at the edge of Gabe's property and was sitting up in a tree, taking pictures of the house. And her.

The story broke the day Tyson was supposed to return to Idaho.

With a sigh, he sat in the office of his Malibu home and stared at the stack of newspapers sitting on the desk before him. Greg had brought them. And now his agent was on the other side of the desk, pacing and cursing—and not nearly as cocky as he'd been when they left the attorney's office two days ago.

"They all say the same thing," he ranted. "They claim professional athletes are reckless and feel they're above the law. They suggest it's time to do something about 'those who use their fame and fortune to take advantage of defenseless women.' They refer to the Kobe case as validation that this is becoming a recurring problem in professional sports. Hell, they even talk about the rise in sex crimes among college sports teams." He jammed a hand through his hair. "It's not good. It's going to kill your endorsements and hurt the whole damn industry."

Tyson had skimmed a few of the articles.

They were all difficult to get through, but none of them bothered him as much as the one he'd stacked on top: New Live-in Lover for Garnier. It started, "Following a recent accusation of rape, Stingray wide receiver Tyson Garnier has already moved on to a new relationship. The woman now living with him appears to be looking after the son he has with Rachelle Rochester, the woman behind the accusation." The accompanying picture showed Dakota wearing jogging shorts and a T-shirt and carrying Braden in a child carrier on her back.

She looked quite thin, he noticed, and hoped she'd be happy about that—because there wasn't much else in the article that would please her. It painted her as another gullible woman taken in by his "almost hypnotic charm." Which, of course, he employed only when he wanted to lure some young thing into his bed. But the story didn't stop there. It implied that not only was he using Dakota for her body, he expected her to care for the child he'd fathered with the last woman in his life.

Nice...

"We live in a crazy world when a woman

can get away with this, you know that?" Greg said.

Tyson didn't answer. He was afraid if he ever really started to vent, his emotions would get the best of him and he'd wind up hurting somebody.

"Rachelle's psycho, man! Yet everyone is feeling sorry for her and rallying to her defense." Greg pivoted and headed toward the window. "Makes me sick."

The phone rang before Greg could pass in front of Tyson again. Tyson hadn't been accepting any calls. His lawyer had instructed him not to respond to the many journalists who were hot on his trail. He wasn't eager to talk to the press, anyway. They were doing their best to crucify him without even allowing that there might be another side to the story.

He planned to ignore this call, too, but his housekeeper knocked softly before poking her head into the room.

"Mr. Garnier?

"Yes?"

"A man named Howard Schilling insists you speak with him."

Tyson met Greg's eyes. His agent wasn't pacing anymore. He was standing in the middle of the room, looking like he'd just swallowed a golf ball. "Strive Athletic Equipment," he managed to whisper. "It's starting."

Wrestling with the flood of anger coursing through his body, Tyson reached across the desk, punched the blinking light and spoke into the receiver. "Tyson Garnier."

"Tyson, what the hell is going on?"

Dropping his head in his hand, Tyson pinched the bridge of his nose. "I'm being accused of a crime I didn't commit, that's what."

"Of course you didn't rape this woman. It's got to be some kind of money grab, right? But I have to be honest: She's got you by the balls. I don't know how much she wants, but pay her off and do it fast, damn it, before this thing gets any more out of hand."

"I've already given her a million dollars."

"So? That was for the baby. You think I don't know what's been going on?"

A headache started behind Tyson's eyes. "But this isn't about money. It's about revenge."

"Revenge for what?"

"I don't know! For refusing to let her screw up my son's life. For refusing to let her take over my own life."

"Are you telling me you can't solve this

problem, Tyson? Because that's what I'm hearing."

Rocking back, Tyson leaned his head on the soft leather of his chair and closed his eyes. "I'm telling you it's up to the legal system now. I've done everything I can."

"You can sign over custody of Braden!" Greg cried, standing over him.

Tyson opened his eyes and gave his agent a menacing look designed to shut him up. But it was too late. Howard had heard.

"Who's that?" he asked.

"Greg."

"Put him on."

Tyson nearly handed the phone to his agent. Howard and Greg were the ones who usually dealt with the business end of his endorsements, anyway. It was Tyson's job to show up at a few cocktail parties, shake hands and smile for the cameras. But he wasn't going to allow these two men to decide what should happen to a baby in whom they had no real interest. *His* baby. He knew they'd gang up and try to pressure him into giving Braden back to Rachelle, and he wouldn't allow them to do that, not after witnessing firsthand what kind of person she was. "No."

Dead silence met this response. "That's not

the answer I was expecting," Howard said at length, and Tyson thought Greg might expire right there on the floor.

"This is *my* decision," he said, "and I won't allow her to coerce me into giving back a child she wasn't taking care of in the first place. If I did, it'd only be the beginning of future problems, because this isn't really about Braden. It's about me—or she would've called me and begged me to let her see her son instead of refusing to speak with me."

"Come on, Ty—" Greg started, an irritating whine in his voice, but Howard was talking at the same time.

"That's unfortunate. I wish there was something I could do to help you, but…"

He was backing away from the situation, getting ready to drop the ax. Tyson could feel it. He stood up, trying to prepare himself for the blow. Once Strive pulled their support, the others would follow. "There is," Tyson interrupted. "Stick by me, Howard."

The other man clicked his tongue. "I wish I could, Ty. But you know how it is. In advertising, perception is everything."

Tyson's headache grew to new dimensions. "If perception is everything, how about giving off the perception that you believe in me?

That you won't allow a liar and a cheat to make you scramble and run for cover?"

Evidently, his words made some impact because Howard didn't respond right away.

"You still there?" Tyson asked.

Howard let go of an audible sigh. "You've got a week, Tyson. If this nightmare doesn't end by then, there's nothing I can do," he said and hung up.

As Tyson put the phone down, Greg's mouth went as round as his eyes. "You saved Strive?" he breathed.

Tyson rubbed his temples. "Unless something changes, I just postponed the inevitable."

Chapter 14

Grandpa Garnier: If you're riding ahead of the herd, take a look back every now and then to make sure it's still there.

Dakota fingered the package in her purse. She'd had to drive to Boise to pick up Tyson today, so she'd asked Hannah to watch Braden and left a little early. Tyson had mailed her her second paycheck, and she was planning to do some shopping with it. She needed to buy some clothes that fit her. And she wanted a new outfit for the party—something stunning, if possible. But once she'd arrived in Boise, she'd spotted a Planned Parenthood clinic, and it was almost as if the Ferrari had turned into the parking lot of its own accord.

After spending the whole two hours she'd reserved for shopping in a six-by-eight cubicle, getting her blood pressure checked and receiving advice about safe sex, she had a month's worth of birth control in her possession. She wasn't sure she'd ever need it. She couldn't imagine getting that intimate with one of Tyson's friends at the party next weekend. But the clinician said she wouldn't be fully protected until she'd been on the pill for five days—and it seemed pointless to sacrifice a good shopping trip unless she was going to make use of what she'd just gotten. So she'd gone through a drive-through restaurant to get a glass of ice water and swallowed her first pill. Now she was officially a modern woman, prepared to be as spontaneous, sexually, as any other modern woman. But she had no clothes for the party, and she was out of time. Providing it was on schedule, Tyson's plane had already landed.

"Oh well, a girl's gotta have priorities," she muttered as she turned onto the road leading to the airport.

Tyson was waiting in front of the terminal when she arrived. Dressed in worn jeans and an Abercrombie T-shirt, he was wearing a baseball cap, a pair of sunglasses and sporting a goatee—and he didn't look happy.

Dakota didn't typically like facial hair. But Ty could've shown up in an ape suit and she would've found him attractive.

"God, I'm falling in love with him," she said hopelessly, trying to shake off the sudden "sinking in quicksand" sensation that came over her as she pulled to a stop.

"Where were you?" he asked, shoving his seat forward so he could stow his bag behind it.

She didn't want to tell him she'd spent two hours at Planned Parenthood and started on the pill, as he'd suggested. She was still in denial about maybe needing the protection. "Shopping for clothes for the party."

His irritation immediately cleared and the scent of male and leather that lingered in the car grew stronger as he climbed in. "Find anything?"

"No." She shot a second glance at his goatee and touched her chin so he'd know what she was talking about. "Going for a new image?"

"More or less. It's not much fun to be recognized right now." He frowned as he strapped on his seat belt, and she knew he had to feel as though he had a big target painted on his back.

"Is Braden with Hannah?" he asked.

Dakota adjusted the air-conditioning vents. "Yeah."

"When do we have to be home?"

She checked for oncoming traffic, then merged into the passing lane. "She didn't give me a set time."

"Maybe I'll call her to see if we can stay in Boise for another couple of hours."

Dakota felt her eyebrows inch up. "What for?"

"Unless we want you wearing a pair of Wranglers, we'll have a lot better chance of finding you something to wear here than in Dundee. And I'm starved."

"You're going to need more than one outfit," Tyson said, marveling at the amount of weight Dakota had lost.

"I'll pick up a few things when I get the chance." She hiked up her old jeans as she came around the front of the car, but two steps later, they sagged low again, hitting her a little below the hips like before.

When she passed him, he grabbed a handful of loose fabric and pulled her backside up against his front. "A slight tug would drop them to your ankles," he murmured in her ear. He'd just wanted to rile her up a little, see her blush. Oddly enough, he'd really missed her while he was gone, spent most of his time thinking about her. But she didn't act the slightest bit ruffled. She leaned into him, causing his knuckles to graze the smooth skin of her lower back.

When she turned her head, their lips were only centimeters apart. "Don't worry, I can keep them up," she said, then she tossed him a cocky grin and pulled away.

Tyson's jaw sagged in surprise. What was this? Dakota was *flirting* with him? *Teasing* him? Judging by the extra wiggle she put in her walk, he was convinced she was.

"You're asking for trouble," he told her as she walked into the store ahead of him. But he liked it. He liked the new Dakota. He liked her *a lot*.

"Can I help you?"

A tall woman approached, wearing a lot of makeup and expensive clothes and offering them a polite smile.

"We're just looking, for now," Dakota said, and the woman nodded and moved away.

Tyson stood watching as Dakota sorted through the racks. Occasionally, she'd pull out a pair of pants or a top, but after checking the tag she'd invariably put the item back.

Finally he reached around her, reclaimed the jeans she'd returned a second earlier and handed them to her. "Try these on."

She lowered her voice. "They're too expensive."

"I want to see them on you." Their eyes met, and Tyson let his hand rest on the bare part of her hip revealed by the pants she was wearing now.

Catching sight of the hanger in Dakota's hand, the woman immediately came toward them. "Those jeans are some that fit really well," she said. "Shall I start a dressing room for you?"

"That'd be great." Tyson intervened before Dakota could refuse and passed the jeans over to her. Then he selected a gray spaghetti-strap top made mostly of lace and a thin, matching button-up sweater. "And these."

The woman's smile widened. "Excellent choices. These will go together perfectly!"

Dakota scowled at him as the woman disappeared into a dressing room. "Those jeans are a hundred and sixty dollars," she whispered. "And who knows how much those tops are! You didn't even look!"

"I gave you plenty of money."

"But I'm not going to let you pay for my clothes."

"Why not?"

"Why should I?"

"Because the party was my idea. And I want to decide what you wear."

"*You* want to decide?"

"It's a small concession to make," he said with a wink.

A leery expression darkened Dakota's features, but she grabbed another top, a black one, and ducked into the dressing room while the salesclerk held open the curtain.

"Did you get the package I sent you from L.A.?" Tyson called after her.

"What package?"

Evidently not. He was sort of glad about that. The way they were flirting with each other, the bra and panty gift wouldn't come off like the favor it was intended to be. "Never mind." It'd come tomorrow or the next day. Hopefully, he could snag it and throw it away.

"What package?" she asked again, but he didn't answer. He was too busy trying not to gawk at the sliver of bare back he could see through the crack between the curtain and the wall.

"Those jeans will be stunning on her figure," the salesclerk predicted, folding her arms.

Tyson nodded and grabbed for a magazine. But even though the salesclerk had warned him, he wasn't prepared for the sight Dakota made when she emerged from the dressing room. The jeans were tight and low—a definite improvement on loose and low—and showed off her feminine curves to perfection. He liked the way she looked in them, but the gray sweater was made of such thin fabric he could almost see through it, and the lacy undershirt showed a lot of cleavage.

"What do you think?" Dakota turned in a circle.

His mouth had gone so dry he had to swallow, hard, to be able to speak. "The jeans might work, but we definitely need a new top."

She and the salesclerk exchanged surprised glances. "You don't like this one?" Dakota asked, disappointment threading through her words. "You picked it out."

"It looks different on."

The salesclerk looked offended. "What do you mean? It's lovely!"

Tyson refused to let his gaze fall below Dakota's neck. He knew how his friends would react to seeing her in a top like that. They'd be more than eager to spend some time with her. But what if they didn't realize she needed more than someone to show her a good time?

"That top will only bring the wrong kind of attention," he said.

"What are you talking about?" Dakota asked.

The salesclerk smiled nervously. "I'll give you two a few minutes alone," she said and hurried across the room.

"Tyson?" Dakota said when the woman was straightening racks beyond earshot.

He lowered his voice. "There won't be a man in the place who'll be able to take his eyes off you."

"You're kidding me, right? Isn't that the point?"

It *was* the point. Originally, anyway. But she needed the *right* man, someone who would love her and take good care of her. *Any* red-blooded heterosexual male would want a few minutes alone with her after seeing her in that outfit. "Just take it off. We'll find something else."

Her eyebrows knitted in apparent confusion. "I don't understand. You tell me I'm too conservative, that I need to take some chances. So here I am, taking chances. This isn't even a big chance. This top has a sweater over it, for heaven's sake. And I've already gone too far?"

"It shows too much."

"It only shows a little!"

"That sweater…*clings!*"

"Clings," she repeated, shaking her head. "That's what this kind of sweater is supposed to do. Good thing I didn't tell you I went on the pill today!" With that she pivoted and headed back to her dressing room. The chain scraped across its track as she jerked the curtain closed, but he couldn't let the argument end there. Didn't she understand he was trying to help her?

Getting up, he went after her before she could remove anything. "You don't get it," he said as he slipped inside.

Her troubled gaze met his in the mirror. "What I get is this, Ty. You need to decide what role you want to play in my life. Do you want to be my employer, my social director or my overprotective big brother?"

Turning her around, he used one finger to tilt up her chin. "You know what I want."

"No, I don't!"

"I want *you*. I want to be your lover," he whispered.

Her liquid chocolate eyes looked deep enough to drown in. "You turned me away."

He ran his thumb across her bottom lip, slid the tips of his fingers down the column of her throat. "I'm damn proud of that. It was one of my better moments."

"*Better* moments? You humiliated me!"

He let his fingers continue their downward travels and curl around one full breast. "I gave up what I wanted because of what you want."

Her eyelids lowered to half-closed, and she put a hand on his chest as if to steady herself. "And what do I want?"

"A husband. A family."

She said nothing.

"Am I right?" He hoped she'd deny it. Then maybe he could justify letting their relationship develop in a different direction. But she didn't.

"Eventually."

Knowing he had only one more shot, he flicked his thumb over the tip of her breast. He was no longer playing fair, but he was getting desperate. "And for now? Are you interested in a brief but torrid affair?"

Standing on tiptoe, she brushed his lips with hers. He thought that meant she was going to tell him yes and brought his arms around her so he could kiss her more deeply. He craved the taste of her like he'd never craved another woman—but she broke away before their tongues could meet.

"What?" he said, feeling deprived.

"I couldn't survive brief," she said intently. "Not with you."

Before he could formulate a response, the voice of the salesclerk came from outside. "So…how are you doing in there? Are you going to get the whole outfit?"

Tyson stepped out to respond. He didn't want to get the tops. They were too sexy. Or maybe not. It wasn't the tops that were bothering him—it was the intent behind Dakota wearing them. His idea to pass her off to someone else might have been a good one in theory, but it wasn't so easy in practice.

"You won't find a prettier outfit," the salesclerk said with an encouraging smile.

With what Dakota had done to her body, and what she'd had to work with from the beginning, anything would look good. But Tyson didn't want to sit around, watching her try on a dozen different items. Seeing the clothes come on and off that many times would only make it harder for him to keep his hands to himself.

With a sigh, he handed the salesclerk his VISA. "You win."

"So you're on the pill?"

Dakota glanced at the tables closest to them to make sure Tyson hadn't been overheard. "Do we have to talk about this in a restaurant?"

"I'm just asking."

She noticed that he hadn't eaten very much of his clam chowder. "I thought you were hungry."

"Not so much anymore." He added pepper to his soup. "Are you going to answer me?"

"Yes."

"Yes, you're going to answer me? Or yes, you're really on the pill?"

Taking the package from her purse, she slid it across the table. "Here. You can see for yourself."

He didn't seem particularly pleased. "Where'd you get this?"

She leaned closer to him so she wouldn't have to speak very loudly. "There's a Planned Parenthood here in town. I drove past it, realized what it was and turned around."

He added additional pepper to his chowder, which was already more black than white. "You're serious about this party."

She sat up straight and ate another bite of her salad. "What do you mean, *serious?*"

"You thinking you might…you know, finally do it?"

The waitress came by to fill their water glasses. Dakota waited until she moved on to respond. "I'm twenty-six. I figure it's time to do *something.*"

"With someone else."

Dakota didn't want to contemplate that, couldn't even imagine it. But she also couldn't imagine how badly it'd hurt when Tyson left if she didn't at least *try* to protect herself from falling any further in love with him. He'd had a lot of relationships; she'd had very few. She was at a distinct disadvantage. "I don't think we should talk about this," she said.

"I want to know."

"If the situation is right, and the timing is right… I guess. Maybe. I'd like to meet someone someday who might actually fall in love with me. And sex is part of that."

"You have to be careful, Dakota."

"That's why you're in charge of quality control."

He frowned. "What's quality control?"

"Introducing me to the right kind of guy. You mentioned a Quentin Somebody. You thought we might be good for each other."

"Quentin won't work."

He stated this so authoritatively, she stopped eating. "Why not?"

"He's too…ready for marriage."

"Isn't that a *good* thing?"

"You don't want to commit to the first guy you meet. Besides, I don't like his mother. I've met her, and she's too bossy. You wouldn't want an interfering mother-in-law, would you?"

"You didn't mention his mother before."

"It didn't occur to me. Besides, that was back when this idea seemed like a good one."

Wariness crept up on Dakota. "What's changed?"

"I don't want you to get hurt."

"That's why you're introducing me to other men, isn't it?"

He hesitated, so she jumped in again. "At any rate, I don't have a better plan. And aren't there other guys who'll be coming, guys who don't have meddling mothers?"

"I guess."

"Who?"

"John Sykes, Danny Carruth—"

"John looks cute on television," she said, taking another bite of her salad.

"You watch football?" He sounded inordinately pleased.

"I'll sit through a game or two with my father every once in a while."

The "pleased" moment passed. "You think John's cute, huh?"

"Sort of."

"How cute?"

"Just…cute, okay?"

"Well, John won't work."

"Why not?"

He used the pepper again. "He's too big a baby. Whines about everything."

"And Danny?"

"Danny weighs over three hundred pounds." More pepper. "He's going to die of a heart attack before the age of fifty. You don't want to be a young widow, do you?"

She reached out and took the shaker away from him. "I can't pine for you forever, Tyson."

He shot her a disgruntled glance. "I'm only asking for a few *weeks*," he said sulkily.

When she laughed, he responded with a boyish grin that nearly melted her resistance right then and there. She had a feeling she'd pine forever, regardless. But she had to do *something* to save herself. If they canceled the party, she wouldn't meet anyone new, and after Tyson moved away, her life would go back to the way it had been before he arrived.

She couldn't face that dismal prospect. Not after she'd had it so much better.

"Come on," she said, using a conciliatory tone. "I went to a lot of work for this body. I might as well see if anyone likes it."

His smile vanished and he grabbed for the pepper. "Are you *trying* to ruin my lunch?"

"Maybe."

He didn't ask why. Dakota knew he didn't need to. They both understood the reason already.

Tyson frowned at the scar on his knee. He had less than five weeks before he had to report to Los Angeles, and he wasn't ready. Because of some torn cartilage, which seemed to be taking forever to heal, he was in the worst physical shape he'd ever been in. And he wasn't making a lot of progress.

Lance, the trainer Gabe had lined up, was hunkered down to examine his leg, his face showing concern. A tall, soft-spoken man with blond hair and blue eyes who preached against fast food and trans fat, he took his job seriously. "Is it bothering you already?" he asked.

"Just a few minor twinges," Tyson said.

"Then why are you frowning?"

Tyson peeled off his sweaty T-shirt and threw it at the hamper in the corner of Gabe's gym. "I don't know."

Lance rocked back on his heels, resting an elbow on his own knee. "You're distracted. But who wouldn't be with what you're going through?"

Tyson shrugged, letting the trainer believe it was the problems he was having with Rachelle that were bothering him. But now that he was tucked away in the mountains and the rest of the world seemed to be moving on without him, his lack of focus had just as much to do with Dakota. She was different since he'd come home. Despite her rejection of his offer for a brief but torrid affair, she was acting a bit reckless. And that tempted him to be reckless, too.

He remembered the way she'd brushed up against him this morning while reaching around him for the sugar, could still feel the soft give of her breast as it came into contact with his arm. When he'd moved to get out of the way, she'd curved her lips into a taunting, purely feminine smile.

She knew she was driving him crazy; she was doing it on purpose.

"Let's do another circuit." Lance tapped him on the shoulder, and Tyson forced himself to move. He needed to burn off as much testosterone as possible.

Tyson was in the family room watching some football DVDs his coach had sent when he heard the doorbell. Dakota answered and told someone thank you. Then there was the rumble of a big truck pulling out of the drive, and his stomach sank.

"The packages you sent from L.A. have arrived!" she called.

He'd guessed as much. Thank goodness Lance was gone. "The big one's for Braden."

"You sent something to Braden?"

The surprise in her voice did nothing to improve his mood. "Even ogres like me have an occasional weak moment."

She came to the doorway and waited until he turned to look at her. "Should we bring them in here so you can see us open them?"

"No." The last thing he needed was to watch Dakota pull that sheer bra and those "barely there" panties from the box.

"You *are* being an ogre," she said. "You've been grumpy all day."

"I'm busy." He skipped back ten minutes or so on the DVD because he hadn't been paying attention to it. He was busy but not with what he should be doing. He was busy wanting something he couldn't have.

"Fine." She took Braden, who'd crawled into the room as she left. From there, Tyson heard no response to the packages. No noise. No nothing.

He tapped his fingers on the leather couch, wondering what she thought of what he'd sent. "Do you like it?" he asked at last.

"Braden loves his stuffed dog. So do I. I've never seen one quite so big."

He waited but she didn't continue. "And you?"

"I don't know," she called back. "I didn't open it."

"Why not?"

"I'm pretty busy myself."

"Fine," he said. "Bring the gift to me, then. I'm not going to give it to you."

She appeared in the doorway. "You're taking it back?" Her voice sounded far less strident.

"That's exactly what I'm doing." He wasn't about to have her wear that lingerie for someone else, regardless of his intentions when he'd bought it. He suspected he hadn't purchased it for the sake of someone else to begin with, but that was more self-analysis than he considered wise at the moment. Some things were better ignored than explored.

"Here." She walked over and dropped the box on the couch. "I didn't want it anyway."

Right. Her disappointment at losing the gift was as easy to read as her stubborn pride. "You're making this difficult," he said.

She narrowed her eyes. "I'm making *what* difficult?"

Pausing the DVD, he put the box in his lap, intending to hide it or burn it or…something. "Living in the same house."

"I'm cooking and cleaning and taking care

of Braden. How is that making anything difficult for you?"

"You know what I mean."

"No, I don't."

Tossing aside the box and the remote, he got up and closed the distance between them. She retreated as he advanced, but soon backed into a wall, and he put one hand between her and the door before she could move to the exit. "You're punishing me for not being able to give you what you want."

"You're imagining things."

"No, I'm not." He arched an eyebrow as he gazed down at her. "But I think you should take this as fair warning."

"Fair warning of what?"

He kissed her hard, as he'd wanted to kiss her in the dressing room. "I'll only let you push me so far."

She was breathing heavily, from anger *and* excitement if she was experiencing anything close to what he was feeling. "Before…?"

"Before I carry you upstairs and have you begging me to show you what making love is all about."

They stared at each other for a long time. Then she wet her lips and seemed to soften. "Why would that be so bad again?"

He longed to pin her against the wall and kiss her hungrily, to let that act lead to its natural conclusion. But he didn't want to be too rough. Dipping his head, he touched his lips to hers, barely letting their tongues meet, using everything he'd ever learned about kissing a woman to coax her into changing her mind. He thought he might be getting close when the tension went out of her body and she sighed in satisfaction. "It wouldn't be bad," he whispered. "It'd be good. Damn good. I promise."

"*This* is good," she murmured, and she was right. The desire that flowed through him was more intoxicating than liquor.

Her arms went around his neck, and when his hands slipped under her shirt, she didn't stop him. At the feel of her soft flesh, he pulled back to catch his breath. He needed to calm down, take his time, make sure she enjoyed every second as much as he did. But he was feeling a little shaky and out of control, which was a new sensation for him.

"God, I want to make love to you," he whispered.

When she looked up at him, her eyes were large, luminous, beautiful. "Do it."

His heart pumped faster. "I'll be gentle. I promise."

"I know you will."

"And afterward, you'll be okay, right?" He cupped her breast as he'd longed to do that day in the dressing room. "You can take what we're about to do in stride?"

Doubt entered her eyes. "How can I take it in stride when I've never done it before?"

"It's…it's an attitude. Just an attitude." One she clearly didn't possess. *Damn it!*

"I don't know how I'm going to feel."

That admission caused his conscience to start nagging him again. He didn't want to leave Dakota any worse off than he'd found her, didn't want to ruin the beauty of her trusting heart. "Dakota, I have to make sure you go into this with your eyes open," he explained. "I can show you a good time and… and I can provide you with some nice things before I go, which I plan to do anyway, but I can't give you any more than that. You have to understand, okay?"

She caught the hand that was cupping her breasts and moved it away. "You're saying you want to make love to me but you don't love me, right?"

"I'm saying…" What was he saying? He

could feel what he wanted getting away from him, but didn't know how to stop it without being an insensitive jerk. "I'm saying it can't go anywhere after whatever happens here."

"I see." She nodded as a small, rather forced-looking smile curved her lips. "I'm sorry, I guess I'm just not...cosmopolitan enough to look at it the way I should, after all," she said, and then she slipped away.

Tyson stood where he was, trying to let some of the emotion drain out of him, but it didn't seem to be going anywhere. *Give it time. Get a grip.* She was right to have stopped what was happening. She deserved more. And when it came time for him to fly home, he'd be damn glad he didn't have anything to seriously regret.

But that didn't stop him from feeling like shit right now.

Chapter 15

*Grandpa Garnier: Speak your mind
but ride a fast horse.*

Dakota sat on her bed, trying to recover from the maelstrom of emotions assaulting her. When she closed her eyes, she could still taste Tyson, still smell him. And even though he'd made it crystal clear that his feelings did not echo hers, she still wanted him.

"Quit being an idiot," she told herself. "How many times does he have to warn you to guard your heart?"

At the bottom of the stairs Braden was starting to fuss. He'd probably seen her storm past him and done what he could to follow. She should've brought him up with her, but she'd been too upset to think of anything except getting away from Tyson.

"Da…da…da!" he babbled. That was usually all it took to bring her running, but she wasn't thrilled about the possibility of bumping into Tyson again. Surely Braden could wait a few minutes, let her regroup.

"Da… DA… DA!"

"Hang on, sweetheart," she muttered. "I need a minute."

What was she going to do? It was stupid to compound her problems by wishing for something she could never have. If she wanted to improve her life, she had to forget Tyson and find someone else, someone who was emotionally accessible.

Getting up, she fingered the outfit hanging in her closet, the one she planned to wear this weekend. Hopefully, she'd meet someone at the party. It'd be easier to get over Tyson if she could distract herself with another relationship, even if that relationship only widened her circle of friends. She hadn't realized how limited she'd allowed her life to become. Maybe she had to stay in Dundee and take care of her father, but she could change other aspects of her life. Reach out. Have fun. Spice things up. Without money and without freedom, she'd fallen into such a terrible rut.

Braden wasn't fussing anymore. Hurrying into the hall to make sure he was okay, she saw Tyson lifting him off the bottom stair. Their eyes met as he glanced up at her, but Dakota refused to feel anything. He was her employer, she told herself firmly. If he was also kind enough to introduce her to some teammates, she was going to take advantage of the opportunity. She was losing her perspective only because being with a man like Ty had made her almost painfully aware that somewhere along the line she'd quit really living. She'd gone through the motions, but she hadn't had any real hope or happiness, hadn't *felt* anything anymore.

At least nothing like what she'd experienced since coming to the cabin. Now she was feeling the flipside of those missing emotions—disappointment and pain. But she supposed she had to accept the bad along with the good.

She hesitated, wondering whether she should go down and take the baby. But Braden seemed happy in his father's arms.

And Tyson acted as if he had the situation under control. He stared at her for a second, then carried the baby back into the living room.

The phone rang while Dakota was standing in the hall, and she hurried to her room to answer it. Thanks partially to the photo of her taken at the cabin, other members of the press had placed Tyson in Dundee and a few of the more tenacious reporters were trying to contact him. Because of that, Dakota had been fielding all incoming calls, and it became her job to tell everyone he wasn't available for comment. But this time Tyson answered the phone himself. She heard him say hello just as she picked up the handset.

"Mr. Garnier?"

"Yes?"

Dakota had already started to hang up so that she wouldn't be eavesdropping when she jerked the phone back to her ear. It was Mrs. Cottle, who owned the pharmacy. Dakota hadn't immediately recognized the voice because Mrs. Cottle sounded so uncharacteristically hesitant.

"Is there any chance I could speak with Dakota?" she asked.

There was an almost imperceptible pause

on Tyson's part. But then he said, "Sure, I'll get her."

"I'm already on the line," Dakota said.

There was a click as he hung up and Mrs. Cottle spoke again. "Dakota?"

"Yes?" She sank onto the bed. "Is everything okay at the store, Mrs. Cottle?"

"Everything's fine. It's just… Well, I'm not even sure I should be bothering you, to tell you the truth. At bingo last night, everyone was saying how great it is that you're finally out from under your father's thumb, at least for a while. I'm happy about that, too. You know I don't like what's been going on. But you've been such a good daughter to Skelton. It seems to me you'd want to know if…if…"

Dakota tensed. "If what? Is something wrong?"

"I don't know. Maybe. Your father wasn't looking too good when he came in to the store last night. Matter of fact, I've never seen him look worse."

Dakota winced beneath an avalanche of guilt. She hadn't visited her father yesterday, even though he'd called to tell her he needed his pain medication refilled. She'd arranged a ride for him and gone to Boise to pick up Tyson instead. Then she'd stayed for shopping and dinner—and had gone to bed feeling a little relieved that she hadn't had to deal with him for one whole day.

"Did he fill his prescription like he was supposed to?" she asked.

"Yes. And he promised me he was taking all his pills. But... I think he should go back to that specialist in Boise and see if something else is wrong."

Feeling the weight of the constant care her father needed settle more firmly on her shoulders than ever, Dakota switched the phone to her other ear. "You're probably right."

"I can take him to Boise if you're too busy, but I thought you should know."

Her father wasn't Mrs. Cottle's responsibility. Maybe Dakota had temporarily gotten lost in her hopes and dreams, but she was beginning to come out of the fog. "No, I'll ask Tyson for the day off and take him myself." She knew Tyson wasn't going to like having her gone, especially since she couldn't take Braden with her. But she needed to spend some time with her father. He'd been having a rough go of it lately. Maybe the aches and pains he'd been complaining about had been real, not exaggerated to make her feel guilty for abandoning him, as she'd originally believed.

"That won't be a problem?" Mrs. Cottle asked.

"No, of course not."

"I'm sorry to be the one to deliver bad news."

"It's better that I know."

"I think so, too. We miss you around here, you know. Can't wait for you to come back."

Dakota tried to say the same thing. She missed the Cottles. They were salt-of-the-earth kind of people. But she couldn't claim she missed working for next to nothing at a small, hometown pharmacy. Half the time she zoned out so she wouldn't lose her mind performing the same monotonous tasks day in and day out. "You've been good to me," she said. "Thanks for calling."

"You're welcome. Let me know how it goes, okay?"

"Okay." When Mrs. Cottle hung up, Dakota slowly returned her handset to its base and sat staring at the wall. Her father had state help to cover most of his medical care, but the gas to drive him back and forth to Boise, the wear and tear on a car that was already worn out and the missed work would cost her.

A creak in the hall alerted her that someone was coming. Then Tyson appeared in her doorway, still carrying Braden, who squealed in excitement when he saw her and started squirming to get down.

"Everything okay?" he asked.

"I have to take my dad to the doctor in Boise."

Tyson put his son on the floor and leaned against the door frame. "When?"

Braden crawled directly to Dakota and demanded to be picked up. She obliged and his chubby face broke into a triumphant smile because he'd attained his goal.

"As soon as I can set it up."

"What's wrong with him?"

"I don't know exactly. Could be that his liver's getting worse. It hasn't been functioning right for some time now. Or it could be his blood pressure." She kissed Braden's round cheek, drawing from the good feelings he engendered. "It could be anything, really."

"Do you want to take the Ferrari?"

"No, thanks."

He straightened. "How are you going to get there, then?"

"My car can make it." She hoped. "Do you want me to line up someone to watch Braden?"

"How long do you think you'll be gone?"

"I'm going to stay with him until I can get him to the doctor, if that's okay. I might need the rest of today, and tomorrow."

Tyson scratched his neck, obviously not happy. She initially thought he was worried about losing her help with Braden, but what came out of his mouth indicated otherwise. "Nights aren't your father's best time, Dakota."

"I'll be fine."

He nodded. "If that's what you want."

"Should I ask Hannah or someone to help with Braden?" she repeated.

"No, I've got him," he said and left.

Without Dakota, the house was quiet and lonely. Tyson had come to Dundee believing he craved privacy, but he was beginning to realize that he craved *intimacy*—the kind that went beyond sex. Having Dakota around, gardening, cooking, listening to music, playing with the baby, made the place more comfortable in the same way an overstuffed recliner surpassed a hard cane chair when it came to watching television. Somehow, he was content when she was at the cabin—and oddly unsettled when she wasn't.

I'm just worried about what could happen to her. Skelton might be sick, but Tyson had witnessed firsthand the mean gleam in the old man's eye. If he went after Dakota again, there was no telling what damage he might do, because she wouldn't run or—he thought about that cut on her arm that had taken so long to heal—even tell anyone what was happening. She believed she had to make the best of the situation without involving others.

"I don't like that she's there," he said to the room at large. But what could he do about it?

Rubbing the stubble on his chin, he got up and traipsed to the kitchen, where he nuked some of the left-over lasagna Dakota had in the fridge and chased it with a glass of milk and an extra-large piece of chocolate cake.

"She's really got to quit making desserts," he complained. He was the only one who ate them. But they were comforting, too, sitting on the counter beneath a cake cover, waiting for him.

A noise made him pause with his fork halfway to his mouth. Was the baby waking up? Tyson found himself almost hoping he was.

Now that he and his son knew each other better, having Braden around beat being alone. They'd had a surprisingly good day together.

Tyson couldn't hear any crying or baby babble. Nothing except the usual house sounds. Braden was probably out for the night. According to Dakota, he often slept clear through until breakfast.

Of course he would tonight, now that Tyson could use the company.

Pushing his empty cake plate aside, Tyson finally grabbed the phone and did what he'd been wanting to do all evening: he called Dakota. It was late, and he knew she might already be asleep, but he couldn't relax until he knew everything was okay at the trailer park.

The phone rang several times. There was no answer, but at least he didn't get the notice of disconnection he'd gotten last time.

On the tenth or eleventh ring, he hung up.

"She'll be fine," he told himself. Surely he could count on the disgruntled neighbors to step in if need be. But a small voice at the back of his mind said, "The way they stepped in when he cut her arm?"

"Shit." Leaving the kitchen, he took the stairs two at a time.

Braden was sleeping on his stomach with

his butt in the air. The baby looked so content Tyson hated to disturb him. But he couldn't leave him here alone, and he couldn't stand not knowing what was happening with Dakota.

"Come on, bud. Let's go see what's up with your favorite girl."

As he lifted the baby into his arms, Braden's eyes opened and a big, sleepy smile stretched across his face.

"Don't do that to me," Tyson said, but he was smiling right back.

The mobile home park was dark except for the flicker of a television in one of the first trailers.

No lights on in the Brown home could be a good sign, Tyson thought. It was nearly midnight, after all, and they were likely asleep. But if Dakota was sleeping, why hadn't the ringing phone awakened her? She got up with Braden if he so much as whimpered. And she was home. That was her car in the ramshackle carport.

He parked as close behind her Maxima as he could. He wasn't sure what time the bar closed in town, but he didn't want to take the chance of the Ferrari being sideswiped as someone negotiated the narrow, gravel park road.

Braden was asleep. He'd drunk half a bottle of formula and dropped off immediately afterward, and didn't seem bothered by the fact that they were no longer moving. Removing him from his car seat, Tyson put him over one shoulder. Braden squirmed and twisted until he made himself comfortable, finally settling with his cheek against Tyson's neck as Tyson carried him to the door.

If Dakota was asleep, he didn't want to wake her just so she could tell him she was okay. He'd see for himself if he could slip inside and take a look around. But he was hesitant to do that without an invitation, so he knocked softly.

No response.

He tried the handle.

Bingo. As he'd expected, folks at the trailer park weren't too worried about intruders. Only a really dumb crook would bother burgling one of these homes. Anyway, if Tyson had his guess, whatever violence occurred in Dundee was pretty much limited to domestic disputes.

Stepping inside, he closed the door behind him and was instantly swallowed by a much deeper darkness—along with the smell of bacon and onions. He smiled. Dakota had been cooking again.

The digital clock on the microwave blinked the time: 11:43. All the blinds were drawn, and the green numerals provided the only illumination.

Everything appeared to be okay so far, but the memory of that cut on Dakota's arm motivated Tyson to keep checking. After getting Braden up and driving forty minutes in the middle of the night, he wanted to be sure.

Needing his hands to feel his way around, he laid Braden on the couch and used two chairs to create a barricade so that he couldn't roll off. Then he heard something: a low murmur. Was someone awake?

He walked down the hall toward the bedrooms and paused outside the first door, which was closed. The noise was coming from inside. Now that he could hear it more clearly, he realized it was a television. He hadn't seen the flicker of the picture because this bedroom was on the rear of the trailer.

Giving the door a gentle rap, he opened it.

Dakota's father sat in a recliner almost identical to the one in the living room, facing a television perched on the dresser. But he wasn't watching it. The angle of his head suggested he was asleep, and a deep snore confirmed it. Behind him, a rumpled bed was pushed into the corner to make room for such a large chair.

The stench of cigarette smoke hung thick in the air, suggesting Skelton had been busy chain smoking not too long ago. But he was out now, probably in a drug-enhanced stupor, judging by the bottle of sleeping pills sitting on his dresser.

Tyson backed out of the room and continued on to the next door, which was also closed. This had to be Dakota's room. Hopefully, she was safe inside.

Not wanting to wake her, he didn't knock. He simply opened the cheap, lightweight panel that served as a door and peeked in, but without a television, he couldn't see anything. Slipping inside, he made his way over to the bed, where he eventually encountered a warm lump beneath the blankets—a lump that stirred when he touched it.

"Dad? Is it you? Are you sick?" she mumbled.

Relief washed through him. She was fine. "It's me," Tyson said.

"Ty?" The surprise must've chased away

some of the grogginess, because her hand suddenly moved up his arm to be sure. "What are you doing here? Is Braden okay?"

"Of course."

"Where is he?"

"Sleeping on the couch."

"*My* couch?"

"I made it so that he can't roll off."

Her hand fell away and the sheets rustled as she sat up. "What's wrong?"

The fact that she wasn't at the cabin. The fact that he'd been worried about her. The fact that she hadn't answered. "Nothing. Go back to sleep."

"But I don't understand."

"I was only making sure you were safe." Suddenly feeling the exhaustion he should've felt hours ago, he longed to get into bed with her and pull her into his arms. Instead, he straightened and started to move away.

"You drove all the way down here and now you're going back?" she asked.

He hesitated at the door. "Do I have another option?" he asked, suddenly hopeful.

"I can make you a bed on the couch—no, wait, Braden's on the couch." She started to get up. "I guess I could make you a bed on the floor beside him."

Tyson wasn't thinking the floor sounded too comfortable. Especially when Dakota was in here. "Not the best offer I've ever received," he said dryly.

She drew close but didn't touch him. He knew what would happen if she did. Maybe she did, too. "You could use my father's bed. He has to sleep in a chair."

Tyson scratched his head. He'd already seen that bed. And the man snoring next to it. "The floor will work."

Chapter 16

Grandpa Garnier: Don't go wakin' snakes.

"Dakota, call the police!"

Wrestling with the last vestiges of sleep, Dakota opened her eyes and blinked at the ceiling. At first she felt a little disoriented—she could hear Braden *and* her father, so it took a minute for it all to fit into place. Then she realized she was home, in her old room. She could tell by the water damage in the corner, which ran down the wall.

"Dakota?" Her father again. It was his bellowing that had awakened her.

"What?" she called back.

"There's a strange man and a baby in our house."

She rubbed her face. No need for alarm. Her father was just being rude to Tyson. "Lighten up, Dad," she shouted.

"Okay, the baby can stay but the man has to go."

"You're real hospitable, you know that?" Dakota heard Tyson say.

Dakota pushed herself out of bed and stumbled into the living room in her pajama bottoms and tank top before the two could really square off. "That's enough," she said, but Tyson didn't appear to be taking her father too seriously. He was still halfway in the bed she'd made him, propped against the couch, his hair sticking up in crazy directions, and he had Braden in his lap.

"Hi, sweetheart." She offered the baby an inviting smile.

Braden responded by squealing and kicking his legs, but he didn't climb off his father's lap and crawl over to her, which was a surprise.

Tyson's eyes gleamed in triumph as Braden grabbed his T-shirt with both hands and smiled at her while laying his head on Tyson's chest. "Guess he likes it where he is."

"He'd come to me if I called him," she said.

Tyson arched one eyebrow. "I don't think so. I think he's finally figured out that I'm a pretty nice guy."

She'd figured that out a while back, but it hadn't made life any easier. "I'd prove he likes me best, but I need to make breakfast right now. You hungry?"

He tried to smooth down his hair. "Starved."

"I didn't invite you to stay for breakfast," her father said.

"You didn't invite me to stay the night, either," Tyson responded. Then he flashed them both a cocky grin. "Yet here I am."

Her father glanced at her while jerking a thumb at him. "You like this arrogant son of a bitch?"

So much it scares me. "A little," she said.

"Why?" he asked.

She let her lips curve into a teasing smile as she shrugged. "He's got a cute baby."

Her father nodded. "I guess I have to give him that."

Tyson spent the morning at Dakota's, where he'd actually grown quite comfortable. It was difficult to forgive Skelton for what he'd done to Dakota—especially as he couldn't be trusted not to do it again—but seeing him together with his daughter made it easier to understand why she remained so devoted to him. Apparently he only got out of hand when he drank. But unfortunately he drank far too often.

He and Braden left the trailer park about the same time Dakota and Skelton left for Boise. On their way out of town, they visited Gabe, where Braden crawled around while Tyson and Gabe talked football. Then they dropped by the pharmacy to find a soft toothbrush for Braden's very first tooth, and a few other items. About halfway home, Braden started reaching for Tyson, wanting to be released from his car seat, and finally broke into a full wail when his demands weren't met. His face turned red and everything, but somehow Tyson remained calm. He knew Braden was just hungry and tired.

Braden cried himself to sleep only minutes before Tyson turned into the driveway of the cabin. "Of course," he muttered. But an inexplicable warm feeling washed over him when he finally lifted Braden from his seat and the baby gave a wounded hiccup and burrowed into his shirt.

"Poor baby," Tyson said, and because Dakota wasn't there to see him, he let his hand come up and rub his son's soft back. "Maybe you're not so bad, after all, eh?"

"Tyson, where the hell have you been? I've been trying to reach you all afternoon."

Just back from a jog with Braden, Tyson grimaced at the sound of Greg's voice. Had he known the caller was his agent, he probably wouldn't have left his son in the garage, still strapped inside the jogger, so that he could hustle into the cabin to answer the phone. Every time Greg called, Tyson's problems grew a little bigger. Maybe Greg wasn't the *cause* of the bad news—only the proverbial messenger—but Tyson was trying to enjoy a few days of denial. Reality would hit soon enough.

"I went running." He carried the phone back with him to get Braden.

"How's the knee?"

"Not bad." Not great, either, but Tyson still hoped for the best. "What's up?"

"I have some positive news."

Tyson perched Braden on his hip as he

went back into the house and filled his water bottle, which he'd drained on the long, exhausting run. "Rachelle has recanted?" he said sarcastically.

"No…"

"Then what?"

"One of the waitresses at the restaurant where you met Rachelle, a girl by the name of Mindy, is going to be a big help to us."

"How?"

"She said she heard Rachelle bragging that she'd met you and that you were coming back to get her after her shift."

Tyson let Braden down to crawl around while he took another drink of water. "What does that prove?"

"I'm not finished yet. Are you ready for this?"

At the excitement in Greg's voice, Tyson slowly lowered the arm that held the water bottle. He could barely breathe. "More than ready."

"Rachelle told her she was going to 'ride you all night long.'"

He blinked, hesitant to hope for too much. "You're kidding."

"Isn't that great? It proves that she *wanted* to

get in the sack with you, man, that she *planned* on it before you could even approach her."

Tyson stared out the window at the dappled sunshine and pine trees, his heart beating faster than when he was running. "You think that'll be enough?"

"I can't say for sure, but I know things just got a hell of a lot better for our side. I've already called Howard. With that kind of news, he said he could give us a few more days to iron this out. And if you keep Strive, you'll keep most of your other endorsements. They've been waiting, following Strive's lead."

Tyson thought about reclaiming the peace and confidence he'd experienced before Rachelle. Was it possible? Could this whole thing simply go away? He'd still have Braden, of course. There was no going back *that* far. But somehow having a son didn't seem as bad as it had before. "Wow," he said. "That's incredible."

"It *is* incredible. We're back in business, big guy. It's only a matter of time before this nightmare is over. I'm taking Mindy's statement to the police right now. I think the D.A.'s going to want to see it before he decides whether or not to press charges."

"That detective… Donaldson? He's not going to want to let go of this."

"Fortunately he's not the one who decides."

Tyson nodded as all the ramifications of this latest development sank in. He wouldn't have to start the season under the terrible cloud of suspicion that hovered over him now. The media fervor would die down, and he could focus on improving the strength and mobility of his injured knee.

And finding a good man for Dakota, of course. But that suddenly seemed easier, too, now that he was about to shake loose of his other problems. He'd been happy before, right? He'd simply go back to the way things were.

Smiling in unadulterated relief, he called Quentin Worrack to make sure he was still coming to the party. Tyson wasn't sure why he'd told Dakota that Quentin's mother was so meddlesome. Now that he really thought about it, Mrs. Worrack didn't seem all that bad.

What was this?

Dakota took the Dundee Pharmacy bag from her dresser at the cabin and sat on her bed as she sorted through it. Fingernail clippers. Chap Stick. Nail files. Ponytail holders. Toothpaste. Deodorant.

Where had all this stuff come from? Mrs. Cottle sometimes encouraged Dakota to help herself to a few essentials from the drugstore—as a benefit of working there—but Dakota couldn't imagine her employer had sent home a bunch of personal hygiene items, especially with Tyson. So what did that mean? That Tyson had *bought* them?

When she'd come down the hall, she'd peeked around the corner and noticed that his door was open a crack, too, which meant he was probably awake. But she'd wanted to change her clothes before letting him know she was back. When they'd gone to the doctor's earlier, her father had accidentally burned a hole in the sleeve of her blouse with his cigarette while she was trying to help him get back into the car, and she was exhausted and wanted to get comfortable.

Returning the drugstore items to the dresser, she shed her clothes in favor of a pair of sweats and a T-shirt, planning to go to bed as soon as she made sure Braden and Tyson were okay. Tyson had left several messages on her home recorder while she was in Boise, but he hadn't picked up when she tried to return his call, so she'd hurried back to the cabin instead of staying another night with her father. She figured he must've been having trouble with Braden and needed her.

A quick check of the baby's room seemed to confirm that. Braden wasn't there.

"Oh, boy," she muttered and hurried to Tyson's room.

"Come in," he called when she knocked.

She stepped inside to find him propped up in bed, wearing only a pair of basketball shorts. She could smell the dampness of a recent shower, could see that Tyson's hair was still wet. And Braden was lying on Tyson's bare chest, fast asleep.

Tyson himself seemed perfectly relaxed, which only added to Dakota's confusion. What was going on? Why had he been so eager to reach her? And if Braden was asleep, why hadn't Tyson put him in his crib? He always handed off the baby to her as soon as possible.

"Is everything okay?" she asked uncertainly.

Tyson grinned. "Better than okay."

Obviously something had happened while she was gone. "What does better than okay mean?"

"Greg called earlier."

"That's your agent, right?"

"Yeah." Tyson shifted, being careful not to wake Braden. "He thinks the whole Rachelle issue will soon be a thing of the past."

"How?"

"She happened to tell another waitress at the restaurant where she worked just what she wanted from me."

"Money?"

His expression turned a little self-conscious. "Not that part."

"What other part is there?"

He opened his mouth, then closed it again. "Never mind."

"Tell me. What'd she say?"

"That she…wanted to…you know, have some fun."

It wasn't often that Dakota saw Tyson at a loss for words. Fortunately she was beginning to catch on. "You mean put another notch on her bedpost?"

He chuckled. "You are so old-fashioned."

"You're the one who couldn't say it."

"I just figured you wouldn't want to hear it."

True, Dakota thought. Which was why she focused on working through the implications of this new development. "That should help convince people you didn't force her. But what's to stop her from claiming she changed her mind once you guys reached your place, and you wouldn't let her? You know Donaldson will believe whatever she says."

"Hey, are you trying to ruin my night?" He side-armed a pillow at her, which caused Braden to readjust his position. "It's the first good news I've had. I'm celebrating here."

Dakota managed a contrite expression. "Oh, right. Well, maybe she's not that smart. Anyway, it's a start, huh?"

His smile softened. "Yeah, it's a start. I feel high even though I haven't had a single drink."

She knew how badly the scandal had embarrassed and hurt Tyson, was pleased that the newspapers might not feel quite so free to characterize him as a predator in the future. "You want me to put Braden in his crib?" she asked, moving to the bed. She wanted to lift the baby into her own arms. She'd missed him, so much that it worried her. What was she going to do when Tyson took him and went back to L.A.?

He shook his head. "No, he's okay for now."

Another surprise.

"How'd it go at the doctor's?" he asked.

Dakota thought about the time she'd spent with Skelton. They'd enjoyed themselves, almost like old times. He hadn't even tried to make her feel guilty about leaving him to come back to the cabin, as he had in the previous two weeks. Hadn't balked when Terrance showed up. But he was ill. There was no getting around that. "Okay, I guess. He doesn't look good, and he doesn't feel good, but the doctor insisted he's no worse off than before."

"I hope the trip brought you some peace of mind, at least."

"It did. A little."

"How'd the car run?"

"Rough."

"We've got to find you another car."

He said this more to himself than to her, but she didn't want him to feel responsible for helping her. "Someday. For now I think I'll get the oil changed." She grinned. "Thanks for the paycheck."

"I owed it to you." His attention shifted back to the television. "Have you ever seen *The Last Samurai*?"

On TV, Tom Cruise was wearing a kimono

and watching himself do a kata. "No. Is it good?"

"One of my favorites." He motioned to a spot next to him. "Watch it with me."

She perched on the edge of the bed, hesitant to get too close for fear she'd forget everything she'd learned about herself over the past few days. "I found some interesting objects on my dresser," she said, still curious to learn where they'd come from.

He didn't glance away from the television. "I bought that stuff earlier, thought you might be able to use it."

"Ponytail holders, razors and deodorant? Are you trying to tell me something?" she joked.

When his eyes met hers, he was more serious than she expected. "Only that I care about you."

She didn't know what to say. Maybe he cared, but not enough. What he'd said before was evidence that his visit to Dundee hadn't made much of an impact on his life—that it had been nothing more than a voluntary time-out—while it had changed everything for her. Her world post-Tyson would never be the same.

"Thanks," she murmured and stood up before that meager offering could entice her into forgetting that "caring" wasn't love. "So...now you're all set for when you go back, eh?"

"Yeah." Lowering the volume on the television, he fiddled with the blanket. "Will you be going with me?"

"Even if I didn't have my father to worry about, I don't think that would be good for either one of us, do you?"

He seemed to think about it for a moment. "Sometimes I can't imagine leaving you behind."

"And other times?"

"I realize that I need to focus if I want to play football this year. I have to overcome a knee injury, adjust to being a father, repair my public image and salvage what I can of my endorsements. And I won't be able to concentrate on all that if I'm wondering what to do about you."

"What to do about me?" she echoed.

"When and if I should move on. How to do it without hurting you. What to do if I can't move on as easily as I have in the past. All of it."

"I see. Well, I wouldn't want to distract you from what really matters," she said and walked out.

Chapter 17

Grandpa Garnier: No matter who says what, don't believe it if it don't make sense.

Tyson was still feeling euphoric when Friday rolled around and the party began. Taxi after taxi had delivered friends he hadn't seen for weeks—in some cases months. And he'd just received word that the police wouldn't be pressing charges against him. Mindy's statement might not have been enough had Rachelle been content with arguing as Dakota guessed she might—simply claiming she'd changed her mind about sleeping with him and he'd refused to take no for an answer. But if she'd considered that easy lie, she hadn't been willing to rely on it. When she heard about Mindy's statement, she arranged a meeting with her old colleague, where she promised Mindy a tidy sum to change her story—a bribe Mindy recorded and turned over to police.

Tyson didn't know Mindy very well, but he was eternally grateful for her help and honesty. He'd sent her a gigantic bouquet of flowers as a thank-you because that tape did what nothing else could. Even Detective Donaldson had to admit Rachelle wasn't the injured party she pretended to be. It was the detective's call that dotted the *i* in *victory* for Tyson. Greg had been the first to pass along the good news, but Donaldson had called shortly afterward and offered Tyson a rather contrite apology, which was big of him considering his arrogance during their meeting.

The only thing really bothering Tyson now was the way Dakota was acting. After that night in his room when she'd walked out, she'd thrown herself into cooking a gazillion side dishes for the upcoming barbecue and taking care of Braden, but she'd been avoiding him the whole time. If Tyson got in the Jacuzzi, she went to bed. If he went to bed, she got in the Jacuzzi. If he worked out, she stayed clear of the gym and cleaned the kitchen. If he handled calls and paperwork in Gabe's office, she worked out.

Even tonight. *Especially* tonight. Tyson had invited Hannah and Gabe to the party, but they were expecting their oldest son home for a visit and had offered to keep Braden overnight at their place instead. They wanted Dakota to relax and enjoy herself without any distractions, they said, and she seemed to be taking advantage of the opportunity. Every time Tyson looked at her, she was smiling and laughing with someone else. She was dancing a lot, too. They'd pushed the furniture to the edges of the living room to create a dance floor.

"It appears your nanny is having a good time."

Tyson turned to see that Elaine had walked up behind him. The girlfriend of one of his best buddies, Hank Chapman, the center on the team, she was easygoing and affable, well-liked by the whole group. She was perceptive, too, judging by what she carried in her hands.

"How'd you know I wanted a beer?"

"It wasn't your thirst that brought me over."

"What's that supposed to mean?"

"You're staring."

"I'm what?"

She took a drink from her own frosty bottle, then tipped it toward the dancers. "It's true. When you're not flipping burgers outside, you're watching Dakota as if someone might throw a bag over her head and carry her off."

Evidently, he'd been feeling so good about everything else that he'd dropped his guard where Dakota was concerned. "I just want to be sure she's comfortable," he said. "She doesn't know anyone here but me. Gabe and his wife couldn't come."

"She seems to be fitting in."

They both watched as Quentin Worrack asked Dakota to dance—for the third time. Quentin teased her by swinging her around before going into an old-fashioned dip, and for the first time, Tyson realized that Dakota had lost even more weight. Or maybe it was those distracting jeans and that top he'd bought her, doing a little *too* much to set off her newly improved figure. If he'd thought she looked sexy in the shop, she looked downright scandalous in a crowded room. None of the other women had her earthy beauty, and the guys certainly noticed. Although there

were other women wearing much more revealing clothes, Tyson knew he wasn't the
only one having a hard time keeping his eyes
off the cleavage showing above the gray lace
of Dakota's undershirt.

"You think she likes Quentin?" he asked
above music playing so loud the whole house
pulsed to the rhythm.

"What do you want to hear?" Elaine replied with a laugh.

"Yes," he lied. "I'm trying to set them up."

Confusion clouded Elaine's eyes. "You're
kidding me, right?"

"No. They're perfect for each other."

"How so?"

"He's ready for marriage and babies. She's
ready for the same thing."

"And you're not—is that it?"

He stretched his neck, feeling a little uncomfortable. "I've already got Braden, of
course, but I'm not feeling particularly domestic."

"Marriage could interfere with football."

He took a pull from his beer. "A lot of guys
who play football are married, and they do
fine. I just can't picture myself settling down
at this point, that's all."

"You're afraid of the commitment."

Tyson wanted to deny that he had such a typical "guy" phobia, but he couldn't. "I've never met anyone I want to spend the rest of my life with," he said simply. "That's a big decision."

"Too big for you to ever make?"

"I've been in enough relationships to see how the passion and desire to be together fades with time."

She studied him. "God, I'm glad I'm in love with Hank and not you," she said.

"I'm being realistic."

"You're being cynical."

"Maybe I've been hanging around Greg too long."

"But you like her," Elaine said.

"Sure, I like her."

"How much?"

"What do you mean? I want her to find the right guy, someone she can love and be happy with."

"You're sure."

He smiled as confidently as possible. "I'm positive."

She shrugged. "Okay. I think I can help you out. The guy we brought with us? Hank's friend from high school?"

Tyson's eyes focused on a man he'd spoken with earlier, who was across the room. Tall, with dark hair and blue eyes, he looked as pretty as some of the women. "Joe Something or Other right? You've brought him to other parties."

"Joe Beck." Elaine toasted the object of their conversation, and Joe tilted his head in acknowledgment.

"What about him?"

"He thinks Dakota's beautiful, would love to spend some time getting to know her."

Tyson nearly told her that they'd never be right for each other, but caught himself before the words came out, knowing he wouldn't have an answer if she responded with a *why?* "He hasn't even asked her to dance," he said, attempting to make idle, unconcerned conversation.

"Because he's convinced he'd be invading your turf." She eyed Tyson carefully. "I told him he was wrong, that you'd be with her if you wanted her. But he disagreed. He said you've been subtly marking your territory all night. So I started paying more attention, and that's how I caught you staring at her."

"I'm not marking my territory," Tyson said with a grimace. "Dakota's my nanny, nothing more."

"So I can assure him you're not interested?"

Tyson hesitated. Quentin was a nice guy, but with a blockish head and slightly crooked nose, he wasn't nearly as good-looking as Hank's friend from high school. He wasn't nearly as savvy, either, or Quentin would've noticed the same nuances. But if Tyson had his guess, this Joe fellow might actually be someone Dakota could get excited about.

Wait. That was what he wanted, right?

"Is he a good guy?"

"*I* think so."

"What does he do for a living?"

"He's an investment broker, remember? I've told you that before. We're clients. So are a lot of the other guys on the team. He's hoping you'll invest with him, too. I think that's why he wanted to come tonight. You're his latest prospect."

"Is he any good at what he does?"

"He's great."

Tyson frowned. "Do you know what his mother is like?"

"His *mother?*" she said with another quick laugh. "I think you've had one too many, Ty."

"This is my first." He lifted his bottle as he spoke, suddenly realizing that one beer would never be enough to see him through this evening, not with ideal men like Joe Beck sniffing around Dakota. "I'm just being careful. I don't want to see her hurt."

"She looks like she can handle herself to me. Judging by the way you're acting, she's managed to stay out of your bed."

He refused to give Elaine any indication of whether or not she was right. "There's got to be something wrong with him," he said, still hoping to find some legitimate complaint against Beck.

Elaine gave him a playful jab with her fist. "Jeez, Tyson. He's not asking to marry her, you know."

Problem was, Tyson could imagine it happening. What wasn't there to like about Dakota? And he could see some of the other women in the room casting admiring glances at Joe, guessed he'd be at least a small temptation to Dakota.

That acknowledgment punctured the bubble of pleasure and relief Tyson had experienced since he'd escaped the hangman's noose. But he couldn't let Dakota fall back into her old life, which would happen if she wasn't involved with someone.

"Who am I to object?" he said at last and

downed the rest of his beer. Then he left the room so he wouldn't have to watch and drank another three bottles in the Jacuzzi.

Dakota knew the moment Tyson left the room because it was as if he took all the fun with him. The laughing and talking and music felt completely empty, made her chest hollow. But she kept smiling and nodding and dancing. This was a party, after all, and she wasn't about to reveal that she was more miserable now than before it had started.

"Excuse me."

Dakota turned to see a man with dark, curly hair, a movie-star smile and laughing blue eyes.

"I'm Joe."

"I'm Dakota." She offered her hand, and felt the warmth of his fingers close around hers.

"Nice name."

"You can probably guess where it came from."

He raised an eyebrow. "You were born in North or South Dakota?"

"Conceived in North Dakota, while my parents were on their honeymoon."

He stepped out of the way as someone passed through toward the kitchen, but continued to focus on her. "I can think of better places to spend a honeymoon."

"They wanted to visit as many states as possible."

"Did they make it to all of them?"

"No. They ran out of money after driving through four," she said with a laugh.

"But they were too in love to care, right?"

"My father was in love, not so sure about my mother." She'd spoken to Consuela a few times, but they were virtual strangers. Having left the United States twenty-four years before, Consuela's English had deteriorated to the point that Dakota could hardly understand her, and even without the language barrier it would've been difficult to communicate. Dakota had never been able to forgive her mother for abandoning them. Although Skelton had taken care of Dakota and loved her, he'd never completely recovered from the divorce. Dakota sometimes wondered if his drinking problem stemmed more from losing Consuela than the injury that kept him from being able to work. She also wondered what her life might've been like had her mother kept the promises she made when she married Skelton.

"Your parents are no longer together?" Joe said.

"No."

"Neither are mine. But my grandparents just celebrated their fiftieth, so I guess it's possible for love to last."

Dakota smiled. "What do you think the secret is?"

"Commitment. But it has to be a fierce commitment, or it won't survive life's bigger challenges."

"In sickness and in health, in poverty and in wealth," she murmured.

"I guess it's not such a secret, after all, huh?" His smile showed a row of straight white teeth as he offered her his hand. "Would you like to dance?"

Forget Tyson... Forget Tyson... Forget Tyson...

Dakota was doing her best. She had the attention of a very handsome man who was treating her as if she was the only woman in the room. She knew she should be enjoying every minute. Yet all she could think about was the wide receiver who'd walked out the back door an hour ago.

Give up on it already. He'll never return your feelings.

"Dakota?"

Joe had said something about his investment business. "I'm sorry." She shook her head. "The music's so loud. What was that?"

"Would you rather go out back, so we don't have to shout?"

Now that she'd complained about the music, Dakota didn't feel she could refuse. But Tyson was out back, or at least he'd headed that way when he left.

Was he still there? No telling. Most people had already eaten, but he could be grilling more steak, chicken or burgers. Or he could be in Gabe's old workshop where they'd set up tables for poker. He could even be around front, talking football or cars. There were people everywhere. Most would head back to Dundee at the end of the night and stay in the town's only motel. Hank and Elaine would stay at the cabin until Sunday.

"Sounds good."

"Why don't you put on your suit?" he asked. "We could get in the Jacuzzi."

When she'd taken her father to Boise the previous day, Dakota had purchased a black-and-white polka dotted bathing suit for the party. It was a relatively inexpensive one-piece, but she thought it was cute. "Sure. I'll be right back."

"I'll meet you in the water," Joe said.

Which seemed like the perfect plan—until Dakota walked out and realized that Tyson was in the Jacuzzi, too. With a beautiful woman sitting on either side of him.

Dakota knew that Joe was looking at her, but she couldn't feel his gaze the way she could Tyson's. Tyson's almost burned her as it traveled up her legs, over her hips, waist and breasts to her face. The other women were both wearing bikinis, but in that moment Dakota felt as if her own rather conservative suit revealed everything. The tips of her breasts began to tingle, and her cheeks grew hot before she could even sink into the water. Worse, the yearning inside her was so strong she feared everyone would see it.

"Having fun?" Tyson said, toasting her with a bottle of Samuel Adams.

Joe had brought out a couple of beers. Dakota picked one up and tipped it toward Tyson. "Most definitely. You?"

"Time of my life."

"Wonderful."

The women sidled closer to Tyson. Dakota had met them earlier. Apparently they were friends of one of the guys Tyson had invited. But that guy—Peter Somebody—wasn't around now.

Joe flashed his straight white teeth, then clinked the neck of his own beer bottle against Dakota's. "Here's to professional football."

"Why football?" Tyson's voice was thick enough that Dakota wondered if he'd had too much to drink. She could understand how he might get caught up in his recent good fortune. Judging by how close to him his female friends were sitting, they were eager to help him celebrate in any way they could. But other than the slightly slower speech and eyelids that were half-lowered, he showed no signs of inebriation.

"Because I'm a big football fan, excited that the season's about to start, of course," Joe said. "And now that she knows you, I'm sure Dakota's a fan, too, even if she wasn't before."

Dakota didn't comment because she wasn't sure she could call herself a true fan. She knew it was silly, but she was jealous of Tyson's career, because it was more than a vocation to him. It held first place in his heart, and no one, especially a poor woman who couldn't even leave the small town in which she'd grown up, would ever be able to compete.

"When do you have to return to L.A.?" Joe asked.

Beads of water rolled over Tyson's pectoral muscles as he hooked his arms over the lip of the Jacuzzi and studied Joe beneath his lashes. "Same time as Hank," he answered as if Joe should've known that all along.

"Of course."

Dakota cleared her throat, but the other women didn't seem to notice the strain between the two men.

"I can't wait till you come home," one of the women purred. "It's been such a *boring* spring with the team scattered all over the country."

Tyson didn't respond, but this comment seemed to identify the woman as a groupie. Maybe she'd come at the invitation of someone else, but she definitely had her eye on Tyson.

Surely he isn't stupid enough to get involved with someone like *that,* Dakota thought. But the way he was acting, she wasn't sure. He'd talked about being careful, but that seemed to apply only to her.

Maybe he was drunk, after all.

Tyson set his bottle on the side, his attention firmly fixed on Joe. "So what do you think of my nanny?"

Joe slid his glance Dakota's way. "I think she's amazing. What do *you* think of her?" he countered.

Tyson chuckled softly and brought his beer to his lips again. "She's great with kids. Looks damn good in that suit, too."

The women on either side of him exchanged a predatory glance and sat a little higher as if to make the most of what they were—or weren't—wearing. But Tyson didn't seem to notice.

Neither did Joe. "It's more than her body that interests *me*," Joe said.

Dakota squirmed uncomfortably as Tyson seemed to mark the inflection of his voice. "I'm glad to hear it," he said. "Because if it wasn't like that, I might have to break your jaw. And I wouldn't want to do that to a friend of Hank's." He smiled as if he was joking, but it was a challenging smile, not one that reached his eyes.

"Tyson!" Dakota said. "You're not my big brother."

"I don't think he has any illusions about that," Joe said wryly. Then he got out of the Jacuzzi and offered her a hand to help her out, as well.

They were gone. Tyson couldn't find them anywhere. After Dakota and Joe had left, he'd sat in the Jacuzzi another half hour, fighting the impulse to get out and search for them. Resisting turned out to be pointless, though, because it only took another two beers to change his mind. Abandoning the two women in the Jacuzzi, he moved around the party, looking for his nanny and her new love interest. And when he couldn't find them, the jealousy that had been eating away at him since Joe first asked about Dakota began to burn like acid in his stomach.

Maybe the handsome, smooth-talking Joe was everything he appeared to be. But Tyson couldn't sit back and watch another man make a move on Dakota. Somehow that kind of thing was easier to contemplate when it was only a possibility.

Hank bumped into him as Tyson walked

around the poker tables in the workshop. "What's wrong?"

"Nothing." He tried not to scowl as he scanned the crowded room, but that was almost impossible when he didn't find what he wanted.

"You look like you're ready to kill somebody."

Whether he resorted to violence would depend on what he found. If Joe was truly interested in Dakota *as a person,* he wouldn't need to be removing any clothing just yet.

The images that bombarded Tyson made him cringe. God, and he'd been the one to encourage her to start the pill. *Do you think what I've got is enough to...you know...revive my love life?* she'd asked. *Hell, yes! And now you've got the protection, too.*

"Have you seen Dakota?" Tyson asked a teammate's brother.

"Who?" the guy asked in confusion.

"My nanny."

"I didn't even know you had a nanny."

"Never mind." Brushing past him and Hank to go outside again, Tyson circled Dakota's garden and walked toward the front of the house. But Elaine saw him from the patio and intercepted him.

"They went on a hike," she said.

Tyson didn't ask how she knew who he was looking for. He nodded briskly, so he wouldn't respond to her smug "Aha! I know you care" smile, and strode through the gate. But once he was in front of the house, he realized it didn't make sense to go any farther. He could comb the forest all night and not find them. They could've gone anywhere.

The only thing he could do was wait.

Chapter 18

*Grandpa Garnier: Love your enemies
but keep your guns oiled.*

Tyson was sitting on the porch in one of
Gabe's homemade chairs when Dakota and
Joe returned. She didn't see him at first. It
was dark, he was in the shadows, and she
was too busy talking to Joe about his Italian grandmother. But then Tyson moved—
and she jumped and immediately let go of
Joe's hand.

"Tired of the party?" Joe smiled as if the
uncomfortable exchange at the Jacuzzi had
never taken place.

Tyson didn't answer.

"Ty?" Dakota said, confused by his stony silence. But he didn't respond to her, either. Getting up, he walked inside and slammed the door.

She turned to Joe. "I'm sorry. He's not normally like this."

"I know."

"I can't imagine what's gotten into him."

Joe grinned. "I can."

She waited, expecting him to elaborate, but he simply took her hand and started toward the house. "Don't worry about him. He'll get over it."

Dakota attempted a smile as Joe's fingers entwined with hers. But the slamming of the door seemed to echo in her soul, tempting her to go after the man she really wanted. What was wrong with him? He should be happy! He'd been cleared of Rachelle's accusations. And this whole party was his idea.

Anyway, it was very unlikely she and Joe would ever become an item. She was so in love with Tyson she couldn't really give Joe a fair chance. But there wasn't any reason they couldn't be friends. Joe was intelligent, confident, gregarious.

She needed to come out of this summer with *something* different, something hopeful....

"I feel like dancing," she said.

Joe nodded in approval. "Good girl."

Dakota put everything she had into having a good time. She laughed, she talked, she ate, she danced—and ignoring the sensible voice that usually caused her to limit her alcohol, she drank. Soon she no longer had to fake that she was having fun. She felt like she was walking on clouds, unreachable by reality or pain. Even the knowledge that Tyson would soon be leaving Dundee and taking Braden with him had lost some of its razor-sharp edge.

She deserved one night, didn't she? One night to cut loose and enjoy everything Tyson had introduced her to before he left and it all disappeared.

Tyson was drinking, too, probably just as much. But alcohol didn't seem to be having the same effect on him. Whenever she caught sight of him, he was scowling darkly, and that scowl had never been darker than it was right now while he watched her dance with Joe again.

"Having a good time?" Joe asked, drawing her attention back to him. Either Joe was oblivious to or ignoring Tyson's cold stare, because he didn't acknowledge it.

Focusing on the song that was playing—"Bring it on Home to Me" by Little Big Town—Dakota decided to ignore Tyson, too. What could he say about her behavior? Maybe she was a little tipsy, but she and Joe weren't dancing that close. "Yeah. I'm glad you came."

"So am I." He placed a kiss on her forehead. "You'll have to come visit me in L.A. sometime."

She blinked up at him in surprise. Her mind told her to agree. There wasn't any reason not to. Technically, she was available, had been hoping to meet someone tonight. And yet she felt as if she'd be leading him on. Her heart was already committed. "Joe, I… I think you're really nice, but—"

He held up a hand. "You just want to be friends."

She winced. "That's a tired line, I know. I'm sorry, but in my case it's sincere. I can't offer anything more. At least right now."

"Because you're in love with someone else?"

Her eyes sought Tyson again. "How'd you know?"

"I'd have to be an idiot to miss the way you and Tyson constantly search the room for each other. He's nearly breathing fire over there." Joe chuckled. "That's pretty tough to miss, too."

"Actually, I think he's upset that I'm not interested in the guy *he* picked out for me. He can be sort of…protective."

"You really think that's what's going on?"

"Don't you?"

"Not at all. If he was setting you up with someone, I'm betting it was with a guy who couldn't offer him any real competition."

No one could offer Tyson any real competition. That was part of the reason Dakota was so upset. There wasn't anything wrong with Joe. She should've jumped at the chance to get involved with him. Instead, she'd already backed away.

"He's trying to placate his conscience by pretending he's not standing between you and happiness," Joe continued. "In reality—and this could be strictly subconscious—he wants to put you on a shelf just in case he changes his mind."

Dakota wasn't sure Joe was right, but he

sure sounded confident of his analysis. "You should be a psychologist."

"If you look at the situation objectively, it's not that difficult to read."

"Tyson won't change his mind about me."

"He could. He's definitely tempted." Joe cocked an eyebrow at her. "He's about ready to punch me out, isn't he? That's not a mild reaction."

"If you already knew all of this, why did you invite me to L.A.?"

He turned her so that she couldn't see Tyson anymore. "Because, unlike Tyson, I'm not afraid of what you could mean to me. And I don't have a problem with waiting."

"He's going to break my heart," she said miserably.

"I think you might break his, too."

"No. I don't mean that much to him."

"Wanna find out?"

"How?"

"Simple. Kiss me. Kiss me like you'd kiss Tyson if he were holding you right now, and let's see what he does."

"He won't do anything. No woman means that much to him."

"You won't know until you test him."

The song started coming to an end. "What

do you get out of this?" she asked as they slowed to a stop.

He grinned. "A kiss."

She rolled her eyes. "You could get a kiss from just about any woman you wanted."

"Maybe you're the only woman I've asked in a long time. Anyway, it's time for him to fish or cut bait."

"Fish or cut bait," she repeated. That same cliché held true for her.

Tugging Joe into a small alcove, where someone would have to be specifically watching to notice, she pressed her lips to his. At first it was hard not to draw away. His mouth was warm and soft, but it wasn't Tyson's mouth. Only when she closed her eyes and let the wine she'd drunk help her imagine it *was* Tyson did she feel any desire. Then, parting her lips, she kissed Joe deeply, letting her fingers bunch in his hair.

They were both breathing hard when they parted. "Wow," Joe said. He looked a little stunned. But Tyson was nowhere to be seen.

Tyson didn't reappear for the rest of the evening. Dakota continued to go through the motions of socializing and playing hostess, which she felt obligated to do in Tyson's ab-

sence, but she wanted everyone, including
Joe, to go home. By the end of the evening,
when all guests were in bed or had used taxis
to take them to the motel in Dundee, and
she'd finished cleaning the kitchen, it was
nearly two o'clock in the morning.

On impulse, she called home. Her father
had been doing better about keeping his
promise to stay sober. Or maybe it wasn't
his willpower that deserved the credit. His
health had been so bad lately he didn't feel
like eating or drinking. But after what she
considered a pretty disastrous evening, she
missed him. Maybe she was trying to force
too many changes in her life. Maybe, even
before Tyson left, she should move home.
Watching Braden during the day but sleeping in the trailer at night would help keep
her head on straight. Maybe, in a few weeks,
she could even dredge up the desire to see
Joe again.

The phone rang four times. She was about
to hang up. Her father slept in fits and starts
and was often awake at odd hours of the
night. But if he happened to be resting well,
she didn't want to disturb him.

"'Lo?"

At the sound of his deep, scratchy voice,

Dakota brought the receiver back to her ear. "Dad? Did I wake you?"

"No. But it's late, isn't it? Gotta—"

"Two," she answered to save him the trouble of using the TV remote to find out. He had a clock in his room, but he piled so much on the dresser he probably couldn't see it.

"What's wrong?" he asked.

"Nothing," she lied. "How are you?"

"The same."

"Is the pain in your back getting worse?"

"Sometimes better or worse isn't that easy to distinguish. It's just there, always."

Because of me. "I'm sorry. Sometimes I wish…"

"What?"

She finally put into words what she'd thought so often in secret "…you hadn't been able to rescue me that day."

"Then you could've died!" he said. "Don't *ever* talk like that."

"But it's not fair. You told me to stay away from the construction. I can still hear you warning me."

"You were only a child. Kids are curious. If I hadn't taken you with me, it wouldn't have happened."

"You had to take me. I was too little to stay home alone."

"I should've waited for Regina or another baby-sitter or...*something*. I could've lost you...." Although his words dwindled off, Dakota heard a silent *"too"* at the end. He'd lost her mother long before the accident. She'd wounded him maybe as irreparably as the piece of wood that fell on him from twenty feet above. "Anyway, that's a trade I'd make again, in a heartbeat," he added gruffly.

Dakota's throat tightened at those words. She couldn't speak right away, so she was grateful when her father didn't push her for a response.

"You need anything?" she asked at length. "Braden's staying with Hanna and Gabe tonight. I could come home. Bring some of the leftover food we've got here. I made potato salad."

"Isn't Tyson around?"

"I think he went to bed a long time ago."

"You should be in bed, too. Anyway, it's starting to rain here. I'd rather not have you out driving in it, especially at this hour."

He sounded like the old Skelton, the admonishing and cautious parent she'd known before alcohol had become his crutch.

"It's good to talk to you again," she said softly.

He didn't point out that they talked every day, didn't ask what she meant. On some level, she believed, he understood. "Get some sleep, okay? I don't need anything."

"Dad?" she said before he could hang up.

"What?"

"I love you."

"I know. I thank God for you every day," he said and the line went dead.

Dakota dashed a hand across her wet cheek. The alcohol she'd had earlier was making her feel weepy, she decided. And she hadn't had much sleep this week. She'd been so busy avoiding Tyson, taking care of Braden and getting ready for the party, she'd been on the go constantly.

"Everything will look better in the morning," she promised herself. She hoped that would be true of the whole evening. Even the memory of having kissed Joe just to make Tyson jealous, which seemed terribly desperate now that her reasoning skills were less impaired. But when she climbed the stairs, she didn't go straight to her room. She saw a sliver of light beneath Tyson's door and couldn't resist knocking.

"Go away," he said, but she poked her head in anyway.

He was sitting on his bed, fully clothed, watching television. At the motion of the door, his gaze cut her way. A muscle twitched in his cheek, but he didn't say anything.

A voice in Dakota's head warned her not to go inside. If she waited until morning, her conflicting emotions might possibly disappear, or at least come into sharper focus. She felt like she was dangling at the end of a very thin string, swaying in the wind. She'd fall, and she'd fall hard if she wasn't careful. But she couldn't shut the door on the wounded expression that entered Tyson's eyes when he saw her.

"Everyone who was planning on leaving has left," she said, acting as if she'd merely come to report on the party.

He didn't reply.

"Hank and Elaine are sleeping in the guest room above the garage."

No response.

"I cleaned up. We're good to go for breakfast, when everyone returns."

Nothing.

Finally Dakota sighed and gave up the

false cheer. "Are you just going to sit there and stare at me?"

"Where's Joe?" he replied.

She flashed back on that kiss and felt her face flush. "He went to the motel."

The muscle flexed in Tyson's cheek again. "You didn't have him stay?"

"No."

Looking sleepless and upset with his hair standing up on one side, he watched her closely. "Why not?"

She took in the definition of his powerful shoulders, the flicker of emotion in his eyes, the sensual mouth that currently formed a hard line. "How can I make love with him when the only person I really want is you?"

His Adam's apple moved as his gaze swept over her, and her heart began to pound. She'd laid it all out there, bared her soul. Now she didn't know what would happen. She thought he might warn her, again, that he'd be leaving. But he didn't. Her confession seemed to be all that was necessary to snap his restraint.

"Let's do it this time," he said.

Dakota was so nervous she could barely get into the pretty bra and panties that Tyson had given her as she left his room. He'd told her she didn't have to wear them unless she wanted to, but she definitely wanted to. In them, she felt prettier, sexier. Still, she'd never owned such revealing lingerie, let alone worn it for someone. And her weight loss was so recent that she wasn't completely confident in her body. Was she thin enough? Would he find her attractive?

She felt so exposed—physically and emotionally.

"Dakota?" He was right outside her door. Obviously she was taking too long, but breezing into his room wearing nothing except a sheer bra and a thong seemed so brazen. She'd been trying to figure out whether or not she should cover up with the clothes she'd had on before, or use a robe.

"Yes?"

"Is something wrong?" he asked.

She drew a deep breath. "No."

"So…why are you still in there?"

"I'm just wondering—" she shot another glance at herself in the mirror "—am I supposed to wear something over this?"

His low chuckle was filled with relief. "Why? I'll just have to take it off. I prefer you skin to skin." His voice had deepened, grown rougher. "Can I come in?" he asked when she didn't immediately open the door.

Reaching over, she flipped off the light. "Sure."

The door opened, and she steeled herself for the moment he'd see her in the sliver of light from the hall. But it wasn't as frightening as she'd anticipated. He stared at her with his mouth agape, his eyes moving over her as if he couldn't take in her appearance quickly enough. "You're beautiful," he breathed.

She smiled, no longer quite so self-conscious. "What made you buy this stuff?" she asked.

"The desire to see you in it." He came in and closed the door behind him.

Emboldened by the sudden and complete darkness, Dakota stepped toward him. She craved Tyson's hands on her body, his mouth hungrily devouring hers. Every nerve seemed to scream for the same thing, so loudly she couldn't hear above the cacophony of need.

He touched her first at the bare curve of her waist. His hand rested there lightly, as if he was afraid he might spook her if he didn't calm her first. Then his mouth found hers, giving her a chaste but tempting kiss. "You're all I've been able to think about."

She parted her lips, prepared for something far deeper, and he groaned as she encouraged him. Moving his tongue over hers, he explored her mouth in a thorough, searching kiss that left her weak at the knees. "And you taste every bit as good as I thought you would."

Finding the bare skin beneath his shirt, Dakota slipped her fingers up and over the muscular contours of his chest. She'd imagined doing this at least a million times, but the reality of touching the man she loved so powerfully and so hopelessly was better than she could've dreamed.

This was what she'd longed for—and what she feared. She'd fallen for a man who would never offer her what she was willing to offer him. But she couldn't think about that now. Heady desire seemed to spread through her veins like sweet, thick honey.

His nipples puckered beneath her touch, and she heard him suck in a quick breath. "This won't be easy," he said.

"What won't be easy?" she murmured. So far, it was the easiest thing in the world, everything she wanted.

"To go slow, to not get carried away." His hand was on her breast, stroking her through the thin fabric of her bra, which made it difficult to think. "I don't want to hurt you."

"It won't hurt for long, right?"

"I'm hoping it won't hurt at all." Tyson's hand moved lower, making her squirm at the intimacy of the contact.

"It's okay," he whispered. "Relax."

Relax? Was he kidding? "That's asking a bit much. I'm not sure I can even breathe."

"That's part of the fun. You like it, right?"

Closing her eyes, she let her head fall back. "I like it."

His razor stubble grazed her neck as he kissed her there. "Tell me what you want, Dakota. Tell me you want me as bad as I want you."

She caught his face between her hands. "I do," she answered earnestly.

He stared down at her as he slipped aside her thong. "Where, Dakota? *Where* do you want me?"

She couldn't answer. Her whole world seemed to be tilting on its axis, leaving her boneless and weak and completely dependent on him. He didn't give her time to respond, anyway. Using one arm to support her, he kissed her again while using his other hand to search out everything he'd denied himself. "Here?" he asked, and thrust his finger deep.

She gasped at the heady rush of pleasure that slammed into her.

The muscles in his body tensed in response, and he paused to rest his forehead against hers. He didn't explain, but she got the impression he was struggling not to lose control. "You're perfect," he told her, his voice strained as if he hovered somewhere between pain and ecstasy.

She undid the top button of his jeans, but he stopped her before she could touch anything more than the straining zipper. "Not yet."

"Why not?" she murmured, slightly dazed.

His hand slid her panties aside once again, more confidently and possessively this time, as though he'd already done a little exploring and had every right to claim the new territory as his own. "Because it's your turn."

"Can't we both have our turns together? Isn't that how it works?"

His laugh held no humor. "If I didn't want you so bad, maybe we could."

At least she wasn't in this alone.

Dakota was already soaring inside—gliding, spinning, dipping and gathering speed.

Tyson was at the center of it all, both the cause and the reason. She'd never felt so physically or emotionally out of control.

Picking her up, he carried her into his room and deposited her on the bed. Then he stripped off his clothes and lay next to her.

The feel of his skin against hers was every bit as heavenly as she'd imagined. She let her hands delve into his hair, raked her nails gently across his back and breathed in the scent of wood and evergreen that lingered on him.

"This feels so good," she said. "*You* feel good."

"Take these off."

When she obediently wriggled out of her panties, he acted as if he wanted to roll her beneath him immediately. But he stopped her when she tried to slip her arms around his neck, encouraging him to do just that. "Not yet," he told her. The light was on in his room, and she could watch him watching her. He was gazing down at her as if he'd never seen anything more lovely.

"Why not?"

He kissed the side of her mouth. "You're not ready."

She might've argued, but he'd unhooked

her bra, and she couldn't think as his mouth closed over one of her breasts. "Tyson!" she gasped.

He laughed, his breath warm against the wetness he'd created, and moved to her other breast.

She arched into him, seeking more of the titillating scrape of his tongue. The tension inside her was so tight she thought she might explode. "What are you doing to me?" she asked.

But he didn't answer. He didn't have to. His mouth soon left her breasts and moved lower—and a few minutes later, she knew.

Tyson had never used so much restraint. Probably because he'd never been quite so eager to make love to a woman. But the added effort with Dakota was worth it. When her hands fisted in his hair and she moaned his name, he felt a great deal of masculine pride—which quickly gave way to pleasure as he eased himself inside her.

"That's it," he encouraged as her body slowly accepted him. If it hurt, she didn't complain or even flinch. Of course, she'd been through enough in her life that she wasn't the spoiled or delicate type. He was proud of that, proud of her. She was a survivor.

Still, he was taking it so slowly it was almost an agony to him. Watching her carefully, he began to move slowly and gently, trying to read her every expression, her body's responses. "You okay?"

"Yes. Stop holding back," she said. "I want all of you."

He closed his eyes as she wrapped her legs around him, pulling him deeper, and finally gave in to the drive that had been building in him for weeks. Pleased when she eagerly met his every thrust, he finally allowed his body the release it craved. After the most exquisite pleasure blasted through him, he collapsed on top of her, enjoying the musky scent of her sweat-slicked body. But a few seconds later, he roused himself and rolled off so he wouldn't crush her.

"You still okay?" he asked. Sleep beckoned, but he didn't want to succumb until he'd made sure she felt good about what they'd done.

"Fine," she murmured.

After the passion she'd shown him, he'd expected something a little more reassuring than a polite, one-word answer. When she didn't elaborate, he rose up on one elbow and tried to see her face. "You liked it, right?"

She threaded her fingers lightly through his hair. "I liked it a lot. You'll be a hard act to follow," she said, sounding aloof for the first time since he'd touched her.

The euphoria began to dissipate. "A hard act to follow? What's that supposed to mean?"

"It's a compliment. It means it'll be tough for anyone else—in the future, of course—to compete."

He hesitated, unsure why she'd had to bring them both back to reality so abruptly. "We just made love, Dakota. Do we have to talk about other men right now?"

"I wasn't talking about other men. I was merely trying to let you know that you don't have to look back once you go. I'll move on and be perfectly fine."

He didn't know how to respond. She was purposely giving him exactly what he wanted—a brief but torrid affair, no strings attached. But it was a little *too* brief, even for him. "I've already asked you to go back with me."

"I know. I can't leave my father." She got out of bed.

"Where are you going?" he asked in surprise.

"I want to take a quick shower and get some sleep." She made an attempt to search for something—the bra and panties?—but when she didn't immediately encounter them, she gave up. The bedding was so jumbled, they could be anywhere, and he was too shocked by her actions to worry about discarded clothing.

He rubbed his eyes. "What'd I do?"

"Nothing. This is how 'casual' works, isn't it?"

"*Casual?*" he echoed. "You didn't respond as if this was casual."

"I'm new at it. Maybe I'll get better with time." He was pretty sure she was smiling, which seemed to bother him almost as much as her words. "Good night and—" she seemed at a loss "—is 'thanks' appropriate?"

Tyson felt the anger that had boiled inside him earlier return. "Yeah, no problem," he said. "Let me know the next time you're looking to get off. If I'm still around, maybe I can be of service."

"Maybe," she echoed, and she snapped off the light as she left.

Chapter 19

*Grandpa Garnier: Love is like war,
easy to begin but hard to end.*

Dakota charged immediately to the bathroom, shut and locked the door and leaned against it. Her whole body was shaking, even her lips, and her throat stung with the effort of holding back tears, which she could no longer deny. They rolled down her cheeks in a steady stream, but it didn't matter now. She'd done it. She'd let Tyson off the hook before he could even wonder what to do about her.

I had to. It would've come to that eventually, right? And she much preferred their brief romantic interlude to end while they could still like and respect each other. If she hadn't acted right away, there was a good chance he would've awakened in the morning, realized what he'd done and regretted it. He wanted to be free. He'd made that clear from the beginning. Which meant he'd only resent her if she tried to take that away from him.

As difficult as it had been to climb out of his bed, especially on the heels of the soul-moving encounter they'd just shared, she'd managed to make her legs work and her lips smile and her voice sound nonchalant. The past few minutes had cost her a great deal, but it had been worth it to maintain her dignity.

She thought about how gentle he'd been with her, how unselfish, and closed her eyes. She'd never forget tonight, wouldn't let herself be sorry.

Drawing a bolstering breath, she turned on the shower, but she didn't get in. Maybe she wanted Tyson to think she could wash away every trace of him that perfunctorily, but she couldn't. The scent of him lingered on her skin, and she wanted it to remain as long as possible.

Besides the memory, it was all she'd allow herself to take into tomorrow.

Tyson felt a little shell-shocked as he listened to the water run. He wasn't sure how to react. A few minutes earlier, Dakota had been panting his name and clinging to him as if she'd die before letting go. And then... *Is "thanks" appropriate?*

"Wow," he muttered, and scraped his palm over his face.

The water went off, and he found himself waiting for her footsteps in the hall. He was hoping she'd have something else to say to him, so that he'd have the opportunity to convince her to come back and curl up with him. He hadn't meant that parting shot. He hoped she knew that. Even if she had used him, he wouldn't mind letting her do it again. And again.

We're going to have to figure this out. They had very different pasts; they wanted very different futures. But he cared about her. Did it have to be all or nothing?

The light disappeared from beneath the door. She wasn't coming back.

Briefly, Tyson considered going to her, but ultimately decided against it. They needed to talk. But it had already been an emotionally exhausting evening. And if he couldn't give her what she really wanted, he'd only hurt her in the end, right?

Maybe she knew his limitations better than he did.

Joe was at breakfast. Because Dakota couldn't quite meet his eye, she kept herself busier than she had to be making breakfast, serving the guests and cleaning up. She hoped no one would notice how withdrawn she was today, but of course, Joe did. He tried to talk to her on two different occasions, but Elaine drew him away both times.

As difficult as it was to face Joe, it was even harder to face Tyson. What they had shared last night was so intimate—more intimate than anything she'd ever shared with another human being—and it felt strange to wake up and go back to business as usual. Especially when she could've sworn she had a big sign blinking over her head that said, "I had sex with Tyson last night."

"Hey, how come you're the one doing all the work?"

Dakota felt her muscles tense at the sound of Joe's voice. After a quick stint in front of the television, laughing at sports bloopers with a lot of the other guests, he was back. "Breakfast was my idea," she said with a shrug. "Tyson handled the barbecue, I agreed to do breakfast."

Joe insisted on drying off the frying pan she'd just washed. "So...how'd it go with him last night?"

Cheeks burning, she turned and opened a cupboard, ostensibly to put away some glasses. "He went to bed early."

"Come on." In her peripheral vision, she saw him arch one eyebrow. "You're telling me you didn't see him after I left?"

Her hand froze midmotion. Then she closed the cupboard and glanced around, afraid someone else had heard the meaningful inflection of his voice. No one was paying particular attention. Except Tyson, of course. He'd been watching her all morning. He'd even come up behind her once, so close she could feel the heat of his body. His breath had stirred the hair around her ear as he'd whispered, "Every time I look at you, I see you as I saw you when I first opened your bedroom door last night."

Dakota had tried to stifle the shiver his words evoked, but she knew he'd noticed when she met his eyes and he'd given her a slow, sexy smile. She knew what that smile meant—that it was going to take Herculean effort to keep their attraction from getting out of hand again, especially because he was done fighting. He wanted more, and he was letting her know it.

"Dakota?"

She blinked at Joe. "What?"

"That kiss worked, didn't it?"

Dakota saw Tyson give Elaine a "take care of it" look and Elaine moved toward them. But Joe pulled Dakota into the pantry before she could reach them and shut the door. "So...are you two an item now or what?" he asked.

"Dakota?" It was Elaine, knocking on the door.

"Tell Tyson to protect his own interests," Joe called back to her.

"I don't know what you're talking about," she said innocently. "I just came over to tell Dakota how good breakfast was."

"Sure you did. Anyway, she thanks you and will do so in person later."

"What?" Elaine replied innocently.

"You heard me."

They both heard Elaine move away, reluctantly if the pause that followed served as any indication, and Joe turned his attention back to Dakota. "What happened last night?"

"Nothing. Nothing's changed," she lied.

"Then you're still in love with him."

She shrugged. "Pathetic, huh?"

He didn't seem pleased, but he took the news like a good sport. "At least he's interested. I've been to several parties he's attended in the past year, but I've never seen him act that way about anyone else."

"He's too caught up in football to care about a woman."

"Well, if you ever need a shoulder to cry on…" Joe reached into his wallet and handed her his card. "And if you're interested in making money, I could give you a few investment tips at the same—" His words fell off as his eyes shifted to a spot over her left shoulder.

Dakota knew the squeak she'd heard was Tyson opening the door. Ignoring the awareness that skittered down her spine, she nodded. "Sure. I appreciate it."

"Your investment tips are so secret they've got to be shared in the pantry?" Tyson asked dryly.

Dakota grinned at Joe, who winked and shook his head. "See what I mean? I'd better get back to the party. I've got to thank Elaine for tattling."

Swallowing a laugh, Dakota waited until he was gone to face Tyson.

"What was that all about?" he asked suspiciously.

"You heard him. An investment opportunity."

"It had better not be an investment in *you*."

"We're just friends."

His eyes remained wary. "Still playing at casual relationships?"

She lifted her chin. "Getting good at them, actually. I have an excellent teacher."

"You still think last night was casual." As he stepped closer, his masculine scent evoked erotic memories.

"Of course." She swallowed hard. "Casual is all you do, right?"

"That depends on your meaning of the word." He closed the door behind him, and the noise from the breakfast party immediately dimmed. "Casual doesn't mean indifferent, Dakota." Putting his hands on her shoulders, he ran them down her arms. "I care about you. I've already told you so."

In a desperate bid to save her sanity, she told herself it wasn't true. Or if it was, what he felt couldn't compare to her feelings for him. But it was difficult to hang on to that thought when he was so close...lowering his head...kissing the corner of her mouth... pulling her up against him. "Or that I'm not dying to touch you again."

Proof of that was very apparent. "There are people on the other side of that door," she pointed out.

"Which is why I can't go back out there yet." He kissed her more deeply.

"I don't think that kind of kissing will help."

"You're right," he admitted. "God, I can't believe we were stupid enough to invite all these people up here. All I want to do is make love with you. And we're invaded, overrun. But it won't be long before they go."

Dakota tried to drum up some of her resolve. "Tyson, what happened last night won't happen again. Casual means...casual, okay? It means no right to future contact. It means no commitment. I'm your nanny, nothing more." *Please, leave me the chance to recover.*

He watched her steadily. "But you want to make love again."

He'd made it a statement, but she could

tell he was wondering, hoping she'd admit it. "Someday. When I find the right man."

"I don't see Mr. Right on the horizon. So why not enjoy some lesser mortal, someone like me, in the meantime?"

And die a little in the process? "Tyson—"

He silenced her with a kiss that burned all the way to her toes. "Can you honestly tell me you don't want me?" he asked.

"I'm saying I'm stupid to get involved."

"But I'll be leaving soon."

"Exactly!" If he only knew how deeply she was falling in love with him. "Anyway, there're other women to…enjoy."

He had his hand under her shirt, cupping her breast. "I don't want anyone else."

She fought the current of desire threatening to sweep her away. "Someone could walk in here, Ty."

"Which is why we should take this upstairs."

"Right *now?*"

"Why not?" He trailed kisses down her neck. "You've been driving me crazy all morning."

Her restraint slipped a little further. "We were just together last night."

"You left too soon. I hated that."

It had been a major victory. And here she was, backsliding. "What about your friends?"

"They're busy having fun. They'll never miss us."

She laughed, kissed him, then gently nipped his lip with her teeth. "Forget going upstairs." As long as she was going to crash and burn, she might as well create the mother of all bonfires. "Let's take the Ferrari into the mountains."

"You want to make love outside?"

"Why not?"

"You'll get no complaints from me." He grinned as his hands slid down, rounded her bottom. "I'll get a blanket and some wine. You want anything else?"

"Just you."

Sobering, he stared down at her for a long moment. Something changed in his eyes, softened. But she didn't know what it meant and, a second later, he slipped out.

"I can't believe we did this," Dakota said, mumbling as if she didn't have the energy to speak clearly. "We have guests at home."

Tyson had his pants up, but they hadn't been up for long. He opened his eyes and squinted at the dappled sun falling through the pine trees all around them. He felt like he was floating on the wind that was gently buffeting the leaves. "If we don't go back right away, maybe they'll leave," he said hopefully. "I wouldn't mind saying goodbye to Joe."

"Joe's not so bad." She stirred, rolling away from him onto her side. "Anyway, they're your friends. Why do you want them to leave so soon?"

"I have other interests right now." He curled his body around hers, lowering his hand until he found what he wanted, then smiled as he heard Dakota's quick intake of breath.

"Such as…" she managed to say, but the word sounded a little strangled.

He lowered his head to breathe the words into her ear. "Making you writhe and moan and completely lose control. Again."

"I'm too exhausted. It won't work," she said, but it was a halfhearted answer, because he was already getting a good start on it.

"Wanna bet?" he challenged. Then he proceeded to prove her wrong.

"Tell me about your mother."

Dakota was lying on Tyson's shoulder. For the past several minutes, she'd been chastising herself for not getting up and insisting Tyson drive them back to the cabin so she could resume hostessing duties. But she felt so content she couldn't move.

"What do you want to know about her?"

"How long has it been since you've seen her?"

"I was only a baby when she left."

"So you don't remember her?"

She brushed her hand over his washboard abs, the light matting of hair on his chest. "No. I have a few pictures, that's all."

"I'd like to see them sometime."

Dakota didn't answer. The pictures weren't something she pulled out from under the bed very often. The woman in them was a stranger.

"Do you have much contact with her?"

"She's called a few times. Not a lot."

"What does she say?" He ran his fingers idly through the long strands of her hair.

"She asks how I'm doing in heavily accented English. Twice, she invited me to visit her, but even if I could've left my father, I don't know how either of us would've paid the travel expenses. Although she's remarried, her husband works as a truck driver, she works as a housekeeper and they have five kids to take care of. Besides that, she comes from a very poor family, all of whom saved for years to make it possible for her to come to the States so that she could have a better life."

"A life she ended up not wanting."

That wasn't the only thing she hadn't wanted. And Dakota could anticipate the same kind of treatment from Tyson. He was going to leave her, as well—and he was going to take Braden with him.

Sitting up, she began straightening her clothes. "We'd better get back. I want to pick up Braden, don't you?"

"Hey." He took her hands, forcing her to look at him. "Don't withdraw."

"I'm not withdrawing. There's just not much to say about my mother."

"What happened to your parents' marriage, do you know?"

"From what my father has said, too many differences. My mom was a devout Catholic, my father was agnostic—still is. She wanted to maintain the traditions of her homeland; my father wanted her to adopt American traditions. Bottom line, they didn't get along, and she missed her family so much she eventually went back."

"And your father? How long ago did he get hurt?"

"It's been sixteen years."

"He's been in pain that long?"

She pretended to be absorbed in zipping and buttoning.

"What happened?" he asked, watching her.

She didn't want to talk about it. Facing the reason for her father's injury made her feel guilty, even though she'd been only ten years old when she made the mistake that had caused everything. "He just…got hurt."

"How?"

Brushing the twigs from her hair, she used her fingers to comb it into some semblance of order. "It was an accident." Finished, she reached out to help him up. "Let's go."

He hesitated, but finally seemed to accept her reluctance to supply details. "Wouldn't want to keep *Joe* waiting," he said, giving her the evil eye.

She grinned at the jealousy in his voice. Tyson hadn't shaved today. She liked the shadow of beard growth that covered his jaw, the unruliness of his short, thick hair, the mischievous sparkle in his eyes. "Give poor Joe a break."

"If he doesn't back off, I'm going to give him a black eye."

"Why are you so threatened by him?" she asked.

"Because he's just a little too eager to see me gone."

She grew serious as she smoothed a finger over the cowlick above Tyson's forehead. "That doesn't matter. You can take me or leave me, remember?"

He gave her a funny look but he didn't say anything, just held the door while she got in the car.

"Do I look as if we've been messing around?" Dakota asked, sounding self-conscious.

Tyson hid a satisfied smile as he cut the engine of the Ferrari and lowered the garage door, pausing long enough to pick a pine needle out of her hair. "Do you want the truth?"

Twisting the rearview mirror so she could see into it, she attempted to make more repairs. "Not if you have to ask that."

He leaned toward her, making the most of the light shed by the automatic garage door opener, which would shortly snap off and leave them in darkness. "For what it's worth, I think you look sexy as hell," he said and meant every word of it. But maybe that was because it was *his* kisses that had left her mouth a little swollen, *his* razor stubble that had chafed the soft skin of her cheek and neck, *his* hands that had explored every inch of her body.

She eyed the door that led beneath a covered walkway to the cabin. "Why don't you go in and play host while I drive to town, visit my father and pick up the baby?"

Braden. Oddly enough, Tyson was eager to have him back, too. And it had nothing to do with worry. He knew Hannah would be taking excellent care of him. "You're done with the party?"

"I'm afraid our plan has failed miserably."

"You got laid, didn't you?" he teased.

She grimaced. "By the wrong guy."

Sobering, Tyson sat up. He didn't like her response, but he couldn't correct her. He *was* the wrong guy. They'd both known it from the beginning.

"It's okay to have a little fun before you settle down." At least he hoped it'd be okay. He didn't want to hurt Dakota just because he couldn't keep his hands off her.

"Yeah. No worries. This is casual."

There was that word again. But this *wasn't* casual. He knew because he was the king of casual, and what he felt for Dakota was completely different. He'd tried to tell her that. But she wouldn't believe him, and he didn't have a better label for their relationship, so he let it go. "You don't think your father will realize you've been making love with me? You look like you're just about ready to light the proverbial cigarette."

She laughed at the mental image his words evoked. "I'll tell him I was out in the garden, working. He'd buy that excuse before anyone at the party would, after seeing me come in with you."

"Your father's pretty leery of me."

"I know. He warned me not to sleep with you."

"He did?" Tyson felt about two inches tall. He'd been trying to protect her from Skelton, and Skelton had been trying to protect her from *him*. "It's just sex," he said a bit defensively. "It's not like I've been torturing you. You liked it, too, right?"

"It's just sex," she repeated, but her voice sounded a little odd, and she got out instead of answering his question.

"If you'll wait until later, I'll go to town

with you. We could have dinner at the diner. Take some to your father."

"I'd rather go alone, if that's okay."

She was pushing him away again, like last night. He hesitated, uncomfortable with her change of mood, but then he told himself that maybe she needed the space. "Take the Ferrari, at least."

"No. I'll call you when I'm heading back. If I don't arrive in forty minutes, you'll know I got stranded."

"Why not take my car?"

"I just…want to find the old me."

"You haven't changed," he said.

She flashed him a mysterious smile. "Have fun."

He didn't know how to respond. "You won't be gone long, will you?"

"What time do I need to have Braden home?"

"I'd like you both back before dark. I don't trust that hunk of junk you're driving."

"Okay," she said.

He sighed, trying to shake the uneasiness that crept over him as he watched her drive away. Then he went inside. But it wasn't half an hour later that he got a call from the police chief—a call that told him he should never have let her go to her father's alone.

Chapter 20

*Grandpa Garnier: You can never
step in the same river twice.*

Dakota knew something was wrong the
moment she pulled up to her father's mobile
home. The police chief's car sat out front,
the driver's door standing open as if he'd
made a mad dash for the house. Several of
the neighbors stood around, shuffling their
feet, smoking or murmuring to each other.
They watched her pull up and, when she got
out, stared at the ground.

"What is it?" she asked. She left her purse

in the passenger's seat, suddenly unconcerned about such practical matters.

Fanny Duluth, who owned the mobile
home closest to them, exchanged a meaningful glance with her husband. Then her chest
lifted, and she stepped forward. "He's gone,
honey. I found him when I came over to borrow some coffee this morning. He must've
passed right after Terrance left, because I've
called him and he was as surprised as anyone."

He's gone… The words seem to echo in
Dakota's head, bouncing around several
times before they made any sense. "But…"
The rest of her words wouldn't come out.
She'd been about to say, "That can't be true.
I spoke to him last night. He said he was fine,
that he didn't need anything."

But she knew what Fanny said was true.
The man who had been both a curse and a
blessing was no longer part of her life. Just
like that—in the blink of an eye—he'd been
erased. She felt such a mixture of emotions she didn't know how to react, but guilt
seemed to hit her hardest. In her most secret
moments, she'd wished for the freedom this
moment signified and felt that it was her wish
that had caused her father's death.

"Are you okay?" another neighbor asked, concern clouding her face.

Dakota didn't know. "How'd it happen?" she managed to ask.

"Dr. Hatcher's on his way. He'll determine the exact cause of death. But we all know Skelton was sick, real sick. This is a blessing, honey. For both of you."

A blessing... She'd lost her father, the man who'd taught her to tie her shoes and ride a bike and drive. And it was a blessing.

"At least he's no longer in pain. And you're finally free to live your own life."

Dakota lifted a hand as she struggled to swallow past the lump clogging her throat. Her father probably wasn't even cold yet and the neighbors were already telling her how much better off she'd be. "Don't, please," she said and started toward the house.

"I'm not sure you should go in there," Fanny called after her, but Dakota was out of reach before she could do anything to stop her, and the others didn't even try. Some murmured a quick, "I'm sorry, Dakota, real sorry," but they didn't expect an answer, and she didn't give them one. Her thoughts and emotions were too jumbled. She'd been in the mountains making love with Tyson, having the most wonderful time of her life, when her father had died.

Chief Clanahan turned as he heard her step in the hall. "The county coroner's going to have Dr. Hatcher pronounce him dead and determine the cause of death." He came toward the doorway as if to block her from entering Skelton's room.

"I want to see him," she said dully.

He hesitated, then nodded, and allowed her past him.

Skelton sat in his recliner, looking older than she ever remembered seeing him. Someone had turned off the television. She was fairly certain it must've been Fanny, or Clanahan, because that television played 24/7. It was what entertained Skelton when the pain grew too bad for him to sleep.

Dakota wasn't sure what she'd expected to feel in this moment, but it was none of the relief that she'd anticipated—only loss, sorrow. And, ironically, it wasn't the memories of their battles that crowded close, it was the times her father had joined her on a school field trip, packed a little something extra in her lunch, or came out, even though he was in a great deal of pain, to see her perform in a school play.

"God," she muttered, her eyes blurring with tears as she took his gnarled hand. "We were quite a pair, weren't we? And look at us now. Maybe Mom was right to leave."

She felt Chief Clanahan squeeze her shoulder. He was trying to be nice, but he wouldn't have felt so free to intrude on anyone else's grief. She and her father had become a community concern, one in which he'd frequently been involved. Thanks to Tyson, Clanahan didn't know about the knife incident, however. No one did. Dakota was more grateful for that now than ever. Public opinion of her father was already bad enough.

And then she saw it—the bottle that normally held Skelton's pain pills, peeking out from under his bed. It was lying on its side with the lid off, empty.

She glanced up at Clanahan, wondering if he'd seen it, too. But he didn't seem to be searching for anything out of the ordinary. Skelton had been sick for so long, he took what appeared to be a peaceful death at face value.

"Can I have a few moments alone with him?" she asked.

"Sure." He gave her arm another pat, went out and closed the door.

Dakota bent, her chest suddenly so heavy

she could hardly breathe, and retrieved the bottle. Sure enough, it was empty. And it had been renewed just last week. Mrs. Cottle had mentioned it to her when Skelton had filled his prescription.

She covered her mouth, fresh tears burning behind her eyes like hot peppers. "Tell me you didn't do it, Daddy," she whispered into her hand, and then she opened the drawer to find the spiral notebook he used to write down the various items he wanted her to pick up from the store. There he'd listed "ice cream" and "shaving gel," but these had been crossed off. Beneath, in shaky handwriting she found a note.

Dakota—

Please don't feel bad and for heaven's sake don't blame yourself. I know I haven't been a very good father these past years. I'm sorry for that. Really I am. You've been the best daughter a man could want. I won't hold you back any longer. I'm setting you free now, honey. I'm setting us both free. I should've done this a long time ago. Before I could become what I've become.

Live and be happy. For me.

He didn't tell her he loved her—he didn't need to. That was one thing she'd always known.

Dakota sank onto the bed, staring, disbelieving, at the words.

A light knock sounded at the door, allowing her no time to recover. "Give me a minute," she said. Then she jumped up, crumpled the note and hid it and the empty pill container in Skelton's sock drawer. Dundee already thought the worst of her father; she wouldn't add suicide to the memories they carried of him.

"Dakota?" It was Chief Clanahan again. He spoke through the door.

"Yes?"

"Dr. Hatcher is here."

Saying a silent prayer that old Dr. Hatcher, who was a recovering alcoholic himself, would pronounce her father dead of natural causes, she crossed the room and opened the door.

"I'm so sorry, Dakota," he said, giving her a sympathetic frown.

She accepted his condolences with a mute nod and waved him in.

He set the bag he carried on Skelton's cluttered dresser. Parting the drapes, Dakota stared outside, watching the wind bend the weeds behind the house while he examined her father's body. After fifteen minutes, she couldn't take the anxiety any longer.

"Do you know what went wrong?" she asked.

"I'm guessing it was his liver that caused it. We could do an autopsy, if you like, to determine the exact cause of death, but, in my opinion, it'd be expensive and pointless. We all know how ill he was."

"It's my choice?" She continued to gaze out the window, wondering how many times she'd stared out at that same scene as a child.

"You're the one who'd have to pay for it, so yes, it's your decision."

Dakota opened her mouth to reply, but before she could get the words out, someone else spoke.

"I'll pay for one if you want it."

Tyson. Dakota turned to see him standing in the doorway, tense, upset, his eyes eagerly seeking hers.

"No. No autopsy," she said. Encouraged by the calm in her own voice, she repeated Dr. Hatcher's words so no one would question her. "We all know how ill he was."

Everyone also knew about his alcohol

abuse and the bumps and bruises he'd given her. But they'd forgotten the man they'd known before the accident.

That was the man Dakota chose to remember.

For Dakota, the next few days passed in a blur. She spent them sorting through her father's belongings, putting those items that held sentimental value in boxes in a corner of Gabe's father's basement—Gabe had volunteered the space and his parents had quickly promised she could use it as long as she needed—getting the mobile home ready for sale, or rent if she couldn't sell it, and planning and attending the funeral. She would've felt completely isolated and alone, despite the flowers and cards she received and the platitudes she heard daily, if it weren't for Tyson, who was there through it all. He helped her pack and move the boxes, gave input on the decisions for the funeral, and made her eat regardless of her lack of appetite.

His emotional support helped her limp through the worst of the aftermath. He supported her financially, too. He'd surprised her by walking into the trailer one day while she was worrying over a stack of unpaid bills, and had offered to pay them. When she refused to let him, he'd insisted on giving her all her wages in advance, which had enabled her to catch up on the house and car payments, at least. And although the owners of the funeral home wouldn't say who'd stepped forward to help with the burial expenses, she knew that was probably him, too.

They slept together every night, but the one time they'd made love had been like nothing Dakota had experienced with Tyson so far. His touch wasn't fevered or passionate; it was more like a gentle "I'm here," which he'd initiated only after he'd awakened to find her standing at the window. Worried because she wasn't sleeping well, he even got up with Braden if he heard him cry in the night.

A week after the funeral, he stood in the doorway, watching her rock the baby. "How long have you been up?"

"Only a few minutes," she lied.

"You okay?"

"Fine." She could see him in the moonlight streaming through Braden's window. He was wearing nothing but a pair of briefs and a tired expression, but she loved the way he moved, the way he spoke, even his lack of concern over his nudity. She loved everything about him. And that was the problem.

She couldn't imagine living without him or Braden. But she needed to figure out how she was going to do just that.

"I didn't hear him cry," he said apologetically.

Because he hadn't cried. Dakota had slipped into his room and, as she'd looked down on him sleeping so peacefully and thought about how soon he and Tyson would be leaving, she'd had the irresistible urge to hold him in these quiet hours, when Tyson wasn't around to see how difficult it was going to be for her to let go.

"He'll be walking soon," she murmured.

"When do most babies walk?"

"Around a year."

"We'll have to pad every corner."

She didn't respond. She wasn't part of that *we* and she knew it. As the silence grew, he rubbed his eyes, then scuffed one foot against the carpet. "Are you going to L.A. with me?" he finally asked.

It was at least the third time he'd asked her. "No."

Folding his arms, he leaned against the doorjamb. "What will you do?"

She wasn't sure. Contemplating that very question made it difficult to relax long enough to eat or sleep. She had so few options. She couldn't travel very far, because she didn't have the money. She couldn't get a decent job because she had no real education. She couldn't get a college degree because she didn't have any way to put herself through. She knew there were ways around such obstacles, other people overcame them every day, but she couldn't see a clear path yet. "I might move to Portland, work and go to school."

"What about visiting your mother? Now might be a good time to get acquainted with her."

He could let her go so easily. "Not yet. Maybe later, when I'm back on my feet," she said, but her feelings for her mother were too complicated to throw South America into the mix.

"I'll miss you," he said quietly.

She smiled. Didn't speak.

"Most people would say something like, 'I'll miss you, too.'"

She laughed softly. He had no idea. "You'll be fine. You'll have football to keep you busy. And Braden."

Coming into the room, he lifted the baby

from her arms and put him back into the crib.
Then he held out his hand to her.

She kept the smile fixed on her face as she
accepted it, feeling his long fingers curl se-
curely through hers as they walked back to
his bedroom. But, closing the door behind
them, he leaned against it, instead of pro-
ceeding to the bed, and she turned back in
surprise. "What is it?"

"Why not come to L.A. for a few months?
You've never been, right?"

Of course not. She'd never been anywhere.
"No, I need to start plans for going to school."

He crossed the room and slipped his arms
around her, which shortened the T-shirt she
was wearing—his T-shirt—until it no longer
covered her panties. "Why Portland?"

"One of the things I've been thinking about
is someday opening my own European café."

"And for that you'd need to go to some sort
of culinary school?"

"One that does baking and pastry."

"They have that in Portland?"

"They do. I looked it up online yesterday."

"I'm sure they have one in L.A., too." He
kissed her neck, the corner of her mouth and,
pressed against his body and his erection,
Dakota felt the stirring of sexual desire. The

fact that he'd be leaving in two weeks created a sense of urgency that made her desperate to take advantage of every hour they had left.

"Probably," she conceded.

"But that isn't good enough for you?"

"Nope." She couldn't go to L.A., not if she hoped to start her own life. She'd wind up being Braden's nanny, since that was what she really wanted, anyway, and then she'd stay for Braden's sake even after Tyson's eye began to wander and he started to bring other women to the house. But she wouldn't allow herself to suffer the kind of heartbreak that would cause, wouldn't allow their relationship to come to that.

I'm going out with some respect and dignity, remember? It was the one thing she'd promised herself the night she'd given him her virginity.

"Why not?"

"I don't want to talk about it right now."

"Because…"

"I want to make love." She pulled off the T-shirt she was wearing, which succeeded in distracting him.

Turning her toward the moonlight, he smiled as he ran his fingers over her ever so lightly, creating gooseflesh in his wake. "But we have a small problem."

"What's that?"

"Your body is saying yes." He continued his tantalizing exploration. "But…"

"What?"

He stopped toying with her and lifted her chin so she had to look him in the eye. "You're acting a little remote. Are you sure you're okay, that you're ready for this after… everything you've been through?"

She guided his hand back to her. "I'm ready. Just do it hard and fast, so I can't feel anything else."

"Dakota…" His voice held concern, even hesitancy, but a wild hunger had taken hold of her, making her more brazen than she'd ever been. Sliding her hand inside his briefs, she made sure he couldn't remember that he was having reservations, let alone what those reservations might be.

"Now or never," she whispered.

And he gave her exactly what she wanted without further argument.

It was morning, but Dakota finally seemed to be sleeping peacefully. Getting out of bed so he wouldn't disturb her, Tyson pulled on a pair of basketball shorts and went to get Braden, who was jabbering in the next room.

"Hey, buddy, what are you doing up so early?" he asked.

Braden answered with a big smile that showed his only tooth, and Tyson began to wonder how it was that his son got cuter every day. "Come on, I'm hungry. Let's go eat."

Plopping onto his behind, Braden lifted his arms, and Tyson grabbed hold of him and swung him up in the air, chuckling when he squealed in delight. "You like that, eh?" he said, tossing him up again.

Braden's wide-eyed, "I'm too excited to breathe" expression made Tyson laugh and, when he caught his son, he impulsively kissed his round cheek. Braden smelled good. And his skin was so incredibly soft.

Something constricted in Tyson's chest. Closing his eyes, he rubbed his lips against his son's cheek again. Now that he'd had a taste of kissing a baby, *his* baby, he knew there was nothing that could compare to it. "You're addictive," he murmured, holding his son close.

Braden responded by placing a very wet kiss on Tyson's chin, but somehow Tyson didn't find it distasteful. It fact, it made the funny feeling in his chest grow stronger.

"Who would've thought I'd ever be so happy to see you?" he said with a grin, and suddenly he didn't feel so angry at Rachelle. She'd changed his life, all right. But now it felt like she'd changed it for the better.

The doorbell sounded reminding Tyson that he'd set up an early appointment with his trainer. Carrying Braden with him, he dashed downstairs, taking them two at a time so he could reach the door before Lance could wake Dakota. He swung open the door just as Lance was raising his hand to knock.

The trainer's eyebrows shot up, and Tyson imagined himself as Lance was seeing him— standing there without a shirt or shoes, his hair sticking up all over, and holding a baby. "I thought we were hitting it hard this morning," Lance said.

"We are. It won't take me long to feed this guy."

"Isn't Dakota here to take care of him?"

"She is, but… I'm sure you heard about her father. She needs a little time to get back on her feet."

Obviously irritated, Lance glanced back at his car, then at the mat at his feet before finally summoning what he wanted to say. "I can appreciate that, Tyson. I really like Dakota, wish her the best. But I have a full day at the vet clinic. I can't come out here in the mornings if you're not going to be ready. You've been off a week already. Aren't you interested in playing this season?"

The warmth and tenderness Tyson had felt only a few moments earlier disappeared, leaving cold fear in his gut. "Of course I'm interested in playing. That's who I am, what I do."

"It takes a lot of focus and drive to get beyond this kind of injury. I've been as understanding as possible, but now that your problems with Rachelle are behind you, you need to hit it hard. That knee's not ready for the abuse it has to take. If you don't get serious, your football days could be over."

Tyson wanted to argue with Lance, wanted to tell him that he was taking his career seriously. But he'd let himself be distracted by a sexy woman and a cute baby. When had being with Dakota and Braden become more important than playing football? What was wrong with him? Neutralizing the threat of Rachelle's accusations and retaining his endorsements had lulled him into believing everything was fine. But if he wasn't careful, he could still lose his career, and once it was gone, it would most likely be gone for good. Second chances didn't come often in the NFL.

"You're right," he said. "I'm sorry."

"So are we going running?" Lance asked.

Tyson heard Dakota's step on the stairs and glanced over at her. Her hair was as mussed as his was, but she'd taken the time to dress a little better. She had on a pair of knee-length cutoffs and a simple tank. With her golden skin and oh-so-kissable mouth, she looked great. Better than great. The sight of her brought images of last night, which had been memorable indeed. But he had to put his relationship with her, and everything else that had happened this summer, behind him. It was time to get back to work.

"We're going running," he said and stifled the impulse to kiss her good morning as she came to get Braden.

Chapter 21

*Grandpa Garnier: If you're gonna go,
go like hell. If your mind's not made up,
don't use your spurs.*

Dakota wasn't sure what had changed, but she sensed a difference in Tyson ever since that day he'd gone running with Lance. He rarely touched her or Braden, didn't come to her bed at night or lead her to his, rarely even talked to her if he could help it and spent all his time working out, studying football clips or taking care of business in the office. She wasn't sure what kind of business he had, since he hadn't seemed too involved in it before and it was the off-season, but she suspected it had to do with investments of some sort, which he'd apparently decided to manage himself.

He was polite when they happened to bump into each other, but he didn't make any sexual advances. And he started spending a lot of time away—at Gabe's house in town, she realized when she overheard him talking with Lance a few days later. He and Gabe had been training together, trying to get Tyson's knee back in shape.

Dakota couldn't understand what had caused such an abrupt reversal in their relationship, especially when she was beginning to feel so close to him, but it was as if all the tenderness and concern he'd shown her and his son had simply disappeared. He was the man he'd been when they first met: angry, although she didn't understand the reason now that Rachelle was no longer a problem, determined and withdrawn.

Finally Dakota called her best friend, Rita Long. She spoke to Rita barely two or three times a year since Rita had married and moved to Seattle, but Dakota didn't know where else to turn. She needed to talk to *someone*. She felt so isolated, so alone. She'd been expecting to lose Tyson when he went to California, not before.

"Tell me this is a good call," Rita said as soon as she heard Dakota's voice.

"A good call?" Dakota echoed in confusion.

"I rarely hear from you anymore, so I'm guessing you've got big news. Are you getting married?"

Dakota managed a laugh. "That's the only thing you'd consider a good call?"

"No, but you've needed a decent, loving man for years. After everything you've done for your father, you deserve to find one."

Dakota remembered Tyson brushing past her so impersonally this morning and swallowed past the lump in her throat. "Sorry, no wedding."

There was a long pause. "Is everything okay, Kody?"

Squeezing her eyes closed at the sound of her old nickname, Dakota thought of her father and all that had—and hadn't—transpired since she and Rita were in high school together. "My father passed away two weeks ago, Rita."

"Oh, no… I'm so sorry. I know—" her

voice broke "—I know you really loved him. I liked the old guy, too."

Rita didn't know about the violence of the past few years. That was part of the reason Dakota had drifted away from her best friend. She'd been too busy trying to deal with her own problems, knew there was nothing Rita could do but feel sorry for her. Now it was suddenly like old times, as if nothing had changed at all, which somehow prompted her to tell Rita the truth—that Skelton's death was a suicide, which she hadn't told anyone else, including Tyson.

"Your poor dad," Rita said. "Who can blame him? He was in so much pain. But I have lots of good memories of him. Remember when he dressed up like a chauffeur and drove us on our prom date?"

Dakota smiled at the memory, glad her friend had missed the worst of Skelton's downfall. "I do."

Rita sniffed. "So what are you going to do now?"

"I haven't decided."

"Have you met anyone? Is there any reason to stay in Dundee?"

Dakota shoved an image of Tyson out of her mind. He wouldn't be in Dundee much longer. "No. I want to leave. I just don't know where to go."

"Why don't you come here?" Rita asked, her voice filled with enthusiasm. "I have a big home with plenty of room. And there are a lot of young, single guys who sell alarm systems for my husband. We could introduce you to some of them. When you're ready," she added.

"I don't want to lean on you," Dakota said. "I—I need to establish my own life."

"An extended visit won't get in the way of that," Rita argued. "Coming to Seattle will simply give you time to heal, to plan your future."

Dakota remembered the excitement she'd felt at the possibility of seeing California and knew Washington was probably just as nice. Maybe she'd even settle there, find a job, get a cheap apartment and eventually start culinary school.

"Do you think there are good job opportunities up there?"

"You could always work for Tim, if you want. His business is growing so fast, he needs a dependable office manager. The woman he has now is mostly retired and puts in twenty hours a week, max. And the pay's not bad."

She'd be with Rita again, too, get to know Rita's husband, Tim, and her little girl, Meggie.

"Do they have any culinary schools in Seattle?" she asked.

"We can check, but I'm betting there are."

"So you're serious."

"I'll even send you a plane ticket."

"No." Dakota thought of the purchase offer that had come in on her trailer that morning. Surprisingly, it was a good one—full asking price, all cash, with a quick close. It wouldn't make her rich, but it would pay off her loans, give her enough to get to Seattle and carry her until she could get a job. School would have to wait, but she'd have that to look forward to, to dream about. "I'll come as soon as the sale of my father's mobile home is final."

"When will that be?"

"In a few days."

"I'll be waiting."

"Thanks, Rita." Dakota smiled as she hung up. Life wasn't all bad. She still had her best friend.

Dakota was so nervous she hovered at the top of the stairs for fifteen minutes before finding the resolve to go down. These days, Tyson usually came home after she was in bed. That was also true tonight, but she'd been listening for him. She'd heard his car pull up outside, heard the door close quietly downstairs. And now it was time to confront him. The escrow on the sale of her trailer had closed; she had the money she needed.

He must've heard her on the stairs. He looked up from where he sat at the table, but then he jerked his gaze away, focusing on the slice of cake he'd just cut. He'd mostly quit eating the food she made—he wasn't home long enough to enjoy a meal—but she'd baked his favorite carrot cake, hoping he'd pause in the kitchen long enough to sit down with dessert so she could have a chance to bring up the subject that had been on her mind ever since she'd spoken to Rita four days ago.

"Do you have a second?" she asked politely.

He kept his attention on his cake. "Sure," he said, then shoveled a big bite into his mouth.

She tried not to remember the times his eyes had warmed when they landed on her, the crooked smile that made her breathless with anticipation, the way his lips tasted when he kissed her. It didn't matter now. That was over. Tyson was supposed to go to California next week, and because Dakota couldn't take living under their current conditions any longer, she wanted to leave before that.

"I have—" her heart was pounding so hard, she had to pause for breath enough to speak "—a proposition for you."

"A *proposition?*"

She wasn't sure what to make of his voice. Was that wariness she heard?

She licked dry lips, willing herself to continue. She had so much hope riding on the next fifteen minutes. "Y-you've been pretty busy lately."

He shoveled another bite into his mouth. "Football's coming up."

"Right. I can only imagine that the season will be even busier."

A nod acknowledged her words, but he still seemed reluctant to give her much attention.

"Uh, when Rachelle had Braden, you were content to pay her child support and let her take care of him."

At this, he lowered his fork and met her gaze. "He's not going back to her. Ever."

"I realize that, and I wholeheartedly support it." She swallowed hard. "He needs someone who will be absolutely diligent in caring for him."

One eyebrow went up. *"Someone?"*

"I'm just saying your lifestyle isn't really conducive to caring for a baby."

"I get that part."

"So… I was thinking." Now it was her turn to glance away. She moved over to the counter, covered the cake he'd uncovered and finally blurted out what she had to say because she was afraid she'd never get to it if she didn't. "*I* would like to raise him."

He stared at her, but didn't say a word as she rushed to explain.

"You know I'd take excellent care of him—I'd die before I let anyone hurt him—and I'd do what you initially expected from Rachelle, only I'd go one better. I wouldn't expect a dime. Not a single dime. I've found a better job, so I'll be able to get by. Besides that, I'd sign whatever you wanted, make sure he had everything a child needs, no matter what, and we'd *never* contact you. I swear. I have a little money coming in from the trailer, and we'd use it to move away. No one would be the wiser. I wouldn't mention your name to a soul, especially the press. And you could go on with your life as if this summer never happened, as if Rachelle and Braden and me… as if we never existed. Doesn't that sound good?"

He looked like she'd slapped him. Obviously she'd said something wrong. She scrambled, trying to figure out what that might have been so she could make it right and possibly hang on to the child she loved.

"Think about it," she pleaded, kneeling down in front of him. "Football, football and more football. Fame. Fortune. Parties. Women. Lots of women…" Her words dwindled off because the mental image of those women was like a knife in the heart. But she'd already lost him. She didn't want to lose Braden, too.

Tyson reached over and touched her face, his eyes deeply troubled, but she couldn't risk giving him the chance to refuse her. Steeling herself against the pain, she pressed on. "What do you say? I mean, let's be honest. You don't want him. You never have. But *I* do." She tapped her chest to prove her sincerity. "I'd give *anything* for him. Granted, I don't have a lot right now, but I can offer you a release from the responsibility of being a father, freedom, the certainty that he will be well cared for. Those are what you want, right, Ty? I—"

"Stop it." He stood up so fast that the chair nearly went flying.

Dakota blinked rapidly, trying to stem the tears welling in her eyes. "What, then? What do you want?"

"I—I may not be the best father, but I won't give him up."

"You haven't even looked at him for eight days!"

"It's *you* I haven't been able to look at!" he said and stormed out.

Chapter 22

Grandpa Garnier: Love is like a bucking bronco. It takes more guts and determination than most men have to hang on, but it's worth the ride.

Tyson sped down the winding road in his Ferrari, his words echoing in his mind. *It's you I haven't been able to look at.* He hadn't completed that statement. He couldn't look at her because seeing her made him want her, which called into question all the decisions he'd recently made. He knew the direction he wanted to go; he just wanted to put this summer behind him, right?

He wasn't sure. That was what being around her did to him. He had to get away. But as he drove, he began to realize he wasn't running from Dakota. He was running from himself—from the unaccustomed emotions she, and Braden, evoked in him. When he looked at her, he didn't see himself as the young, fit athlete he'd always been. He saw a soon-to-be retired football player, a husband and father who was happy to let the dreams he'd held on to for so long go in exchange for growing old with Dakota.

And that scared the hell out of him. He'd decided years ago that he'd never get married. Marriage was overrated and rarely worked out. Take his mother's multiple experiences, for example.

Besides, even if he changed his mind about tying the knot, he certainly wasn't ready to take that big a step right now, when he was at such a critical point in his career. His knee was coming back. He should have another five years.

He found himself at Gabe's house. But he didn't get out and go to the door. He sat in front, remembering Dakota's plea to raise Braden. He'd longed to be able to return to

Life Before. She'd offered him that, and yet he'd turned her down flat.

He dropped his head in his hands. Why had he said no? Because he could never give Braden up. Not for anything. The little guy had worked his way so deeply into Tyson's affections that the idea of losing him manifested itself as a physical ache.

But Dakota loved Braden, too. And it was entirely possible Braden would be better off with her.

A knock on the window of his door brought his head up. Gabe was in the street, sitting in his wheelchair, frowning at him.

Tyson wished he'd gone someplace else, or left before he'd been spotted, but it was too late. He couldn't avoid speaking to Gabe now.

"What's wrong?" Gabe asked the minute he rolled down his window.

"Nothing. I just thought maybe I left my—" Tyson scrambled for an excuse for showing up in the middle of the night "—wallet here."

Gabe's eyes narrowed. "Your wallet?"

"Yeah. Have you seen it?"

"Not in the house. But maybe that's because it's right there, on your console."

Sure enough, his wallet was sitting in plain sight. Tyson felt his face heat.

"You gonna tell me the real reason you're here?" Gabe asked. "And why you've been coming by so much lately?"

"I told you. It saves Lance from having to drive all the way up to the cabin."

"That's it?"

"That's it."

Gabe edged his chair closer and dropped his voice. "But we already worked out tonight, buddy."

Tyson said nothing.

"It's Dakota, isn't it?"

With a grimace, Tyson shook his head, but Gabe went on, undeterred. "What's going on between you two?"

"Nothing."

"Bullshit. I tried to help with the funeral expenses, but Leo over at the funeral home told me it was all taken care of. Don't suppose you know who paid the bill."

"Nope."

"And I hear the mobile home has already sold. Just like that." Gabe snapped his fingers. "That's odd because real estate, especially *that* kind of real estate, doesn't sell quickly around here. And the buyer's name is Richard Peterson. A guy I've never heard of before. Curious, don't you think?"

Tyson scowled. "Don't mention it to anyone else, okay? Dakota needs some seed money."

"And you're trying to give it to her."

"She won't take it directly. So I paid a friend of Greg's to say he was planning to move here, and gave him the money to buy the damn trailer. No big deal."

"What happens when Mr. Peterson doesn't move here?"

"Dakota will be gone by then."

"So she's going back to L.A. with you?" Gabe asked, sounding pleased but surprised.

"No. She was talking about going to school in Portland. But tonight she mentioned getting a better job."

Gabe clucked his tongue. "You're gonna let her get away?"

Tyson was *really* beginning to regret coming to Gabe's. "Why wouldn't I?"

"Because you're in love with her, Ty. For weeks, almost since you first came to town, Hannah's been saying she thinks the two of you belong together, but I wasn't convinced until I saw you with her at the funeral. Every time you looked at her—"

"I hated that she was hurting, that there wasn't anything I could do to stop the pain."

"I could see that. Why do you think you felt that way?"

"I don't know…sympathy?"

Gabe laughed. "No, that's love, buddy. I've been trying to let you come to it on your own but—" he shook his head "—damn, you're stubborn."

He *was* stubborn. How many times had he heard his grandfather say, "I've owned mules that were downright accommodating compared to that grandson of mine." Tyson had come by that stubbornness honestly. It gave him the grit he needed to compete in the game he loved. But maybe it also, sometimes, got in his way.

"What?" Gabe said.

Tyson realized he was smiling at the thought that his grandfather would be calling him a damn fool right now. "Nothing," he said, but he finally gave up trying to deny his feelings. "You're right. I care about her."

"So what's the problem?"

He sighed as he pulled a hand over his face. "What if it doesn't work out?"

"Then you go your separate ways."

"It's not that simple. There could be kids

involved—there *will* be kids involved because, with Braden, there already is. It could
get...messy."

Gabe shrugged. "You're right. Divorce is
ugly. But does that mean everyone should
give up on marriage?"

"Of course not. But what are *our* chances?
This could be a very stressful year for both
of us. She's recently lost her father, she'd be
moving to a new city, taking on my son. And
my career could fall apart in a few months."

"Trust me, if you have Dakota you won't
care nearly as much. Isn't that what scares
you? You'll be putting your faith in someone
else for the first time in your life."

Tyson glanced away. "My mother never
enjoyed marriage."

"She did with your father," Gabe pointed
out. "She's just never been able to find that
kind of love again. She once told me he'd ruined her for anyone else. But do you think,
if she had the chance to do it all over, she'd
pass up the opportunity to share the years
they had together?"

His mother had married several other men,
hoping to find what she'd lost. None of those
had worked out, but that hadn't stopped her
from trying, again and again. What she'd had

must've been truly amazing. Maybe Tyson had the opportunity to experience the same thing with Dakota. "No, I guess not."

"Think about that, okay?" Gabe said and thumped the door.

Tyson did think about it—all the way home. Did he want to miss the chance to be with Dakota? No. He'd been fighting the truth, but there it was. His grandfather would've been right if he'd been here to call him a fool. Gabe was right, too. He was in love, really in love, for the first time in his life. And maybe that meant major changes and risks and losing a little control, but it was time to lose control, to let go of the skepticism that held him back and embrace the hope that their love could survive even when so many others failed.

When he got to the cabin, he ran up the stairs, suddenly in a hurry to reach her. He wanted to slip into her room, hold her close and apologize. Maybe he'd even propose. The thought made his heart pound and yet…it felt right. He was going to marry her whether he continued with football or not. The idea of that was so new to him, he paused for a moment at the top of the stairs. He was going to get *married. Him.* The same guy who'd sworn a woman could never mean more to him than football had just proven himself wrong.

But when he reached Dakota's room, he found her bed empty. Her drawers were open and empty, too. And she'd taken Braden.

Then his parting words came back to him: *It's you I haven't been able to look at.*

"Shit!" He went charging downstairs, his first impulse to get back in his car and chase after her. She'd probably gone to the trailer she'd just sold, unwittingly, *to him.*

But if she hadn't, he'd be stupid to waste his time going to the wrong place. It was better to focus his search.

Grabbing the phone in the kitchen, he dialed Gabe.

"Hello?"

"She's gone," he said simply.

"I know."

That took Tyson aback. He stopped his frantic pacing and froze in the middle of the floor. "How?"

"She brought the baby here."

"And you didn't call me?"

"I couldn't reach you. She arrived right after you left."

"Braden's okay, then?"

"He's fine. Hannah's rocking him in the other room."

"What about Dakota?"

"I don't know. She didn't say much, just that it was time for her to leave town."

"What do you mean, town? For good? In the middle of the night? In that car?"

"Would you calm down and stop yelling?" Gabe said.

Tyson couldn't calm down. He kept picturing her stranded on the side of a deserted highway and some maniac finding her, hurting her. "Did you ask where she was going?" He had to find her, right away.

"She wouldn't tell us. Hannah thinks Dakota doesn't know, either. She's just…running."

From me. "She didn't say *anything*?"

There was a long pause. Finally Gabe responded, "She said to tell you goodbye."

Tyson nearly staggered as those words hit him—because she meant them. He knew she did, or she would never have left Braden. How could he guess where she was going if she didn't know herself? She could be halfway to anywhere, and there was a very strong possibility he'd never find her.

Then Tyson got an idea. It was a long shot, pure hope, but it was all he had.

"Get over to the cemetery," he said to Gabe. "Right away. Maybe you can catch her. I'll meet you there as soon as I can."

"You think she's at her father's grave?"

"She couldn't leave that old man in all the years she took care of him. If this is really it for her, she wouldn't go without telling him goodbye, too."

When Tyson arrived at the cemetery, Gabe was waiting for him at Skelton's grave, as promised, but he was alone.

Tyson shoved the gear into neutral, stared at the lone figure visible in the headlights and felt sick. How had he been so blind? How had he let this happen?

When Gabe didn't come rolling toward him, Tyson forced himself to turn off the ignition and get out. He preferred not to face Gabe feeling the way he was. He, who'd never understood Gabe's complete devotion to Hannah, now felt as if he'd wasted his only opportunity to have the same thing. But he couldn't leave his friend sitting there in the middle of the cemetery.

Gabe said nothing as he approached. They

stood there together, staring at the fresh mound of dirt that was Skelton's grave. There were still sprays of fresh flowers from the recent funeral, sitting on the headstone, everywhere. The scent of carnations and roses was almost overpowering, especially because it was so much warmer here than up at the cabin.

"I guess I was wrong," Tyson said at last.

"No. Just too late." Gabe handed him a note. "I found this on the headstone."

Tyson's chest burned as he opened it and read. There were only three words. *I'm sorry, Daddy.* "What does it mean?" he asked.

"She never told you?"

"Told me what?"

"About the accident?"

"No. She just said it was complicated."

"I suppose it was," Gabe agreed. "She was only ten when it happened."

Tyson was finding it difficult to speak and even harder to come to terms with all the emotions welling up inside him. "How'd he get hurt?"

"Skelton used to be an electrician," Gabe said. "He was helping to build the new elementary school gymnasium when Dakota got sick and couldn't go to school one day.

He didn't have anyone to watch her, so he took her with him—he had to handle something that needed doing. He told her to stay away from the workers, but she was fascinated by all the activity and wandered too close. Suddenly a piece of lumber fell from where they were putting on the trusses. The board would've hit Dakota and, from that height, probably would've killed her if her father hadn't heard someone yell and shoved her out of the way."

"It hit him instead?"

"Yes."

"And he was never the same afterward."

"Right. He couldn't work for very long, began to fall into debt. Dakota took over more and more of the household chores and financial obligations as she grew older." He shook his head. "Must've been one hell of a childhood. Especially when Skelton turned to alcohol to get him through the day."

"I'm going to find her," Tyson said. "Somehow. Somewhere."

Gabe's cell phone interrupted before he could respond. "You're kidding me," he said into the mouthpiece. "Good. We'll let Tyson go. But if she calls back, don't tell her he's coming."

"What is it?" Tyson asked, the moment Gabe hung up.

His friend grinned at him. "Dakota just called."

Almost too afraid to hope, Tyson caught his breath. "Where is she?"

"Her car broke down a couple miles from town, and she twisted her ankle trying to walk back in the dark. She made it as far as the Honky Tonk, but it's closed for the night and now she's wondering if she can get a ride to the motel."

Tyson let his breath go as he embraced the most complete relief he'd ever known. "I'm *so* glad she wouldn't let me buy her a new car."

"You tried?" Gabe said.

"Yup."

"Oh, brother." His friend rolled his eyes, then gave him a playful swat. "And you didn't know you loved her."

"I know now," Tyson said and started jogging for his car.

Dakota was sitting on the curb outside the bar that provided most of Dundee's entertainment, her ankle throbbing and her heart hurting far worse. She couldn't even run away when she tried, she thought, glaring up at the crudely made Honky Tonk sign, the lights of which had been shut off. Now she'd have to have Booker Robinson tow her Maxima and fix it, and she'd have that much less money with which to move to Washington. But that wasn't the worst of it. By staying in Dundee she risked seeing Tyson again, which she definitely didn't want to do.

Braden was another story entirely, however. She desperately hoped Hannah would bring the baby with her. She missed him already. But she knew that wasn't very likely. It was nearly three o'clock in the morning.

Wincing at the reminder that she'd disturbed Gabe's household twice in the middle of the same night, she stood as headlights appeared. At this hour, the town was virtually deserted, so she assumed it was Hannah. But as the vehicle drew closer, she could tell it wasn't Gabe's wife in her big Cadillac. The sound of the engine was all wrong. And the headlights were too low....

As the car passed beneath the closest streetlight, recognition dawned and Dakota tried to hobble out of sight. She couldn't deal with Tyson right now. But it was too late. He slowed and turned into the lot before she'd made it more than a few feet.

"I hear you need a ride," he said, lowering his window.

She didn't want to look at him. Just the sight of his handsome face would undermine her resolve. "Gabe and Hannah are such traitors," she muttered, and he laughed.

"They know you love me."

She lifted her chin defiantly. "They don't know anything."

"They know I love you," he said, his voice softer now, more serious.

Dakota stopped trying to walk away and turned back to face him. "What did you say?"

"You heard me." After parking, he got out of the car and moved toward her.

"What are you doing here?" she asked. "How do you expect me to react to that after what you said earlier, how you've behaved? And where do you expect this to go? You're leaving in a few days."

"And you're coming with me." Scooping her into his arms, he carried her back to the car and deposited her in the passenger seat.

"I'm not playing games, Tyson. I'm done. You're right, okay? I love you. More than I ever thought I could love another human being. But you were right about me. I can't do casual. I'm leaving and I'm going to establish a new life."

He didn't respond as he got in. Throwing the engine in reverse, he backed up, then swung around to come out on the street.

"Are you listening to me?" she asked.

"I'm listening."

"Then where are you taking me?"

"You'll see."

Dakota couldn't imagine what was going on. Tyson seemed different somehow—and preoccupied. He appeared to be searching for something he wasn't sure how to find.

"What is it?" she asked.

"Mulberry Street."

"Why do you want Mulberry Street?"

"Ah, there it is." He made a U-turn even though the light was red, then hung a left at Mulberry.

"There isn't a motel this way," she said. "Only a few houses and a church."

"It's the church I'm looking for."

"Why?"

He didn't answer her question. "That's it over there, isn't it?"

Dakota expected Dundee Fellowship of Christ to be dark and vacant, but strangely enough, there was a light on inside, and the door stood open. Hannah was sitting on the bench by the sign that announced the times of Sunday worship, and Gabe was in his wheelchair right next to her, holding Braden.

Dakota's heart skipped a beat when she saw the baby. "What's going on?" she asked, completely bewildered.

"Looks like they're ready for us." Getting out, Tyson came around to help her. "Can you manage on your ankle?"

She could barely feel the pain. "It's just a sprain, I'm sure, but—"

"Dakota, I'm so pleased about all this."

Hearing a familiar voice, Dakota looked around Tyson to see Reverend Hernandez approaching. The fatigue showing in his face indicated he'd been dragged from his bed, but he was dressed in his customary tweed jacket and slacks. Only, tonight he had on a tie. "All what?" she said numbly.

"Your marriage to—" He glanced uncertainly at Tyson, and Tyson cupped her chin in his hands.

"To me. Will you do it, Dakota?" he asked. "Will you marry me?"

Dakota didn't know what to say. Gabe, Hannah and her pastor were all watching, smiling as widely as she'd ever seen them. But it was hard to believe that Tyson could be serious.

"I'll take good care of you," he promised. "We'll take good care of each other."

"And look at this baby," Hannah added temptingly.

Gabe rolled a little closer. "He's stubborn, but he's a good man, Dakota."

She shook her head. "But this isn't what he wants!"

"Yes, it is," Tyson said. "I think it's what I've wanted all along. I just didn't know it. Will you do it? Will you take a chance on me?"

Dakota gaped at him and his supporters. He was serious; so were they. "We don't have a marriage license."

"We'll get one tomorrow, along with the rings. And we'll redo the ceremony in Vegas on our way home. Unless you want a big wedding here in Dundee."

"No, not on the heels of my father's funeral."

"That's what I thought. We'll make it official later, then. But I wanted to share this with Gabe and Hannah and thought you might like Reverend Hernandez to do the honors. I know I can't offer you any of the trimmings right now, but I'm offering what really counts. As far as I'm concerned this is the real thing—this is where I make my promise."

His promise to love her and her alone… "But I—" Everything was happening too fast. All she could think about was Rita, sitting in Seattle, waiting to hear that she'd arrived safely as far as Boise. She had to tell her.

"Can I borrow your cell phone?" she asked.

Tyson seemed a little confused by her response but handed it to her, and she dialed.

"Hello?"

"It's me."

"Have you reached Boise yet?"

"No, I—" she felt Tyson's hand, warm and strong, holding her elbow "—I guess I won't be coming, after all."

"Why not? Is it the car? I should've sent you money."

Tyson leaned down and spoke into the mouthpiece. "Don't worry. She's with me."

"Who's *that?*" Rita demanded.

"Tyson Garnier."

"Garnier? As in the wide receiver?"

Dakota stared up at the man she loved. "Yeah."

"You're kidding, right?"

"No."

"What are you doing with him?"

"This is that good call you've been waiting for." Dakota let her lips curve into a happy smile. "We're getting married."

"You're marrying Tyson Garnier, *the* Tyson Garnier?"

"Yeah."

"Do you even know him?"

"I've been living with him for the past two months."

There was shocked silence. "You didn't even mention that when we talked before. When's the wedding?"

"Right now."

"Oh, my gosh! I don't believe it. Dakota, I'm so happy for you—"

Dakota didn't hear the rest because Tyson passed the phone to Reverend Hernandez, pulled her into his arms and kissed her.

"It's true," she heard the reverend say. "I'm going to marry them right now."

Epilogue

Dakota sat with Braden on her lap in the stands of the Los Angeles Stingray's home stadium, next to Elaine and several of the other player's wives, nervously awaiting Tyson's first game. The Stingrays hadn't played him during preseason. They'd wanted to give his knee a little more time to heal. But yesterday they officially moved his name from the list of injured reserve to the active roster and told him he'd be starting today.

She saw Tyson turn and look for her from where he stood with the other players along the sideline. "There's Daddy," she said, and lifted Braden's little arm to wave at him.

Tyson's grin widened when he spotted them, but Dakota could tell he was nervous. His endorsements wouldn't last long if he couldn't continue to perform.

He'll be fine, Dakota told herself. She wasn't so worried about the endorsements. She knew she and Tyson could live off the money he'd already made for quite some time. And they were capable of doing other things if they needed to. She was more concerned with how much Tyson's ability to come back meant *to him*.

The excitement humming all around them made Braden kick his legs and squeal. He seemed to love the atmosphere almost as much as his daddy did.

"Tyson's amazing," Elaine said confidently. "That knee won't put him out of the game."

Dakota nodded. She was actually more frightened that he'd get hurt again. But she never fretted about that aloud. Tyson said it invited bad luck. He always mentioned the things that caused bad luck with a crooked smile, as if he knew he was sounding too superstitious, but there was some underlying belief there that she chose to respect.

Why tempt fate? he'd say.

The 49ers fumbled on third down, and

lost their first possession of the game to the Stingrays. With a final glance in her direction, Tyson slipped on his helmet and jogged out onto the field.

"Wow! Look at your wedding ring," the woman on Dakota's left said. Seemingly more interested in socializing than in the game, she reached over to admire it. But Dakota was too intent on what was happening on the field to answer.

Come on, baby. You're fine now. You're going to be just fine when this is over, too.

The Stingrays snapped the ball and used a running play for their first down. Peter Cohen, the running back, managed to gain three yards, but downfield, Tyson was picking himself up after trying to block the outside linebacker. He'd mentioned that the other team would know of his vulnerability and would be trying to exploit it, to put him out of the game.

"Don't you dare," she muttered.

Elaine patted her right leg. "He's okay. Look, he's getting up."

Drawing a deep breath, Dakota waited for the next down. This time Tyson sprinted to the thirty-yard line, easily beating his defender, and waved for the ball. The quarterback saw him and passed it, but it hung in the air just a little too long, giving the defensive back a chance to catch up. They both jumped at the same time, the defender's back to Tyson's chest as he fought to intercept the ball or at least knock it away. But somehow, it was Tyson who managed to come up with it. The 49er came down off-balance and fell, but Tyson found his feet, dodged the safety who was coming over to help and ran for the end zone.

The official signaled a touchdown, and the roar of the crowd nearly deafened Dakota. "Wow! Tyson Garnier with his first catch of the season," flashed across the scoreboard. Then the band started playing.

Their hero was back, Dakota realized, blinking against the tears filling her eyes.

Only now he was *her* hero, too.

* * * * *

Get 4 FREE REWARDS!

We'll send you 2 FREE Books <u>plus</u> 2 FREE Mystery Gifts.

Harlequin Special Edition books relate to finding comfort and strength in the support of loved ones and enjoying the journey no matter what life throws your way.

FREE Value Over $20

Get 4 FREE REWARDS!

We'll send you 2 FREE Books plus 2 FREE Mystery Gifts.

Harlequin Romance Larger-Print books will immerse you in emotion and intimacy simmering in international locales— experience the rush of falling in love!

FREE Value Over $20

Get 4 FREE REWARDS!

We'll send you 2 FREE Books plus 2 FREE Mystery Gifts.

FREE
Value Over
$20

Both the **Romance** and **Suspense** collections feature compelling novels written by many of today's bestselling authors.

YES! Please send me 2 FREE novels from the Essential Romance or Essential Suspense Collection and my 2 FREE gifts (gifts are worth about $10 retail). After receiving them, if I don't wish to receive any more books, I can return the shipping statement marked "cancel." If I don't cancel, I will receive 4 brand-new novels every month and be billed just $7.24 each in the U.S. or $7.49 each in Canada. That's a savings of up to 28% off the cover price. It's quite a bargain! Shipping and handling is just 50¢ per book in the U.S. and $1.25 per book in Canada.* I understand that accepting the 2 free books and gifts places me under no obligation to buy anything. I can always return a shipment and cancel at any time. The free books and gifts are mine to keep no matter what I decide.

Choose one: ☐ **Essential Romance**
(194/394 MDN GQ6M)

☐ **Essential Suspense**
(191/391 MDN GQ6M)

Name (please print)

Address   Apt. #

City   State/Province   Zip/Postal Code

Email: Please check this box ☐ if you would like to receive newsletters and promotional emails from Harlequin Enterprises ULC and its affiliates. You can unsubscribe anytime.

Mail to the **Harlequin Reader Service:**
IN U.S.A.: P.O. Box 1341, Buffalo, NY 14240-8531
IN CANADA: P.O. Box 603, Fort Erie, Ontario L2A 5X3

Want to try 2 free books from another series? Call 1-800-873-8635 or visit www.ReaderService.com.

STRS21R

Get 4 FREE REWARDS!

We'll send you 2 FREE Books <u>plus</u> 2 FREE Mystery Gifts.

Harlequin Historical books will seduce you with passion, drama and sumptuous detail of romances set in long-ago eras!

FREE Value Over $20

Visit ReaderService.com Today!

As a valued member of the Harlequin Reader Service, you'll find these benefits and more at ReaderService.com:

- Try 2 free books from any series
- Access risk-free special offers
- View your account history & manage payments
- Browse the latest Bonus Bucks catalog

Don't miss out!

If you want to stay up-to-date on the latest at the Harlequin Reader Service and enjoy more content, make sure you've signed up for our monthly News & Notes email newsletter. Sign up online at ReaderService.com or by calling Customer Service at 1-800-873-8635.

RS20